ONCE BITTEN

ONCE BITTEN
STEPHEN LEATHER

PUBLISHED BY

Published by AmazonEncore
P.O. Box 400818
Las Vegas, NV 89140

ISBN-13: 9781612181479
ISBN-10: 1612181473

THE ENDING

How is it that Snoopy starts all his books? It was a dark and stormy night. Yeah, that's it. It was a dark and stormy night. I guess that's as good a way as any of starting it, because that's a perfect description of the weather outside right now, the wind roaring and wheezing like some malevolent monster wanting to force its way in and tear me apart, the rain smashing and splattering against the windows, occasional flashes of lightning shooting jaggedly across the infinite blackness of the midnight sky.

There's another way that'd be just as good, just as pertinent: once upon a time. That's how they start all the fairy tales, isn't it, the phrase providing a clear and present signal that what you're about to read is a figment of someone else's imagination, that no matter how scary the story, you're starting from the premise that it's not true, that it can't be real. Maybe that would put you at ease, if you knew for a fact that it never happened, that I imagined it or made it up. Okay, that's how I'll start it then. Once upon a time, it was a dark and stormy night.

So who am I? My name's Jamie Beaverbrook, and I'll be forty-six years old next month. Maybe. The desk I'm sitting at is considerably older than I am, and it's in better condition. It's one of those big, military looking things with brass handles and legs as thick as a ship's mast. The desk is in front of a large picture window that overlooks the ocean. The Pacific. The chair is what they call a captain's chair, a thick, padded leather seat with a curved back that comes up to about my kidneys. It's on wheels so I can scoot it from side to side. When I decided to use the room as a study, I put the desk facing away from the window, toward the door, so that when I was working I wouldn't be distracted by the view. It's a hell of a view, a view you could die for the real estate agent told me, and she was right, but with both fingers of the clock pointing directly up there isn't much to see just now.

There's a computer on the desk, a MacBook Pro. I'm a big fan of Apple, always have been. On the far left is a swan-necked brass lamp which illuminates the desktop in a pale yellow light. Every now and then there's a flash of white behind me, throwing my shadow across the desk and filling the study with a stark brightness like the flash of a camera, and it's followed a few seconds later by the distant rumble of rolling thunder that I can feel deep down in my stomach. I used to know a way of calculating the distance of a storm, something to do with the difference between the speed of light and the speed of sound. You count the number of seconds that elapse between the lightning and the thunder and then divide by something. Seven. Or six. Whatever. It's been a long time since I cared how far away a storm was, but I still count the seconds. Habit, I suppose. Or instinct.

There's a bottle of whiskey on the desk, half full, or half empty, depending on your point of view. Laphroaig. A single malt. One of the best. Next to it is a crystal tumbler, and that's half empty, too. In front of the glass is a small bottle of tablets, capsules actually, red and green. The cap on the bottle is one of those childproof ones; you have to push it and turn it at the same time. There's a seal on it too, and it hasn't been broken. Yet.

In my hands is an envelope, a large one. It's sealed. I sealed it, almost ten years ago, and across the flap is my signature. Who says doctors have unreadable writing? Yeah, I'm a doctor. A psychologist, really. A criminal psychologist. If you need proof, my diplomas and stuff are on the wall to my right, next to the bookcase. Proof, that's what's in the envelope, or at least it was ten years ago when I sealed it, signed it, and placed it in a safety deposit box in the custody of a bank on Washington Boulevard. I retrieved it this afternoon, half an hour before the bank was due to close.

Lightning flashes, and almost immediately afterwards the windows shudder and there's a deafening crash that makes me jump; I spill some of the whiskey as I raise the tumbler to my mouth. My hands are shaking, partly because of the storm but mainly because of what's in the envelope. It goes quiet then, an unearthly silence, as the eye of the storm passes over the house, the pressure so intense that I can feel my ears pop; I swallow hard. I put down the empty tumbler and refill it, and then I slit open the envelope with a paper knife in the shape of a miniature Spanish sword. The air is thick, too thick to breathe, and my skull feels as if it's going to burst like an overripe watermelon. I look at the clock on the wall and it looks as if it has stopped, as if I've been trapped forever at this single moment of time, like an insect in amber, and then there's a flash as millions of volts are discharged from the clouds and the spell is broken and the second hand ticks again.

I tip the contents of the envelope out onto the desk: a sheaf of photocopied sheets which lie there overlapping like a gin rummy hand, and a black-and-white photograph, six inches by four inches, of a girl. The girl. The picture is a close-up of her face framed by shoulder-length black hair parted in the middle, a young, heart-shaped face, no lines or creases, smiling lips, slightly arched eyebrows that give her an amused look as if you've just tried to chat her up with a line she's heard a thousand times before. The hair on the right-hand side of her head is behind her ear as if she'd just pushed it there before the photograph was taken. Because the photograph is black-and-white and not color you can't tell what color her eyes are, other than that they're dark, but I can tell you that they're black. Really black. Not dark brown, not gray, but pure black, as black as her hair. As black as the night. The eyes look out of the photograph straight at me, accusingly, and when I put it to the side of the papers she still looks at me. Still accuses me.

The name on the case notes, her name, is Terry Ferriman, but later on in the investigation we added the alias Lisa Sinopoli. And a few others. So why are the case notes just photocopies and not the real thing? Because they took the originals away, that's why, along with the digital recordings I'd made of our sessions together. I'd had a hunch that they were going to do that, so I'd run off copies and stuck one set in the safety deposit box rented under a false name. Today was the first and only time I'd been back to the bank because I was never sure whether or not I was being followed. I'd given a second set of copies in another sealed envelope to my lawyer, Chuck Harrison, but they disappeared within forty-eight hours of my handing them over, and he denied that he ever saw them. Good old Chuck. I wonder what happened to him. They never found his body.

The hairs on the back of my neck go up, and I shiver. It feels as if someone is watching me, and I whirl around as lightning flashes. There's a face at the window, a haggard face fractured with worry lines and deep-set eyes, the hair uncombed and the mouth open. My heart leaps and I raise my hands to protect myself, but the figure in the window does the same and I realize that it's my own reflection. So that's how far gone I am; now I'm jumping at shadows. My hands are shaking again, worse than before, and the papers make a rustling noise like dead leaves in the wind. I drop the papers and put my hands under the cone of light thrown by the lamp. I don't remember exactly when my hands began to wrinkle, it was a gradual process, but it's obvious that they're no longer the hands of a youngster; the greenish veins are clearly outlined under the tough, suntanned skin, and the lines over the knuckles are deep furrows that don't disappear when I clench my fists. There are dark brown liver spots and a scattering of moles, and I'm sure they weren't there when I was younger, the sign of skin cells going genetically maverick. The signs of age. God, please God, I don't want to get old, and I don't want to die. I want to stay just as I am. No, that's not right—I want to stay just as I was, when I was thirty maybe. At my peak. Before she came into my life. Her jet-black eyes stare back at me from the photograph, and now her image appears to be smiling.

Anyway, I'm not sure how long I've got, so I'd better get started. How did we decide to begin it? Oh yeah, I remember. Once upon a time...

THE BEGINNING

…it was a dark and stormy night. I wasn't asleep when the phone rang because the storm was rattling the windows and a gate was banging somewhere outside. I groped for the phone. The display on the bedside clock radio said 3:15, and the voice in my ear said it was Lieutenant Samuel De'Ath and what the hell was I doing trying to sleep on the night of a full moon?

"I didn't know it was a full moon tonight," I growled at him. "It doesn't seem like twenty-eight days since the last one." I was lying. I always knew when the moon was full—it was my busiest time.

"Well it is, and the crazies are out in force, my man. The werewolves are howling, the vampires are biting, and the ghouls are ghouling. And the call has gone out for Jamie Beaverbrook, Vampire Hunter."

De'Ath laughed like a maniac. Black De'Ath I called him, partly because of the color of his thick skin, but just as much because of his sick sense of humor. He didn't mind—he could take it every bit as well as he dished it out. I sat up in bed and shook my head to clear it. "What's happened?"

"A throat-biter, picked up in an alley off Sunset Boulevard. Blood everywhere." De'Ath was a homicide detective, so he wouldn't be on the case unless the victim had died. "It's open-and-shut, no doubt about it, my man. All we need is the rubber stamp from you that the perp is sailing on an even keel so that we can get on with the paperwork."

"Can't it wait until the morning?" I asked.

"We wanna strike while the iron is hot, no time like the present, he who..."

"All right, all right, I'll be there, just don't hit me with any more clichés."

De'Ath roared with laughter and hung up. I dressed without thinking, blue jeans and my Mickey Mouse sweatshirt, and then I thought better of it and put on a dark blue suit, white shirt, and red tie and then picked up my briefcase from the study. Might as well look the part.

I went through the kitchen door to the garage so that I wouldn't get wet. I pushed the overhead door open and for the first time saw the moon, hanging over the Hollywood hills like a lone white eye glaring defiantly down at California, daring it to do its worst. It was cold. That was one of the misconceptions I'd brought with me to the United States, that Los Angeles was always hot, that the sun always shone on the beautiful people. Not true—the Los Angeles climate was a desert one, and the temperature plummeted at night. Tourists were often taken by surprise at what a cold city LA was. Literally and metaphorically.

The car started on the third attempt, which was par for the course. It was a prime example of British motoring history, a 1966 Sunbeam Alpine Mark IV, 1750cc or thereabouts, bright red with a black soft top, left-hand drive because I bought it in the States. It leaked a bit when the rain was really bad, and parts were difficult to get when it went wrong, but it reminded me of England and I got more fun out of driving it than I ever did out of the American models. I liked the fact that it was old, too; there was something comforting about the feel of the wooden dashboard and steering wheel and the smell of the leather upholstery. There was a permanence about it; it had been around for almost half a century, and yet it was as good as new, inside and outside.

There wasn't much traffic around at that time of the night, so I was at the station within half an hour. I left the car in the captain's parking space because I was damn sure he'd be safe and warm at home in bed.

While I was driving the rain gave up its halfhearted attempt to soak the streets, though the lightning still flashed somewhere beyond the Hollywood hills.

The moon fixed me with its baleful one-eyed stare as I got out of the car. There was no point in locking it—not because it was parked by the side of a police station, but because the soft top was no deterrent to a thief. A quick slash with a switchblade and they'd be inside. Better to leave it unlocked so they could open it and see that there was nothing worth taking.

De'Ath was talking to two uniformed policemen in the main reception area. As usual, it was barely controlled bedlam, packed with sweating policemen, barking-mad drunks, petulant hookers, and surly teenagers, all of them shouting, swearing, and arguing in any number of languages. "Room F," he yelled at me over the din. "Name's Terry Ferriman."

"I suppose an arrest report is asking too much," I shouted back.

He grinned. "At this time in the morning, what d'ya expect?"

"Coffee?"

His grin widened. "I'll have one sent in. Black, no sugar?"

"That'll be the day," I answered. "White. Two sugars. Lawyer?"

De'Ath shook his head. "Perp hasn't requested one. There's a public defender around somewhere if we need one." He turned his back on me and returned to his conversation.

I picked up a visitor's badge from the main desk and clipped it to my top pocket as I edged between a tall blonde in purple hot pants and halter top and the gold-bedecked black guy in a silver suit that she was screaming at and pushed through the double doors leading to the corridor off which were the interview rooms. There was a line of identical green doors, each with a small observation window at head height, an oblong piece of glass reinforced with wire mesh. Each door had a letter stenciled on it, and F was about halfway along the corridor. I knocked once, and the door was opened by a uniformed woman officer, a blue-eyed brunette, and I thought then how strange it was that they were using a woman guard; then I stepped into the room and saw the girl sitting at a table. I was flustered, and I looked back at the door to check that I was in the right room. The guard saw my obvious confusion, and I said, "Terry Ferriman?" to her. Though I wasn't looking at the girl at the table, it was she who said yes, she was Terry. De'Ath was being a smart-ass, I realized, deliberately not telling me that the perp was a woman. Cancel that, she was hardly a woman—she was little more than a girl. I nodded at the guard, and she closed the door and then stood with her back to it, her arms folded across her chest. I sat down on another plastic chair and swung the briefcase onto the table. "My name is Dr. Beaverbrook," I said to the girl. "I'm a psychologist."

"Pleased to meetchya," she said. "I would shake hands, but, you know..." She shrugged, and I noticed for the first time that her hands were handcuffed in front of her. I took out a small digital recorder and a notebook from the briefcase.

"I'm going to record this interview—it's easier than making notes," I explained as I pressed the recording button.

"For sure," she said. She was wearing a gray tunic and trousers which I guessed the police had given her, which meant that her clothes had been sent to Forensics.

"Your name is Terry Ferriman?" I said, and she nodded. I smiled and tapped the recorder with my pen. "You have to say it out loud; it won't pick up nods."

"Oh right, yeah, for sure," she said, nodding her head. "Your accent is really neat. You're English, aren't you?"

I nodded. "How old are you?" I asked.

She grinned mischievously. "How old do I look?" she said, holding her chin up and shaking her head so that her long, dark hair swung from side to side, her jet-black eyes weighing me up. I'd have put her face at about fifteen, smooth white skin and gleaming Californian teeth. Her lipstick was smeared across her right cheek as if she'd wiped it roughly with the back of her hand. Her body I'd have put at eighteen, maybe nineteen. They'd obviously taken her underwear because when she shook her head I could see the ripple of her breasts under the tunic. She caught me looking at her chest and smiled. "How old do I look?" she asked again.

I felt my face redden, and before I could answer there was a bang on the door and the guard opened it to let in De'Ath carrying two cups of coffee, one in each hand, with a file under one arm. His teeth were clenched, and he grunted as he put both Styrofoam cups down on the table so hard that liquid spilled and pooled around them. "Yah! They're hot," he cursed. He waved his hands in the air and swore. He pointed at one of the cups. "That's yours, white and sweet, just like your good self," he said to me.

"Whereas yours is black and cool, I bet," I replied, and he laughed.

"Man, you are one slick Englishman," he said. "Almost makes me wish we never got our independence."

"Yeah, yeah, yeah," I said. "Can we get on with this, please?"

"Sure," said De'Ath. He looked over at the girl. "Professor Van Helsing introduced himself?" he asked her. "He's the man who's gonna tell us if you're sane or not, so be straight with him, d'ya hear?"

She nodded, wide-eyed.

"Has she been charged yet?" I asked him.

"It's coming," he said. "Paperwork's taking time. They're out in force tonight. When you've finished with her, there's a guy in room B who reckons that Satan told him to go and stick up a liquor store and shoot the owner's wife in the face." He leaned against the wall and sipped his coffee.

"Okay, I'll be along when I've finished here." I pressed the pause button on the digital recorder and sat and looked at him because there's no way I was going to start questioning the girl while he was there. He finally got the message and left us alone. Alone with the woman guard, that is.

"He called you Van Helsing." Terry said.

"It's his idea of a joke."

Her brow furrowed.

"Professor Van Helsing. The vampire hunter. The one that went after Dracula. In the book. By Bram Stoker."

"Oh, right, sure, yeah," she said, and her manacled hands went up to her mouth and touched the smear of lipstick. Except that I realized that it wasn't lipstick—it was dried blood. I started the recording again.

"Terry, I'm going to ask you some questions, okay? Just relax, they're not tricks—I'm not trying to catch you out or anything. Trust me, okay?"

"Sure. Fire away. Hit me with your best shot."

"What day is it, Terry?"

"Friday."

"What month?"

"August."

"What year were you born?"

She smiled. "What is this, *Wheel of Fortune*?" she asked.

"Just help me out, Terry. Answer the questions and then I can go home to my bed. When were you born?"

"Twenty-five years ago," she said. "Or thereabouts." She was a lot older than she looked.

"Who is the president of the United States?"

"Don't know, don't care. I never vote—it only encourages them." She giggled and put her hands up to her mouth again. There was dried blood on her hands, too.

"What's the capital of the United States?"

She grinned. "Los Angeles," she said. She watched me scribble her answer in my notebook and held up her hand, waving it to stop me. "I was joking, Jamie. Okay? I was joking. Washington is the real capital. Washington DC."

I sat back in the chair and gave her a stern look. Or tried to anyway. She wasn't supposed to be using my first name. It didn't show the proper respect, you know? "This is serious, Terry," I said.

"Oh, for sure," she sighed. "For sure it is." She leaned forward and looked at me intensely with her jet-black eyes. "The black guy, now he's serious, Jamie. He's trying to bring me real grief, but you? You, Jamie, you're a pussycat." She smiled and winked. "Fire away."

"Can you name three cities beginning with the letter D?"

"Detroit, Dallas, Durham."

"Durham?"

"Yeah, Durham. It's in England."

"I know, it's just a strange city to think of, that's all." She shrugged.

"Have you been there?" I asked.

"Oh, sure," she sighed, and I wasn't sure if she was joking or not.

"What's your favorite food?"

"Are you hitting on me?" she said coyly.

"No," I said.

"Lasagna. What's the point of these questions?"

"They help me assess your state of mind. What was the last film you saw?"

She looked up at the ceiling, thinking. There was dried blood on the underside of her chin, a thin streak as if she'd run a bloody finger gently along it and left behind a trail. She lowered her eyes and caught me staring at her neck. "TV or movie?" she asked.

"Doesn't matter."

"*Casablanca.*"

"What's your favorite color?"

She looked down at her gown. "Well it shitfire sure ain't gray," she said. "Black, maybe. Yeah, I like black."

"Which weighs the most—a pound of coal or a pound of feathers?"

"Shoot, Jamie, we did that one at school. They're the same."

"Which would you rather have, a dog or a cat?"

"Neither."

"You don't like animals?"

She shrugged. "Don't like, don't dislike. Neutral."

"Do you know why you're here?"

"Yes."

I waited, but she didn't expand on her answer; she just sat back and looked at me. "Will you tell me why you think you're here?"

"They, like, think I killed a man."

"And did you?"

"Are you a psychologist or a detective?"

"Fair point," I replied. "How do you feel?"

"About being here?" I nodded. "Scared, I guess. Confused. A bit, like, angry. Yeah, angry, for sure."

"Why haven't you asked for a lawyer?"

"I haven't done anything wrong."

I asked her a few more general knowledge and current affairs questions, and then I switched off the digital recorder and put my pen in the inside pocket of my jacket. "Okay, Terry. That's it. I told you it'd be painless."

"Is that all?"

"That's the first bit over." I picked up my briefcase, opened it, and took out my MacBook and switched it on. It asked me for my password, and I typed it in.

"Okay," I said. I moved my chair next to hers and swiveled the computer around so that we could both see the screen. I looked up at the guard and asked her if she'd take the cuffs off Terry.

"I'll have to check," she said and went out, to look for De'Ath I guess and to get his blessing.

"You really should ask for a lawyer," I said to Terry.

She shrugged. "I haven't done anything," she said. "I mean, like, it's their problem, not mine, you know? Their mistake. I'll be back on the streets before you know it. I'm cool, you know?"

"I can recommend a good lawyer. If you change your mind."

She smiled and nodded. "Thanks, Jamie. But no thanks."

The guard came back with two uniformed officers, which I reckoned was piling it on a bit thick because the girl was showing no signs of aggression and she certainly wasn't on angel dust or anything else that was going to give her the strength of ten men, or even one. One of the men stood by the door, his hand on the gun in his holster. The female guard unlocked Terry's handcuffs while her companion went and stood behind us.

Terry massaged her wrists.

"Better?" I asked.

"Yeah, thanks. What do you want me to do?"

"Okay, this is just another test, just like the questions I asked you before, except this time they're on this screen. All you have to do is to make choices."

"Multiple choice questions?"

"That's right, just like you did at school. Each question will give you a choice of two answers, yes or no. You use the mouse to indicate your choice." I showed her how to use the mouse, and she nodded. I pressed the start button, and a single line of type flashed up on the screen.

"I prefer cold weather to hot weather," it said. "This is an example," I explained. "If you prefer cold weather to hot weather, you indicate yes. If you prefer hot weather, you indicate no. It's as easy as that. The machine will ask you five hundred questions. Some of them will be very straightforward like this one, and others might seem a little strange. But you must answer yes or no.

You can't pass or say both, or neither. You must pick the answer that is closest to the way you feel."

She nodded, her eyes fixed on the screen.

"There's no time limit, but try to answer the questions as quickly as possible. You must concentrate. No daydreaming, okay?"

She looked at me with her unblinking black eyes and grinned. "For sure, Jamie, it's no great intellectual challenge, is it? How do I, like, start?"

"I'll do it," I said. "You ready?"

She nodded, and I set the program running and moved my chair away to let her get on with it. I leaned back in my chair and watched her deal with the questions. She crouched forward slightly, her jet-black hair falling across her face. She seemed at ease with the mouse, and her eyes remained fixed on the screen. The clicks of the mouse being depressed were fairly evenly spaced, three seconds at the most. Five hundred questions, three seconds a go, one thousand five hundred seconds in all. Twenty-five minutes.

When she finished she looked up at me and held up her hands like a child showing that they were clean.

"Finished," she said in a singsong voice. "Did you make up all the questions?"

"Most of them," I answered.

She shook her head from side to side and sighed. "You are one weird dude," she said. "Totally, totally weird."

"What did you find strange?" I asked as I pulled the computer toward my side of the desk.

"The ones about, like, death. And killing. And the fact that every question was asked twice, but, like, in reverse. Why was that?"

16

"To check that your answers are consistent," I said. That's what I told her, but that was only part of the reason. The time difference between the question being flashed on the screen and the mouse being pressed was also important. It gives a clue as to how much thought is being put into the answer, or how much confusion it has caused. And the time taken to deal with the same question when asked in reverse is even more significant. That's what the computer program does, compares the answers and the time intervals with profiles of more than a thousand case histories. And then it gives me the information I need to make a judgment on her sanity.

"To check that I'm not lying?" she said.

"Something like that," I said. "But if you've done nothing wrong, Terry, you've nothing to worry about."

"Have you finished, sir?" the female guard asked me, and when I said I had, she pulled the girl's arms behind her and handcuffed her again.

"Does she have to be handcuffed all the time?" I asked.

"It's procedure, sir," she answered.

I stored Terry's answers in a new case file and then ran a sorting program through them. It flashed "WORKING" for a minute or so, and then the word "DONE" came up. It only took a few minutes, but the program represented more than ten years of my life. I'd started the research as part of a post-doctorate project trying to come up with a computerized version of the Rorschach inkblot test. I got myself into a dead end on that one, and I'd switched to the more easily computerized question-and-answer psychological evaluation systems, such as the Cattell Sixteen Personality Factor Questionnaire and the Graduate and Managerial Assessment system. In the past, interpretation of the tests required a hell of lot of experience, and the results were as much down to the examiner as to the person taking the tests. That's where the Beaverbrook Program scored: by allowing the computer to grade the results, it did away with the personal foibles of the guy doing the interpretation. I did a couple of papers on the computerization possibilities, and they were well received. I managed to attract extra funding from a couple of mental health charities, and I went on to the second stage of the research—developing a subsidiary program which would assess the validity and reliability of the individual tests. The normal way of testing was to repeat the tests, or variations of them, on several occasions and then to compare the results and run them through a standard error of measurement equation. What I was trying to do, though, was to come up with a one-off evaluation system, something that would act as a sort of litmus test, an instantaneous verdict: sane or insane. I eventually came up with a variation of the Spearman-Brown Prophecy Formula which took the results of one test and effectively split them in half and treated them as if coming from parallel tests. It took the world of psychometrics by storm, I can tell you, and lost me a lot of friends. No one likes to be told that a computer can do their job faster and more efficiently, especially psychologists with twenty years of clinical experience.

I asked for the results in graph form, and the screen cleared and then horizontal and vertical lines sprouted from the bottom left-hand corner followed by diagonal wavy lines that represented the parameters within which previous cases suggested normal personalities would lie. A small flashing star marked Terry's profile. Dead center. This girl was more stable than I was.

"Am I, like, okay?" she asked.

I smiled. "You're fine, Terry."

She grinned. "Can you do me a favor now?"

"Depends what you want," I told her.

She nodded her head sideways, indicating her arms handcuffed behind the chair. "Can you get them to take these off me? They hurt, for sure, and my nose, like, itches."

"I'll try," I said, getting to my feet and picking up the briefcase. "I'll ask De'Ath."

"Don't go yet," she said. "Scratch my nose for me first. Please."

"Are you serious?"

"You don't know how shitfire serious, Jamie. It itches like you wouldn't believe."

She smiled and nodded, looking earnestly at me like a dog asking for a bone. I sighed and reached over and scratched her slowly on the tip of the nose. She groaned quietly, her eyes closed.

The door banged open, and I flinched. "You finished?" De'Ath asked.

I felt my cheeks go red because I was sure he'd seen me touching her and there was a supercilious smirk on his face.

"Yeah, I'm done," I said. I nodded at Terry and went to the door, which De'Ath held open for me.

"Jamie?" she said, and I looked back at her.

"Thanks," she said, and winked at me.

De'Ath followed me out into the corridor. "Well?" he asked.

"She seems fine to me," I said. "Though it might have been a help if you'd told me beforehand that she was a girl."

He laughed. "I must've forgotten," he said. "Sorry 'bout that."

"What did she do, Samuel?"

"Stabbed a guy in the heart. Then slashed his throat. When we found her she was crouched over him, lapping at the blood. We haven't found the murder weapon yet, but it won't be long. And what we don't want is for her to spring some vampire story on us, you know. Now, is she sane or not?"

"As sane as you or I," I said. "Or at least as sane as I am. You I'm not sure about."

"That's all I need to know, Doc."

"And Samuel?"

"Yeah?"

"Don't tell people that my name is Van Helsing. It's not funny."

"You know what your problem is, Beaverbrook? You have no sense of humor, that's what."

"From you, dumb shit, I take that as a compliment. Now who's this other guy you want me to see?"

De'Ath took the file from under his arm and opened it. "Name's Kipp, Henry Kipp. Six priors, five of them armed robbery. He's..."

"Come on, De'Ath," I interrupted, "you know you're not supposed to give me information like that. I'm only supposed to make my judgments on the basis..."

"Okay, okay, stay calm, man. Forget what I said."

"You're always pulling dumb stunts like that, so don't tell me to forget it," I said. "These people deserve a fair hearing, and for that I have to be completely impartial."

Our argument was cut short by the swinging doors being banged open and a gruff voice echoing down the corridor. "Well if it isn't Batman and Robin."

I turned to see a barrel-chested, white-haired man in a dark blue suit, his cheeks flaring red. Captain Eric Canonico. Not one of my greatest fans. He pointed at me and yelled at me with his head slightly back, his booming voice echoing off the walls of the corridor. "And who the fuck gave you permission to park in my spot, Beaverbrook? Who the fuck told you to leave the Batmobile in my parking space?"

"I didn't think you'd be in this late, Captain," I said.

"Yeah, well you thought wrong, Batman. But it's not the first time you've been wrong, is it? Now get that pile of shit out of my space and park it somewhere else."

He lowered his accusing finger and transferred his fiery gaze to De'Ath. "Has Mr. Wonderful here seen the girl?"

"Yes, Cap'n."

"And?"

"She's okay."

"So have you started the interrogation yet?"

"Just about to, Cap'n."

"And the victim?"

"No ID. No wallet. Stripped clean. We're running his prints through the computer and checking missing persons."

"Keep me informed. I'll be in my office."

The doors banged shut, but Canonico's presence lingered in the corridor for a few seconds like a bad smell.

"He's never forgiven you, has he?" asked De'Ath.

"Never has, never will. What room's Kipp in?"

"B. What do you think of the girl then?"

"Young. Pretty. Innocent."

"You, man, would never make a cop."

"De'Ath, I wouldn't want to. Not in a million years. By the way, she wants the cuffs off."

"Procedure, Doc. She's in on suspicion of homicide, and a nasty one at that. The cuffs stay on till we're sure she's safe. All you can tell me is if she's sane or not, not if she's likely to scratch my eyes out with her fingers. Leave her to the professionals. And save your pity for the victims."

"Why the blood?"

"Blood?"

"On her mouth. And her hands. I thought you said Forensics had been over her?"

"They have, swabs and scrapings and samples. They're down at the lab now."

"So why hasn't she been cleaned up?"

"Man, this is a police station, not a dry cleaner's. She can wash up later; right now I've a homicide to investigate. You concentrate on Mr. Kipp. After you've moved the Batmobile."

"Don't call it that, De'Ath. I hate it when you do that."

De'Ath's laughter boomed around the corridor as he knocked on the door to the room where Terry sat. When it opened I saw her over De'Ath's shoulder. She looked up and smiled weakly at me, and then the door closed, blotting her out.

I went outside and moved my car and then went to see Henry Kipp. He was as sane as I am, possibly saner. He'd gone into a drugstore on Olympic Boulevard run by an old Polish couple. He'd clubbed the old man over the head with the butt of his sawed-off shotgun, then taken a couple of hundred dollars from the cash register. The woman had begun crying, and Kipp had forced the twin barrels of the gun into her mouth and told her to stop. Then he blew her head off.

"The voices told me to do it." Kipp laughed, showing a mouthful of bad teeth.

"What sort of voices?"

"Devils," he said. "Devils in my head. They tell me what to do."

"Male voices or female voices?"

"Male."

"Like your father?"

"I never heard my old man's voice. Long gone before I wuz born."

He had closely cropped hair and a nose that had been broken so many times that it was almost flat against his face. His hands were square with nails bitten to the quick, strong hands that he kept making into fists as he tapped away at the mouse. He banged it so hard that it rattled, and he ground his teeth as he answered the five hundred questions. He breathed through his nose, the heavy snorting of a wild animal. But he was sane, the program said. Aggressive, amoral, cruel, and as nasty a piece of humankind as you're ever likely to meet, but sane. Sane according to the Beaverbrook Model, which at that stage was all that mattered. He was, without a shadow of a doubt, lying about the voices. Some amateur lawyer he met up with doing a previous spell in the slammer had probably told him that insanity was a good defense, but the manic laugh and the staring eyes didn't fool the program. When I ran it, the blinking star that represented Kipp's psyche was well within the boundaries of what the court accepted as sane. A bit lower and to the left of Terry's, but sane nonetheless.

The door to room F was closed when I went back down the corridor, and I stopped and put my ear to the wood and listened. I could hear De'Ath but not clearly enough to tell what he was saying. I left him to it.

The storm was all but over when I left the station and climbed into my car. As I started the engine, I saw that someone had hung a small rubber bat from my aerial. It was probably De'Ath. Canonico didn't have that sort of a sense of humor. He would have broken the aerial off and slashed my tires—that was more his style. I let the bat wave in the wind all the way home.

THE NIGHTMARE

The alley was dark, so dark you wouldn't believe it. It was narrow, so narrow that if I were to put my arms out to the sides like a crucified man my fingers would touch both walls. I looked up and the walls seemed to go on forever, so high that they seemed to meet in the air miles above. I couldn't see the sky, not even a strip of star-studded blackness, and I couldn't see the moon, but I knew it was up there somewhere, lurking like a hunting leopard. There was a scuffling sound somewhere up ahead, but I couldn't see anything. In the distance I heard the whoop-whoop of a siren, and I turned around to look back along the way I'd walked, but I'd come so far that I couldn't see the streetlights anymore. The scuffling was repeated, as if a rat was rooting through a trash can. The floor was uneven and littered with rusting tins and rotting fast-food containers, and here and there were puddles of dirty water. I moved slowly down the alley, holding my hands out in front of me because I was worried that I might walk into something: something cold and clammy. There was a ripping noise, the sound of material being torn by impatient hands, and then something whacked against my legs and clung to them like a pleading child. I jumped back, but it stuck to me; I kicked out, but still it wouldn't let go. I reached down to grab it, and my hands met wet paper. It was a newspaper, blown down the alley by the midnight wind. I shivered and pulled away the scraps of wet paper, crumpling them up into waterlogged balls and throwing them to the side.

I could hear a slurping noise, the sound of an animal drinking. No, not drinking. Lapping. Like a cat feeding from a saucer of milk. Lap, lap, lap. My trousers had become damp below my knees where the wet paper had stuck to the material and rivulets of water trickled down to my ankles. I moved toward the noise, peering into the blackness, but all I could see were the trash cans and the untidily stacked cardboard boxes waiting to be collected. High up above me I heard a window grate open and then slam shut, but when I looked up there was nothing there, just two sheer, blank walls.

Ahead of me I could finally make out a shape, a gray lump on the floor like a man in a sitting position, legs sticking out, bent at the waist, head slumped against his chest, the slurping noise coming from his throat as if he was having trouble breathing. I wanted to speak, to ask if he was okay, if he needed help, but the words wouldn't come and I walked forward. As I drew closer I realized I wasn't looking at one form but two, one lying down on the ground, the other crouched over him, with its back to me. I moved to the side, and I saw the figure on the ground—I assumed it was a man, but there was no way of telling for sure because it was just a shape—with its legs pointing in my direction, one arm flung out to the side, the other obscured by whatever it was that was kneeling over him. The slurping was louder. It sounded less like a cat feeding and more like two lovers kissing, soft, wet, squelchy sounds and swallowing noises, the sound of flesh against flesh.

Something within me wanted to cry out, to try to stop whatever was happening on the floor of the alley, but I wanted to see exactly what was going on. I wanted to get closer. The two shapes became clearer as I moved toward them. The figure on the floor was lying on its back. It was a man, wearing a suit of some dark material and shiny black shoes. His socks were dark but sprinkled with white triangles. The material around the knees of the trousers was torn as if he'd been dragged along the ground. The shape looming over his neck was wearing a glossy leather jacket with the collar turned up and jeans that could have been blue or black, and boots with silver tips on the toes. The heels of the boots were clearly visible because the figure was on its knees, bending over the head of the man in the suit.

The snuffling noises stopped suddenly, and the shoulders of the kneeling figure stiffened as if aware that I was watching. Its head began to turn slowly. I tried to move away, but my feet seemed to be fixed, as if they'd sprouted roots that had wormed their way into the ground and were holding me fast. I saw a cheek first, alabaster white, a smooth curve from the eye to the chin, and then a curtain of hair swung across and that was all I could see as the head continued to turn. And then, as the figure began to rise and turn at the same time, only then did I see her face. Terry. She was wearing a black leather motorcycle jacket zipped up to her neck, steel zips running at an angle across her chest and others marking where the pockets must have been. She smiled up at me and raised her right hand to her mouth. There was a streak of something along her right cheek, something wet that glistened as she moved, and her fingers touched it, rubbed it, and then carried it to her lips. Slowly and sensuously she licked her fingers with the tip of her tongue, one by one. I couldn't take my eyes off her, and she smiled as if she knew how firmly I was trapped. I was in her power. Totally.

"I knew you'd come," she said, and she took another step forward. For the first time I could see the head of the man lying on the floor. His mouth was wide open as if he had been trying to scream, but I doubted that any sound would have managed to pass the drawn-back lips because the throat had been ripped messily open as if the flesh had been hacked and gouged with a dull knife. Or teeth. He looked dead, his eyes blank and lifeless, but there was blood pooling in the hollow of his throat and it bubbled and frothed as if he was trying to breathe through what was left of his windpipe.

"Look at me, Jamie," she whispered, and I found myself doing as she asked. "Forget him. He's nothing." She licked her fingers again and then reached forward and pressed them to my lips.

They tasted salty and vaguely metallic. She stood up against me so that her jacket brushed against my chest. I hadn't realized until that moment how short she was. The top of her head barely reached my chin, and she had to tilt her head back to see my face, the action stretching the skin taut across her cheekbones and making her look impossibly young, a child with a smeared face. "You have to want to give yourself to me, Jamie. You have to want it deep within your soul. That's the way it works. You have to offer yourself. Nothing less. Do you understand?"

I nodded, my heart pounding in my ears. *Durr-rum, durr-rum, durr-rum.* She pushed her middle finger between my lips and gently rubbed it along my teeth as if daring me to bite.

She raised herself up on her toes, tilted her head to one side, and pressed her lips against my neck, just below my left ear where I could feel a vein pulsing in time to the rhythm of my heart. She kissed me softly, and I felt her tongue probe the skin. It rasped along my flesh as if it were the tongue of a cat and not that of a girl, and then she shifted her head back as if waiting for something. "Once bitten," she said, and I could feel her breath with each word. Then she lunged forward, sharp teeth fixing onto my neck like a cheetah going in for the kill.

I jerked back my head involuntarily, and my eyes opened; I was in my bedroom, my legs tangled up in the quilt, the pillows scattered on the floor. My skin was bathed in sweat, yet my mouth was dry and swallowing was an effort. I staggered to the bathroom and filled a glass full of water. I used the first mouthful to swirl, rolling it around my tongue and spitting it out into the washbasin. I switched on the light above the bathroom mirror and looked at my reflection. Bleary eyes stared back at me, deep-set and worried, small red veins flecked through the whites, the pupils dilated as if I'd taken something. I hadn't. I opened my mouth wide and pulled back the skin on my face. It made me look younger. I relaxed, and the wrinkles and the years came back. Thirty-five going on fifty. I moved my head from side to side half expecting to see bites, but the skin was unmarked. I rubbed my hand across my chin, feeling the stubble of growing hair. I could remember when all I had to do was to borrow my father's electric razor to shave the fuzz on my upper lip about once a month, then once a week, then daily. But it was only in recent years that the stubble would appear in the middle of the night. A sign of being an adult, I guess. A sign of age. Now if I was going anywhere in the evening I looked scruffy unless I shaved again.

I took another mouthful of water and gargled with it, and when I looked down to spit it out I saw that the first mouthful was red. Blood red. I turned on the taps, and it swirled away down the plughole; the second time I spat it was clear, just water and phlegm. I checked out my mouth in the mirror and couldn't see any cuts or abrasions. Just teeth and metal fillings. Another sign of a decaying body. I filled my mouth and spat again, but there was no more blood.

I took a glass of water back with me to the bedroom and lay down on my side, facing away from the window, and tried to get back to sleep. Images of the girl and the alley kept filling my mind, her smile, her eyes, and the blood. I could hear my own heartbeat in my right ear, which was pressed against the pillow. *Durr-rum, durr-rum, durr-rum.* The sound of my lifeblood coursing around the veins and arteries of my body, the tubes that were already silting up with cholesterol and fat globules and all the rest of the detritus that was floating around in my tissues. *Durr-rum, durr-rum, durr-rum.* The constant reminder of my own mortality, a fist-sized hunk of tissue in the center of my chest upon which my whole being depended. Without its seventy-odd squirts of oxygenated blood every minute there would be no more Jamie Beaverbrook. I wondered what it must be like to have a heart attack, to feel the pump splutter and jerk and stop, and to know that the end was coming, that the brain was being starved of life-giving oxygen and that it would soon all be over. The empty blackness stretching ahead forevermore. No more Jamie Beaverbrook.

The train of thought depressed me, as it always did. The morbid thoughts of my own mortality usually came at night, when I was alone in the dark. I shifted my head to try to get my ear off the pillow so that I wouldn't have to listen to my accusing heart counting off the beats that represented the time I had left. Seventy beats a minute, forty-two hundred every hour, one hundred thousand or so every day. What was that a year? More than thirty-five million beats. So how many did I have left if I lived for fifty more years? I did the sums in my head, and it came to about 1.8

billion. *Durr-rum*, minus one. *Durr-rum*, minus two. *Durr-rum*, minus three. This wasn't like counting sheep and easing myself into sleep—this was chipping away at my life bit by bit, alone in a double bed, and the thought filled me with cold dread.

I moved my head again, and this time I felt my right shoulder grate as my arm moved in the socket, the sign of cartilage wearing thin from too many games of tennis and squash. It never used to make that noise, the sound of bone against bone, or maybe it was only recently that I'd noticed it. The cartilage in my knees made cracking noises when I got up, and occasionally my hips would pop if I turned suddenly. *Please God,* I prayed, *don't let me get old, and don't let me die. Let me stay as I am right now. Or if you're feeling extra merciful, let me stay as I was five years ago, when I was in my prime. When I was young.* I took a deep breath, and I could hear the air rushing down into my lungs; when I breathed out it made a wheezing noise like the wind whistling through the branches of a dying tree. What must it be like, I thought, to stop breathing? That was the way people usually went when they died, I guess—the lungs stopped functioning first, then the heart, and only then would the brain start to realize that it wasn't getting freshly oxygenated blood like it was supposed to, like it had been for the past God knows how many millions of heartbeats. Would the body panic, or would it go quietly and surrender peacefully to the infinite oblivion?

I tossed and turned, but I couldn't sleep—not because I wasn't tired but because dark, depressing thoughts kept slipping into my mind and pushing out everything else. Thoughts of sickness, of aging, of death. I switched on the television at the foot of the bed and watched a detective show where two young women private eyes in expensive convertibles cornered a drug ring and survived two car chases and a shoot-out without smudging their makeup. It depressed me even more, so I went to the kitchen and got myself a Budweiser and drank it in bed, propped up with pillows because I didn't want to lie down and listen to my heartbeat anymore.

THE APARTMENT

I don't remember falling asleep, but I must have done because the next thing I remembered was waking up with my neck at a painful angle on the pillow and two empty bottles of Budweiser on the bedside table. The television was on, and a blonde with too much lipstick was telling me that there had been seven murders in downtown Los Angeles and the police were expecting more, what with it being a full moon and all. It was seven o'clock in the morning, an hour or so before I normally got up, but I showered, shaved, and dressed and sat down at my desk with a cup of coffee and a couple of apples. My briefcase was on the desktop where I'd left it the night before, and I opened it and took out my MacBook. I normally write up my reports in my office, but I wanted to make an early start because it wasn't going to be too long before the phone rang, not if there had been seven homicides overnight. I was one of four psychologists employed by the LAPD, but one was in the hospital having her breasts lifted and another had gone skiing in Aspen, which meant double the workload for me and the other guy left behind, Anton Rivron.

The department insisted that all homicide suspects were examined by a psychologist as soon as possible, and had done since the early nineties. It was supposed to be in the interests of justice and all that fair play crap, but it was little more than a cost-saving exercise. There was no point in mounting a full homicide investigation if the perp turned out to be insane. It was far easier, and cheaper, to set the shrinks on him and have him locked away in a secure mental institution and throw away the key rather than trying to pin down a motive and opportunity and all that sort of stuff they do on television. And if the perp wasn't mad, then it was important to get a psychologist's report on him in the file right from the start of the investigation, so that when the homicide detectives had finally put a case together the defense didn't simply try to con the jury into believing that the perp had been temporarily a few sandwiches short of a picnic.

It used to happen a lot—perps would sit in their cells and wait until the Homicide boys had put together a watertight case, and then they'd start talking to themselves and rolling their eyes or claim to have amnesia or any one of a dozen tricks that they thought would get them out of prison and into a mental hospital where they'd stay until they could either persuade the authorities they were cured or they could manage to escape. And the waiting was a hell of lot more comfortable in a hospital than it was in a high-security prison.

What the department needed was someone who could make a snap, but accurate, decision on the mental stability or otherwise of suspects, which would tell the detectives the best way of proceeding with the case. They'd headhunted me from England to set up the system and recruit the three psychologists who worked with me on a consultancy basis. I'd been working at the University of London on a computer system which could assess a person's sanity and compare it with models of various mental disorders. I'd first got interested in the field after following the work of

Professor David Carter at the University of Sussex, whom the British police called up whenever they had a serial killer or multiple rapist they couldn't catch. He'd come up with a way of drawing psychological profiles on computers based on the clues found by police. By giving the police the profile of the man they should be looking for, he made their job a hell of a lot easier. I started to get interested in what happened at the other end of the investigation, after they'd been caught. For my doctorate I developed computer models of various mental disorders and criminal tendencies based on the better part of a thousand interviews I carried out in prisons and mental hospitals in the United Kingdom, and then I began working on a computer program which from simple questions and answers could be used to ascertain a person's mental state. It took many years of work, but eventually I worked it up to the point where it could be used with a considerable degree of accuracy. I produced several well-received scientific papers and went on a couple of lecture tours, and then one day I got a phone call from the London office of an American headhunting firm. Three months later I was in Los Angeles earning five times what I had been paid as a post-doctorate researcher.

The move to Los Angeles made a lot of sense, both from a personal point of view—I'd always been an Americophile—but also because it was the perfect place to research into sociopaths and psychopaths and a host of other mental abnormalities. Put simply, there were more lunatics per square mile in Los Angeles than anywhere else on God's green earth, and I reckoned that while drawing an obscenely high salary I'd also be able to churn out a fair number of research papers. That's the way it worked out, too. Mind you, there was a downside. I lost my daughter, and my wife left me, and she set a lawyer on me who had all the sympathy of a rottweiler with an exceptionally low IQ. And I picked up a nickname. Jamie D. Beaverbrook, Vampire Hunter. Don't you just love America?

The nickname came about because the first case the LAPD gave me was a homeless guy in his sixties who had strangled another homeless man during an argument over the ownership of a supermarket trolley. The guy was claiming that voices had told him to do it, but the program pronounced him sane. As a detective was taking him back to a holding cell, the homeless guy attacked him and bit a chunk out of his ear and started screaming that he was Dracula and that I was Van Helsing. I ran him through the program a second time just to be sure, and the guy *was* sane—albeit with a major alcohol and drug problem—but from then on pretty much the entire LAPD blamed me for the detective's mangled ear.

I did the Kipp report first and printed it out on the laser printer. I slotted the sheets into a blue cardboard folder and wrote "Kipp, H." on it and then went and got another cup of coffee from the kitchen. I put the cup on the desk, and then I went to fetch the morning paper. I sat on the sofa and begin to read it, and then I realized that my subconscious was playing for time, trying to defer the moment when I'd start to put together the report on Ferriman, T. Why was that, I wondered. Because she was so pretty? So young? Because she looked so helpless, and yet, at the same time, so in control of herself?

I flipped the paper closed and sat back at the desk. I called up her file on the computer and went through the answers she'd given. They were the answers you'd expect from any well-balanced young woman—not too aggressive, not too self-centered. The sort of girl who'd make a good friend or lover. It took me twice as long to finish the report on her than I'd taken over Kipp. It wasn't that she was a more complicated case—it was more that

I was finding myself trying to always portray her in a good light, then realizing that it might look as if I was being biased in her favor, so I'd go the other way and be too hard on her. The whole point of the Beaverbrook Program was that it was supposed to take the emotion out of the judgment. The verdict should be totally objective, and it almost always was, yet in her case I was having to constantly force myself to be neutral. And all the time the image of her in my mind was the girl in the alley in the black leather jacket, her lips against my neck. No, I didn't mention the dream in my report. Once bitten…

I was printing it out when the phone rang. It was De'Ath calling, wanting to know how I was getting on.

"Just finished," I said, and I held the receiver by the side of the laser printer so that he could hear for himself. "How's the investigation?"

"Which one?" he said, though he knew full well that I wouldn't be asking about Henry Kipp, Esq.

"The girl," I said.

"Yeah, the girl," he said. "To be honest, Doc, it ain't going so well."

"I thought you said it was open and shut."

"Yeah, didn't I just? We got the report back from Forensics, and it was his blood on her face and hands, no doubt about it. But there was no blood on her clothes. Yet he was covered in it. He'd been stabbed in the chest and slashed about the throat; there should have been red stuff all over her. And there's still no sign of a murder weapon."

"What's her story?"

"Now she's saying that she found him in the alley and was trying to give him the kiss of life. Can you believe that? Blood streaming from his throat and she's trying to give him the kiss of life!"

"Who was the guy?"

"Still waiting to hear from the bag 'em and tag 'em boys. They're gonna take his prints and run them through the computer. Look, Doc, I wanna see her report as soon as possible."

"No sweat, but I don't think it's going to be of much help. She's not a crazy—far from it."

"Yeah, yeah, I'm sure. Can you bring it around?"

"Half an hour, is that okay?"

De'Ath groaned. "Oh, man, can't you come by now? Look, I tell you what, we've just got a warrant to go and check out her place—why don't you meet us there. Anytime after ten, okay?"

I agreed eagerly, too eagerly maybe, but I was intrigued by the girl, and I thought that a visit to her home might provide some sort of insight that I wouldn't get from simply talking to her. I finished the printing, put on a tie, and was outside her apartment block by ten thirty.

It was a four-story modern block on North Alta Vista, close to Sunset Boulevard and, I realized, fairly close to where she'd been discovered kneeling over the body. I recognized De'Ath's car parked outside, and I walked up the stairs rather than taking the lift to prove to myself that I was in good condition. I was out of breath when I reached the top floor, so I stood in the hallway until I felt better and then rang the bell. De'Ath's partner, Dennis Filbin, a bulky Irishman with a drinker's nose, opened the door, grunted, and let me in.

"Don't touch anything," he growled. He was wearing latex gloves and so was De'Ath, who came out of the bedroom with a worried look on his face.

"Don't touch anything," said De'Ath.

"I already told him," said Filbin.

"He already told me," I said. "You found anything?"

"Makeup, a teddy bear, closets full of clothes. She don't appear to have no bad habits." He sounded disappointed.

"You sound disappointed," I said. "Mind if I look around?"

"Help yourself. Just don't touch anything."

"Can I have a pair of gloves?" I asked him.

"If you don't touch anything, you won't need gloves," De'Ath snarled. "Have you got the report?"

"I've got both—Kipp and her." I handed the reports to him and looked around as he and Filbin read through them. The apartment was small: a lounge with a small kitchenette leading off it, and a bedroom with space for a double bed, a dressing table, and little else. Her clothes were in closets which were built into the wall opposite the bed, and I used a pencil to push one of the doors open. There were lots of clothes hanging up: dresses, jackets, skirts, blouses, mostly cheap and cheerful stuff, the kind you'd expect to find in any young girl's bedroom. There were three framed posters on the wall, all of them movie posters: *Total Recall*, *Gone with the Wind*, and *Bambi*. Eclectic taste, no doubt about it.

There was a fluffy toy rabbit on the dressing table and a black-and-white photograph in an antique gilt frame. I bent down to look at the picture; it was of a young man sitting in a director's chair, obviously taken on a film set because in the background were cameras and lights and a tangle of thick, black wires. The man was in his early twenties, clean shaven with his hair swept back, black and glistening as if it had been oiled. He was looking over one shoulder and smiling as if he knew the photograph would end up in a girl's bedroom. It was a movie star smile, gleaming teeth and sincere eyes. On the back of the chair was the name of the film. *Lilac Time*. And below those words was the name of the star. It was an old photograph, and the cameras in the background seemed to belong to the golden age of moviemaking, maybe before sound, even. To the right of the picture, adjusting one of the lights on a massive tripod, was a man dressed in baggy trousers and a checked shirt wearing a cap like Jimmy Cagney used to wear in his old gangster movies.

I wondered if Terry was a movie buff who liked to collect mementos of old movies, but apart from the three framed prints and the photograph there were no other collectibles around. Perhaps the man in the photograph was a relative. Father perhaps? No, that couldn't be right because her name was Ferriman. Unless she'd changed it. If the man was in his twenties and the picture had been taken, say, in the 1930s, then he'd be in his eighties now. Grandfather perhaps?

"Whatchya looking at?" asked De'Ath's voice from behind me. I straightened up. My spine clicked as I did. It had started to do that a lot recently. Arthritis setting in, I bet.

"The photograph," I said. "A relation, maybe?"

"Yeah, maybe. We've about finished here; you'll have to make tracks."

"Okay, give me a minute or two, will you?"

The bed was covered with a thick, peach-colored quilt, and only one pillow had an indentation in it. For some reason I felt pleasantly pleased that Terry Ferriman appeared to sleep alone. I followed De'Ath back into the lounge. There was a small LED television, a hi-fi, a three-seater black leather sofa, and a matching easy chair. The carpet was short-piled, gray, and featureless, and the walls were white and bare. No pictures, no photographs. There were some books on black metal shelves which ran the full length of one wall, and there were black blinds over the two windows. The blinds were down but open so that lines of sunlight cut through the room and drew bright oblong shapes on the floor. There was a black metal and smoked glass coffee table in front of the sofa, and on top of it were a couple of fashion magazines. De'Ath was right—there was nothing there. No bloodstained knife, no pile of bloody clothes, no manuals on how to be a successful murderer. I could see why he was so disappointed.

The kitchenette was white and spotless and looked as if it had never been used. There was a cooker, a microwave, a small fridge-freezer, and a double stainless-steel sink. There was a toaster, an electric kettle, and a scrubbed wood knife rack in which were slotted black-handled knives. Everything was gleaming. Pristine. As if she'd never cooked there.

De'Ath saw me looking at the clean, white surfaces. "Looks like she eats out a lot," he said. "There's only wine and some fizzy water in the fridge."

"Nothing unusual about that," I said. "You'll find precious little to eat in my fridge." Funny how I kept wanting to make excuses for her. "Nice place," I said.

"Yeah, compact," he said. "Bit small for me, but I guess a girl on her own would be quite happy here."

"Samuel, you know there's a knife missing from the rack?"

"Yeah," he said. "We noticed that."

"No toothpicks," said Filbin as he came out of the bathroom.

"Toothpicks?" I said.

"We found a toothpick stuck in the shoelaces of the victim," explained Filbin. "And there weren't any in his pockets. Could be from the perp."

They took me out into the hall, and Filbin locked the door. While we waited for the elevator, I asked De'Ath where he was going next.

"Office," he said. "We're still waiting for the report on the victim. And I want another talk with the girl."

The elevator arrived, and we got in. "Can I come back with you?" I asked.

De'Ath raised his eyebrows. "You seem to be taking more interest than usual in this case, Doc," he said.

I shrugged. "She intrigues me."

"Man, I am disgusted," De'Ath guffawed. "You must be old enough to be her father." He laughed, and Filbin laughed with him.

"Come on, Samuel. She's only ten years younger than I am."

Filbin shook his head in disbelief. "It must have been a rough ten years," he said. Their laughing intensified, and I was relieved when the doors hissed open and we went out into the sunshine.

"Anyway, God forbid I should split up this laughing policemen act, but is it okay for me to go back to the station with you or not?"

"Didn't you come in the Batmobile?" asked De'Ath.

I sighed. "Yes, I meant that I'll follow you back." I pointed to my car. "I'm parked there."

Filbin used his hand to shade his eyes from the sun. "Nice car," he said. "English, is it?"

"Yeah. Though an American helped design it. That's why it's got fins."

Filbin nodded appreciatively, then frowned. "What's that hanging from the antenna? It looks like a bat."

THE AUTOPSY

There were no free parking spaces in the precinct car park, so I left the Alpine on the road. Most of the cops knew who I was, so I reckoned I was unlikely to get a ticket. De'Ath and Filbin were at their desks by the time I reached the Homicide office. More than thirty detectives worked out of the big open-plan office, and all the desks were grouped in twos so that partners could sit facing each other and answer each other's phones and steal each other's sandwiches. They worked a three-shift system and spent most of the time out on the streets, which meant that there were never more than half a dozen detectives actually in the office at any one time. Filbin was talking into one of the phones, to Forensics by the sound of it. De'Ath saw me listening. "Forensics said they've sent her clothes back," he explained. "Said they're clean and there's no point in hanging on to them."

"What are you going to do next?" I asked.

"Ask her about the knife that's missing from the set in her kitchen. Ask her what she was doing in the alley. You know, Doc, police-type questions, just like you see on the television."

Filbin slammed down the phone. "Jerk," he said.

"That's no way to talk to Jamie D. Beaverbrook, world-renowned vampire hunter," admonished De'Ath.

"I didn't mean this jerk," said Filbin. "I meant those guys in Forensics. Had her clothes arrived? Don't forget to sign for them. Don't forget to send back the paperwork. Teaching their grandmothers to suck eggs."

There was a blue file on Filbin's desk, and I could see a color photograph peeping out. He saw me looking and pushed it across the desk at me. "Crime scene pics," he said. "Not for the faint-hearted."

"Mind if I look?" I said, more to keep De'Ath happy than anything else. He sometimes got a bit ratty if I took liberties.

Both men nodded. I pulled up a chair and sat down. There were a dozen or so glossy photographs, each twelve inches by ten inches. Some were close-ups of the victim's face. He seemed to be about forty years old, his hair in a military-looking crew cut, his eyes blank and staring. There was a savage cut in his throat reaching from his windpipe up to his right ear. Other photographs showed his blood-soaked chest, though it was difficult to see where the knife had gone in.

One of the phones rang, and De'Ath picked it up.

The victim was wearing a suit—not the gray one I'd seen in the dream, but a brown and yellow checked one. He was wearing a red tie, and there was a matching red handkerchief sprouting out of his top pocket. Both were the same color as the blood over his neck and chest. I flicked through the photographs, knowing what I was looking for but not wanting to admit it to myself. One of the pictures was a full-length shot of the body. I could see the brown shoes, and I scrutinized the socks. They were red. They were not black with white triangles. I sighed and sat back in the chair.

De'Ath replaced the receiver. "Coroner's office," he said to Filbin. "Autopsy'll go ahead this afternoon. I'm going to have a chat with young Miss Ferriman. Can you hit the phones and nail down a supplier of those knife sets? What was the brand? Dick, wasn't it?"

Filbin nodded. "Yeah, Dick. Some German company."

"Okay, you know what we want. Number of sets sold in the LA area, and we want a set so that we can identify the one that was missing from her kitchen." De'Ath looked at me. "You still here?" he asked.

"No, I'm a hologram," I answered. "I left an hour ago."

A uniformed sergeant came banging through the door, a large plastic bag in one hand. He dropped the bag on Filbin's desk and thrust a clipboard under the Irish detective's nose.

"You've gotta sign for these," he rasped.

"What is it, my laundry?" asked Filbin.

"Don't fuck with me, Filbin. They're Ferriman's clothes, from Forensics. Just sign your name. You can write, can't you?"

Filbin sighed and took a pen off his desk and scrawled on the clipboard while I reached for the bag. Inside there was a white T-shirt, a pair of black high-heeled boots, white panties and bra, a black miniskirt, and a black leather motorcycle jacket. I took out the jacket and held it up. There was nothing unusual about it. You saw ones just like it every time you walked down the street—big collar, lots of zips, belt around the bottom. You know the sort. The sort she was wearing in the dream.

The sergeant with the clipboard walked away. Over his shoulder he shouted, "By the way, Doc, you know the Batmobile's got a ticket?"

"This isn't a boutique," said De'Ath, and he took the jacket from me and pushed it back into the bag.

"What are you going to do with them?" I asked.

"She's not been charged yet, so she's free to wear her own clothes," he said. He swung the bag off the desk and took it with him to the interview rooms. As he went through the double doors, Captain Canonico came barreling into the Homicide office like a frigate under full steam.

"Beaverbrook, got your crucifix and stake with you?" he bellowed.

"Morning, Captain," I said, my heart heavy.

He charged over to where I was sitting, put his hands on the desk, and loomed over me like a storm about to break. "Have I got a scumball for you," he said. "We pulled him in about half an hour ago. He killed two small boys last night. Tortured them with a soldering iron. And then bit their peckers off. Can you believe that? Bit them clean off and swallowed them. Said it would boost his potency. You know what I'd do to someone like him, Beaverbrook? I'd hack off his balls with a blunt hacksaw and lock him away for life. That's what I'd do. But you, Beaverbrook, maybe you'll think he's just a bit disturbed and that we should put him in a nice hospital somewhere and let him take woodwork classes and go for long walks in the fresh air. Anyway, he's in room C. Why don't you go and get inside his head?"

He pushed himself up off the desk and leered at me. "And the Batmobile's got a ticket again," he said, heading back to his office.

"He's still got it in for you, hasn't he?" asked Filbin as he picked up the phone and began to dial. I didn't reply, just grabbed my briefcase and headed for the interview rooms.

I was in room C for the best part of two hours, and I felt sick when I came out. Sick and dirty and tainted. The man was insane, no doubt about it. The program labeled him as suffering from paranoid schizophrenia, and I knew that Captain Canonico would not take the news kindly. I sympathized with him. I hated child-killers more than any other type of murderer, hated them with a vengeance. If I'd had my way I'd quite happily give the bastard a bimedial leucotomy there and then with a broken bottle, but that's not the way the American justice system works. There were times when I hated the job, and hated even more the people it brought me into contact with. There's no excuse for killing children. None. I went straight to my office and drew up the report and put it in a file and then dropped it into the internal mailing system because I didn't want to be around when Canonico got hold of it.

He'd never forgiven me for what happened a few years back when I was on one of my first cases. The Teen Killers, they called them, two nasty pieces of work who'd ended up in a cell together at San Quentin, both of them serving time for rape. They spent several years telling each other stories of rapes they'd committed and planning what they'd do when they got out. They came up with this great idea, that they'd buy a large van and use it to kidnap and rape girls, but to make it a bit more exciting they'd go out with the intention of getting girls of every age between thirteen and nineteen. It was a sort of game. A contest. A full set, nothing less would do. Their names were Ed Vincent and Ronnie Bryant, but after the third rape the media began calling them the Teen Killers. It was Vincent's idea that the girls should be buggered as well as being raped, and it was Bryant's idea to fit up a video camera and lights in the back of the van so that they could film what they did to the girls. It was never really known which one of them decided that the girls should be strangled with their own underwear because when they eventually came to trial they both blamed each other.

Vincent was the smarter of the two—he had an IQ of 154—and in court Bryant said that he had fallen under his influence and that it was all Vincent's doing. They got caught after the fifth murder. The MO had been the same in each case. The naked bodies were discovered by the side of a freeway with a number written on their back in lipstick. The number was the age of the girl. Within a year of them both being released, they'd killed a thirteen-year-old, a fifteen-year-old, a seventeen-year-old, an eighteen-year-old, and a nineteen-year-old. They'd almost got the set, Vincent told me, and he seemed more upset at missing out on his target than the fact that he was facing the death penalty.

Anyway, to cut a long story short, they were picked up in a bar in Hollywood, and I was called in to run them through my program. You've got to remember that this was some time ago and that the program wasn't as sophisticated as it is now. Or as accurate. It wasn't a bug in the programming—it was more the fact that I didn't have enough case histories input as comparisons. That's what I told Canonico, anyway. Not that it did me any good. I ran them both through the program, and it highlighted a number of mental abnormalities which I reckoned were serious enough to justify the men being held in a secure hospital rather than a prison. Canonico protested and demanded a second opinion; I insisted that any further examinations were carried out in a hospital, and they were put into separate vans and driven over to a secure institution near Santa Ana. There was a cock-up, Vincent escaped, and was on the run for ten days. During that time he picked up a fourteen-year-old girl, manacled her in the back of his van, and filmed himself raping, buggering, and finally strangling her. They caught him in a motel outside Palmdale, watching the video and playing with himself. Canonico forced me to watch the video, right the way through, slapping me around the face every time I tried to get out of the chair and away from the images of pain and terror and the girl's unheeded tears.

He'd never forgiven me for the girl's death, and I didn't expect that he ever would. It wasn't my fault, I knew that, and when Vincent eventually went in front of a panel of psychiatrists they came to the same conclusion as I had and he ended up in a secure mental hospital. Bryant was executed a year or so ago when his appeals ran out.

Filbin was still at his desk working his way through the city's knife retailers, and I asked him if De'Ath was still talking to the Ferriman girl. He shook his head and said that he'd gone to the coroner's office to see how the autopsy on the victim was going. I left the building quickly without bumping into Canonico, which almost made up for the fact that I had indeed been given a parking ticket. Somebody had impaled a clove of garlic on my aerial; I pulled it off and threw it into the gutter. The vampire joke had worn thin a long time ago.

When I arrived at the lab where the coroner was working away on the victim of the previous night's murder, I parked the Alpine next to De'Ath's car. Inside a receptionist told me that De'Ath had gone into the lab where the body was being sliced up and analyzed. I said I'd wait outside because I'd seen more than my fair share of corpses being cut up, and to be honest they always made me feel pretty queasy. I'd never actually thrown up, but why take the risk? After half an hour or so, a gray-haired man in green coveralls came out carrying a digital recorder, followed by De'Ath. De'Ath raised his eyebrows when he saw me.

"I was curious," I explained. "I just wanted to know what the autopsy showed."

"Knife through the heart," said De'Ath. "Slash to the throat came afterwards. We've got a pretty good idea of the shape of the knife that did the damage."

"So what's the plan? Get hold of a knife like the missing one and compare it with the shape suggested by the autopsy?"

"Man, you should be a detective," laughed De'Ath. "I'm not sure how much good it's going to do us. I asked her about the knife. She said that when she rented the apartment the knife was already missing, and she said she could prove it. In one of the drawers of the kitchen there should be a full itinerary of everything in the apartment, dated when she took on the lease. Maybe we missed it. I'm on my way there now." He saw the look on my face and wagged his finger before I could speak. "If you want to tag along, that's okay with me, but don't let the captain find out about it," he said.

On the way out he waved his notebook in front of me. "There is something else you should know," he said. "Victim was drained of blood. Most of it anyway."

"What?" I was shocked, but then I realized that he was probably building up to another vampire joke.

"There was hardly any blood left in his body. Now that's not all that surprising considering that he'd been stabbed in the chest, but there wasn't more than a pint or so in his clothes or on the ground where we found the body. And like I said, the girl's clothes were clean." He stopped by his car and unlocked the door.

"You're not going to tell me he was bitten by a vampire, are you, Samuel?"

He roared with laughter and slapped the roof of his car with the flat of his hand. "You've been mixing with weirdoes for too long, man. You're going over the edge." He laughed again and shook his head. "What it means, Van Helsing, is that he was almost certainly killed somewhere else and then dumped in the alley." He got into his car, still laughing.

As I followed him down the road to Terry's apartment, I could see him still shaking with laughter and shaking his head.

He let us into her apartment, and I waited by the hi-fi while he put on another pair of gloves and carefully went through the draws in the kitchenette. "Yeah, here it is," he said, fishing out a sheet of paper. "A full inventory." He looked at the knife rack and counted them off. Six knives in the rack, six knives on the list. Dated six months ago. He folded the list up and slid it into a plastic bag and put it in his inside pocket. He pulled a plastic carrier bag out of the drawer and carefully put the knives into it. "Right, that's us," he said.

"Give me one minute," I said and headed for the bedroom.

"Don't…" he began.

"I know, don't touch anything," I yelled back at him. I was playing a hunch, don't ask me why, but I just wanted to get the name of the man in the photograph. The film star. Greig Turner it said on the back of the chair, and I scribbled the name down on the back of one of my business cards.

"What are you up to, Doc?" De'Ath asked as I returned to the lounge.

"Nothing. Nothing important," I said. "You fancy a drink?"

He looked at his wristwatch, a Seiko electronic job with lots of buttons. "Yeah, you've talked me into it. I know a place near here, come on."

De'Ath knew a place no matter where you were in Greater California. He locked the bag of knives in his trunk, and we walked to a place on Sunset, a narrow bar with stools and a barman in a green and gold waistcoat and a sniffle like he had an expensive habit. He brought us a couple of cold beers, and we clinked glasses while the barman retreated to a tactful distance.

"So what's on your mind?" De'Ath asked eventually.

"I dunno, Samuel."

"It's the girl, right?"

I shrugged. "Sort of. Maybe. I dunno."

"You're playing with fire, man. She's facing a murder rap, and you're employed by the LAPD. Just be careful, all right?"

I nodded and drank my beer. "Can I talk this through with you?" I said.

"I'm listening."

"She's found over the victim's body, right?"

He nodded. "Right."

"Do we know who he is yet?" De'Ath shook his head. "Okay, so she's found over his body, with his blood on her face. He's been stabbed, but there's no knife around. There's a knife missing from the rack in her kitchen, which might or might not be the same type that killed the guy, but she's got proof that the knife was never in her possession, right?"

De'Ath patted his jacket pocket. "Assuming this list is kosher, that's right."

"There's no murder weapon near the body, and the coroner reckons the victim was killed somewhere else and dumped in the alley. Right?"

"Right," he repeated patiently.

"There was no blood on her clothes, which means she couldn't have been the one who dragged or carried him into the alley. Right?"

"That's a maybe, Doc. But I hear where you're coming from. It would've been hard for her to have done that on her own without leaving a trail of blood and getting it all over her clothes."

I put my glass of beer down on the bar. "But don't you see? No murder weapon, no blood on her clothes—she couldn't have done it."

De'Ath nodded and took a long pull from his glass. He turned to face me, wiping the froth from his upper lip with the back of his hand. "It still don't add up," he said slowly.

"What doesn't?"

"If he was dead before he was taken into the alley, why was she claiming to be giving him the kiss of life?"

"Maybe he was still alive."

De'Ath snorted. "Coroner reckons he'd have died within seconds. Long before he was dumped."

"Maybe she didn't realize he was dead. Maybe she thought she'd be able to save him."

"Yeah, Doc. Maybe. But I think we'll keep her in the cell for just a little while longer. Just to be on the safe side, huh?" He waved the barman over and ordered two more beers. "Tell me, Doc, have you got a thing for this girl?"

"Give me a break, Samuel. There's such a thing as professional integrity, you know."

"Yeah, I guess so. Besides, you're probably old enough to be her father."

"What! Come off it. She's twenty-five—you know that. She looks younger, I know, but she's twenty-five."

"Yeah? So how old are you, Doc?"

"I'm thirty-five, thirty-six next month."

He nodded, as if unconvinced. "I always thought you were older."

"You thought I was old enough to be the father of a twenty-five-year-old-girl?" I looked at my reflection in the mirrored gantry behind the bar, turning my head left and right and examining my reflection. The beers arrived, but I didn't drink mine—I'd lost the taste for it. I went home.

I parked the car and let myself into the house. The quietness took me by surprise, as it always did. I still expected Deborah to be there, watching television, working out in her pink tracksuit, cooking, cleaning. Now there was just silence. I left the briefcase in the lounge and made myself a cup of coffee in the kitchen.

I leaned against the fridge as I took a mouthful of the milky brew, feeling the vibrations shiver through my legs. The phone rang. It was my lawyer, Chuck Harrison, asking if I could go round to his office. I made an appointment for four o'clock. While I had the phone in my hand, I called Peter Hardy. Peter and I arrived in Los Angeles at about the same time, me to run psychological profiles on the city's weirdoes, him to write about them. Well, different weirdoes most of the time—he was a reporter working for Britain's brasher tabloids, shoveling showbiz gossip and West Coast dross across the Atlantic as fast as Fleet Street would pay for it. Only very occasionally did our paths cross professionally, but we spent a fair amount of time getting drunk together. We were both going through painful divorces. Painfully expensive, that is.

"Jamie," he said. "How're the animals? Full moon keeping you busy?"

"Tell me about it," I said. "And I'm fresh out of garlic." I didn't mind being teased by Hardy, he was okay. "Hey, what can you tell me about Greig Turner?" Hardy was a movie buff, always out catching the latest releases, but he was also into old films in a big way. He had an extensive video library in his flat, hundreds of black-and-white classics, most of which I'd never heard of.

"In what context, mate?"

"Films. Some time ago, nineteen thirties I guess. Maybe nineteen forties."

"What was his name again?"

"Turner. Greig Turner."

"Was he an actor, or director, or what?"

"I dunno, Pete. All I've seen is his picture. He was a good-looking guy, so I guess he was an actor. But that's just me guessing."

"You said 'was.' Do you think he's dead?"

"It looked like an old picture—he could well be dead now." I fished the card out of my pocket, the card on which I'd written Turner's name. "He was in a movie called *Lilac Time.*"

"*Lilac Time?*"

"That's what it said. He was sitting in a director's chair, and Greig Turner and *Lilac Time* was written on the back."

"Yeah, okay, I'll check it out for you. Shouldn't be too difficult. I'll get back to you, okay? How's the legal battle of the century going?"

"I'm seeing my lawyer this afternoon."

"Yeah? Me too. Hey, did you ever see the film *Strangers on a Train*? You know, the Hitchcock movie, the one where two guys plan..."

"Yeah, yeah, you do mine and I'll do yours. Thanks, but no thanks."

"If ever you change your mind..." he said. He was joking, I knew that, but it struck a bit too close to home. When I hung up I finished my coffee and paced up and down, unable to relax. I looked at my watch. Three o'clock. One hour to get to Harrison's office. More than enough time. I wondered what the problem was this time. I'd thought that Deborah and I had finally got the money thing sorted out. She'd made it clear that she hadn't wanted the house or the car, just cash, and Chuck had thrashed out a deal with the hard-faced cow she'd employed as a lawyer that had too many zeros on the end of it but which at least left me with a roof over my head. Six years of marriage going down the tube was bad enough, but to see everything I'd earned over the past ten years go down with it was a bit much to bear.

I took the car to a filling station on the way to Chuck's office and checked the oil and water levels and the tire pressure and filled the tank with gas. I arrived ten minutes early, but he didn't make me wait, just had his secretary usher me in and shook my hand warmly. It was, I knew, a handshake that cost something in the region of five hundred bucks an hour. He waved me to a big leather chair that must have cost him at least three hours' work, after taxes, and leaned back in his, steepling his fingers and frowning.

"We have a problem, Jamie," he said quietly.

"We?"

He smiled a little. "I'm on your side," he said.

"I'm listening," I said.

He nodded. "Okay, we've now come to a settlement over community property, over the medical plan, and over the bank deposits and insurance. The other party has agreed to the split pretty much as I outlined at our last meeting. However, I'm afraid that I have to inform you that the other party has now decided to press a claim for cruelty."

"Cruelty?"

"Mental cruelty. Pain and suffering. To the tune of two hundred thousand dollars."

"Deborah says that I was cruel to her? I don't believe it."

"Don't forget that she has employed one of LA's toughest counsels to act for her. Carol Laidlaw is one mean son-of-a-bitch. And a dyke to boot. By the time she's finished she'll have your wife hating your guts, no matter how friendly you started out."

"That's great news, Chuck," I said, unable to keep the bitterness out of my voice. "What are their chances?"

"That depends on how solid their grounds are. Whether or not they'll be able to prove their case in court."

"Cruelty. No way, Chuck. I never laid a finger on Deborah. Never. And as for mental cruelty, God, I can barely remember the last time we had an argument." That wasn't true. I could remember. And I could remember her final words, too.

"You've got to remember that Laidlaw is a real professional at dragging up all the bad things that happened during a marriage. She's not interested in the happy memories, the good things you shared. She wants the skeletons, and she knows exactly how to get them rattling out of your closet."

I didn't like Chuck's imagery—I didn't like it one bit. It had been more than a year, but I hadn't come close to getting over April's death, and I doubted that I ever would. She lived for just four days, all of them on a life support machine, tenaciously clinging to life but with so little chance of success that we almost didn't even give her a name. We spent hours next to the incubator, watching her little deformed body twitch and breathe, her perfect, tiny hands clenching and unclenching.

"What does she want, Chuck?"

"Another hundred thousand."

That would just about clear me out. "Tell her it's okay. She can have it." I'd have to sell the car. And a few other things. Like the house.

"We could fight this, Jamie. There's no need to give up. I had no idea it was going to get this nasty. I should've expected it when she hired Laidlaw. She's a bloodsucker of the first order, a real vampire. She sucks and sucks until there's nothing left. But we can fight."

I held up my hands. "Just leave it, Chuck. Just pay what we have to pay so that I can get on with my life."

He looked pained. "I'll tell you what I'll do, Jamie—I'll offer fifty thousand and see what happens. Maybe I can get her down, get her to accept less." He didn't sound convinced. Maybe I was the one who should have hired Laidlaw.

I stood up and held out my hand to say goodbye. "Whatever you want, Chuck. Just do what you think is best." He shook my hand, and I went back to the car. I was going to miss it. I sat for a while, gripping the steering wheel so tightly that my knuckles whitened, my head full of thoughts of the daughter I nearly had. I missed her so much.

Eventually I started the car and drove home, my mood swinging wildly between sorrow and bitter, bitter anger. I was so busy seething that I nearly tailgated a Mercedes convertible, and I had to practically stand on the brake before I screeched to a halt. A horn honked as the red pickup behind me stopped suddenly, and I waved an apology and tried to clear the bad thoughts from my head.

My heart was pounding in my ears again, and there was a dull pain in my chest like I'd pulled a muscle there.

When I arrived home, I pressed the remote control device in my car that automatically opened the garage door, but I didn't drive in. Suddenly I couldn't face the house or the memories it contained, so I reversed back into the road and drove to the precinct instead. It was early evening, and I figured I might as well wait out the full moon where the action was.

I checked out Homicide before I went to my office, but both Filbin and De'Ath were out. A couple of the detectives nodded hello, and when I walked past, one of them howled like a wolf and the other laughed and I heard the words "vampire hunter."

As usual, De'Ath's desk was hidden under a sprawl of papers and phone books and torn-open envelopes. I dropped into his chair and picked up the phone, pressing numbers at random while I scanned his desk. What was I looking for? I wasn't sure. There were half a dozen active files on his desk and some mug shots of men who looked as if they'd be prepared to kill for a handful of change, and under a large envelope I found a half-eaten ham on whole wheat with mustard. Whatever number I had dialed turned out to be engaged, so I cut the line and dialed my home. I flicked the envelope open and slid out some black-and-white photographs of Terry Ferriman. They weren't the front and side views with numbers underneath like they take when they're processing a perp; they were more casual. She was wearing the leather motorcycle jacket, and her hair was neatly combed. I reckoned De'Ath had arranged for them to be taken so that he could use them to show witnesses and the like without making it obvious that the girl was in police custody.

I took one of the photographs and put it in my briefcase as my voice droned in my ear that I should leave my name and number so that I could get back to me. I replaced the receiver and went upstairs to my office. It was half past six and starting to get dark outside.

The first call came at just before nine o'clock. Two officers had picked up a guy roaming through downtown LA stark naked, bent double and occasionally stopping to howl at the moon. To be honest, that sort of behavior isn't all that unusual in La-La Land, but according to the arresting officers he'd attacked two girls. Tried to bite their tits off, they said. They'd asked him for his name, and he hadn't replied, just grunted and growled. He wouldn't, or couldn't, answer my questions either, which sort of made my job impossible. He refused to sit in the plastic chair and instead crouched on all fours in a corner of the room. The first time I got too close he snapped and spat at me, and two officers wearing anti-AIDS gear bundled him into a straitjacket and held him in the chair.

"What do you think, Doc?" asked one of the men, his voice muffled by the respirator and white hood.

"I think he's on something," I said. "Angel dust, or one of the designer drugs coming out of Cal-Tech. Best bet would be to leave him for a few hours, see if he comes down. And get the medics to run a blood test on him. Once he's seen a lawyer, that is."

The two masks nodded in unison, and I wondered if they were taking the piss because it wasn't my job to examine every screwball junkie they pulled in off the streets. I was supposed to concentrate on the serious cases. I left them to it and went back to the officers. Rivron was there, his feet on his desk, reading a magazine.

"Evening, Jamie," he said, without looking up. "You're late."

"I had an appointment with a wolfman," I replied. "A complete waste of my time. I sometimes think the cops take a perverse pleasure in messing us around."

"Don't let them get to you," he said. I was Rivron's boss, but he was five years older than I was, and it often seemed that our roles were reversed. He'd offer me advice, and more often than not I'd take it because he was a good, solid psychologist and spent a lot more time going over the literature than I ever did. Rivron was one of those guys who faded from the memory seconds after he left the room. He had the perfect face for an extra in the movies; it wouldn't matter how many times he popped up in the background, you'd never remember him. Pretty much everything about him was average.

He'd have made a great criminal; you could just imagine the cops doing the rounds and collecting descriptions at the crime scene—average height, average build, brown eyes, brown hair, no distinguishing features. "Do you think you'd recognize the man again, ma'am?" A pause. A cough. An embarrassed look. "Well, not really, officer, no."

His choice in clothing also bordered on the nondescript—sports jacket, neatly pressed flannels, light checked shirt, loafers, quiet socks. He had his own practice as a psychoanalyst, working out of an expensive office in Beverly Hills. His day job, he called it. Working for the LAPD was his pro bono, you know? Something to talk about at dinner parties with the stars. If I sound bitter, ignore me—I'm just jealous because I don't get to tell movie stars about my tangles with LA lowlifes. Since Deborah walked out, I don't get to talk to anybody about my work.

The phone warbled, and Rivron picked it up, took down a few notes, and replaced the receiver. "Toss you for a vampire?" he asked. "Downstairs in room D. Bit a couple of down-and-outs."

"Killed them?"

He shook his head. "More likely he'll be going down with alcohol poisoning. Or worse."

The phone rang, and I reached for it this time. "You have it, I'll take this one," I said to Rivron, and he sighed and picked up his briefcase. Inside was his laptop computer and a copy of the Beaverbrook Program. He waved as he went through the door, and I waved back.

"Beaverbrook," I said. It was a sergeant on the desk. They had a possession case for me. I started taking notes until it became obvious that he was talking about a teenager caught driving a stolen Rolls Royce.

"You cannot be serious," I said.

"Hey, Doc, possession is nine-tenths of the law," laughed the sergeant, and he hung up. Everyone's a comedian.

So you reckon this whole full moon stuff is a crock of shit, do you? That there's no way a satellite whizzing around the earth can possibly affect the actions of the billions of tiny people going about their business far below? Most scientists will laugh in your face when you suggest that the moon has a direct effect on the incidence of abhorrent behavior, but you ask any police desk sergeant and he'll tell you without a trace of hesitation that when the moon is full, the crazies come out to play. Okay, so maybe they've been influenced by too many video nasties and it's not actually a physical reaction, just a Pavlovian-type response, see the moon and howl sort of thing, but the end result would be the same, wouldn't it? Me, I've done enough basic research to know that there is a statistically significant increase in criminality during the full moon. I've started retesting suspects who were first examined during the full moon, running them through the program a couple of weeks after their arrest and comparing the results. There's a difference. Not much, to be sure—the curves don't shift so that a criminally insane person becomes sane when the moon's on the wane, but there is an effect. Once I've got enough raw data I'll put together a paper for one of the less serious journals, but I already know I'll come in for a lot of stick.

Many people have a gut reaction about the moon, accepting without too much thought that they tend to get drunk easier when the moon is full or that they're more likely to get into an argument or a fight. There are lots of farmers around who reckon that crops grow better if you plant them when the moon is waning rather than waxing. It doesn't matter why; they just believe that it happens.

There is a theory that says the effect of the moon on men is tidal, that it has the same pull on the water in our bodies as it does on the planet's oceans. Water accounts for more than eighty percent of our bodies, so it's possible that the pull of the moon affects the concentration of the chemicals in the body and the reactions they undergo. Another theory reckons it's something to do with the light from the moon, something like seasonal affective disorder which is reckoned to affect about one person in a hundred, mainly women. SAD usually occurs between October and March and is reckoned to be a form of light starvation in people whose hormones can't adjust to the seasonal lack of light. Sufferers tend to get depressed, anxious, and sometimes violent, and they can be helped with a form of light therapy, sitting in front of a light box that gives out ultraviolet light—not enough to tan, but five or six times what you'd get under normal domestic lighting. It works. So if lack of light can affect susceptible individuals, maybe moonlight can change others, in a different way, but a way we don't yet understand. Whatever the reason, the end result is the same. When the moon shines, the crazies come out to play.

I left the precinct at about four o'clock in the morning, dog-tired and feeling dirty, mentally and physically. Someone had hung a garland of garlic around the aerial of my car. I threw it on the back seat. It wasn't funny anymore.

THE RELEASE

I guess I was so wrapped up in my work that I forgot about Terry Ferriman for a day or two. Peter Hardy hadn't called me back about the film star, and I had a lot on my mind, what with Deborah's financial bombshell and all that, but it was mainly work that kept me occupied. Over the nights of the full moon, my team and I worked pretty much around the clock, processing the alleged bad guys. I was on my way in after a hurried lunch with Rivron when De'Ath grabbed me by the arm in the squad room. "My man, your bird is about to fly," he leered.

"My bird?" I replied, totally confused as I usually was when talking to De'Ath.

"Bird. Bat. Whatever. Ferriman, Terry. Ms. Alleged Vampire of this parish."

"What, you're letting her go?"

He grinned. "I thought that would brighten your day," he said. "She came up with a brief, a real high-powered hotshot lawyer, and she managed to get the bail down to six figures."

"That's still a hell of a lot of money, Samuel. For a girl living in a tiny apartment like she does."

"Maybe she's got real rich parents," he said with a shrug.

"Parents are dead, she told me."

"Yeah? I must have missed that in the file. Orphan?"

"So she says. Maybe that's where she got the money."

"Inheritance you mean?"

"Inheritance, or insurance settlement. Any news on the victim?"

"Still dead, last I heard." He guffawed and then repeated the joke to Filbin, who'd just walked up to his desk with Styrofoam cups of coffee for them both. Filbin laughed with him.

"You know what I meant," I said patiently.

De'Ath slapped his desk and laughed all the louder. "No," he said eventually after he'd calmed down. "Still no ID."

"She still here?" I said. "You said the bird was about to fly."

De'Ath wiped his eyes. "She's just getting her things together. You wanna see her?"

"Not really," I lied. The fact was that I did want to see her, though to be honest I wasn't sure why. Yes I was, I was attracted to her, that's why I wanted to meet her, even if it was just to say hello and to ask her how she was. I dumped my briefcase and laptop in the office and then went to the main entrance to the precinct house, knowing that was the way they'd send her out. She was already there, arguing with the desk sergeant, making sweeping gestures with her arms and raising her eyes to the heavens at his answers. The sergeant was Patsy O'Hara, a genial Irish American with five children and a grandchild on the way, and I knew he wasn't normally hard to deal with, so I wondered what her problem was. I looked around for her lawyer, but she was on her own, so I went up to the desk.

"I don't want to go!" she said and banged her fist down on the desk.

"Acting like that won't get you anywhere, young lady," O'Hara said, and I could tell from his voice that his patience was beginning to wear thin. Terry was dressed in the clothes I'd seen in the bag on Filbin's desk: miniskirt, ankle boots with leather tassels on the side, black stockings, and the leather jacket over a white T-shirt. And sunglasses. She looked older than she did when she was just wearing the gray police-issue tunic.

"I just, like, wanna stay here until later, you know? You can't make me go!" She stamped her foot as she spoke.

O'Hara sighed and shook his head. "Ms. Ferrlman, your lawyer has gone to a devil of a trouble to get you released. For the life of me I can't understand why you don't just go."

"Terry?" I said, standing next to her.

She turned and saw me and removed her sunglasses. "Jamie, thank God," she said. "Can you make this guy see sense, please?"

"What's the problem? Lieutenant De'Ath tells me you're free to go."

"That's the problem," she said. "I don't want to go. Not now."

"What do you mean? Is there someone trying to hurt you?"

She looked even more exasperated. "I can't go out in the sunlight, that's all."

I gave O'Hara a hard look. "You set her up for this did you, Patsy? I thought better of you."

He looked pained and held up his hands. "Hey, Jamie, it's nothing to do with me. Scout's honor."

"Did you hang the bat on my aerial, Patsy?"

"That I did not, son," he said.

"Look, I shitfire sure don't know what you two are babbling about, but I just wanna, like, stay put for a few hours," said Terry, putting her sunglasses back on. "Until it gets dark, you know?"

"And as I've already explained to you, young lady, this is not a waiting room," said O'Hara, looking at me for support. "Your lawyer has fixed your bail; you're free to go."

"I can't go," she cried, stamping her foot again.

I took her by the arm. "A joke's a joke, Terry, but that's enough. I don't know who put you up to this, but it's not really funny anymore. I've had far too many vampire jokes played on me over the years." I began edging her toward the doors that led outside. "If you need a lift, I'll happily run you home. But drop the vampire act, okay?"

She was still pulling against me, her feet slipping on the polished floor. "Jamie, I'm not joking. I have a bad reaction to sunlight, honest I do."

"Yeah, yeah, yeah," I said. "Any more of this and I'm going to bring out my crucifix."

She stopped dead, and I was surprised at her strength. For a moment I couldn't budge her. I couldn't see her eyes because of the sunglasses, but I got the impression that she was glaring at me. Then she just as suddenly relaxed as if she'd decided to drop the act. "Okay, Jamie," she said slowly. "Have it your way." She let me escort her to the doors and take her out to the steps that led down to the sidewalk. It was early afternoon, and the sun was bright enough to force me to shield my eyes as I looked across at her.

"See," I said. "You didn't burst into flames."

She smiled and then winced, and then I saw the right side of her face, the side nearest the sun, begin to bubble as if acid had been thrown at it. Her forehead began to go the same way, first breaking out into hundreds of small bubbles and then browning like a pancake on a griddle. She put up a hand to shield herself, and I saw that begin to go brown. I grabbed her by the shoulder and pushed her back inside the building.

"Jesus, Terry, what's happening?" I said.

She was shaking uncontrollably, and I took her to one of the benches at the side of the room and sat her down. Patsy O'Hara came bowling over, asking me what was wrong.

"Is there a doctor here?" I asked him.

"You're a doctor, Jamie," he said.

"A medical doctor!" I shouted at him. "For God's sake, Patsy, I'm a psychologist. I've no idea what this is. Get somebody, quickly."

"Doc Peterson is in testing a couple of drunk drivers," he said. "I'll get him."

He jogged off to the cells while I sat with Terry. The bubbling had stopped, but the patches of brown were still all over her right cheek and her hand, and there were small pinpricks of blood on her skin. "Terry, I'm sorry. I'm really sorry," I said. She just grimaced.

Patsy came back with Peterson. He pushed me away and sat down beside her, holding her head in his hands and inspecting the damage to her cheek. He took off her sunglasses and looked at the skin around her eyes and then checked her hand.

"Vitiligo?" he said to Terry. She nodded.

"Why did you go out in the sun?" he asked her.

She shrugged. Patsy and I looked at each other, and it was impossible to tell which of us looked the more guilty.

"Don't you normally wear sunscreen?" Peterson asked.

"SPF thirty," she said. "It's the only way I can go out during the day. But I didn't have any with me."

"You should have borrowed a hat, then. Or stayed inside. You've seen a doctor about this?"

"Of course," she said. "I've had it since I was a kid."

"Have you tried steroid treatment?"

"Tried it but it didn't do any good. The doctors say the best thing to do is to stay out of the sun."

Patsy went back to the desk. I sat where I was and wished that the ground would swallow me up. Peterson turned to look at me. He was about ten years older than I was, with a great bedside manner which unfailingly put patients at ease. He was a master at handling people, which is why the cops liked to have him in to test the drunks. He had a sympathetic face, oyster-like eyes, and a Mexican moustache which he rubbed occasionally. "You seen this before, Jamie?" he asked.

I said no, and he held Terry's hand in front of my nose. "Vitiligo," he said. "It's an immune disorder which prevents the skin's pigmentation from working normally and makes the skin hypersensitive to sunlight. It's not uncommon—about one in two hundred people suffer from it in one form or another."

"I've not heard of it," I said. I looked across at Terry. "I won't forget," I said to her. She smiled ruefully and put her sunglasses back on.

"Is there anything you can do for her?" I asked Peterson.

"No, the browning will go away on its own eventually," he said. "As to the disease, as I said to…I'm sorry, I didn't get your name," he said to Terry.

"Terry," she answered.

"As I said to Terry here, steroids are about the only long-term treatment, but even that isn't guaranteed. The best remedy is just to stay indoors." He stood up and shook her hand. "Best of luck, Terry. And stay out of the sun, okay?"

"It's a promise, Doc," she said.

As Peterson walked away, I turned to her and put my hand on her shoulder. "Terry, I'm so, so sorry. I had no idea."

"You didn't believe me," she said.

"I know, I'm sorry. It's just that the guys here play so many tricks on me you wouldn't believe it. They make my life hell."

"Jamie Beaverbrook, vampire hunter?"

"That's right. And after a while I guess I think everybody's at it. I apologize, I should have taken you at your word. I won't doubt you again."

"You mean there'll be a next time?" she said, teasingly.

"I hope so," I said.

"Yeah, me too, I guess," she said.

"Friends?" I asked.

"Friends, for sure," she agreed.

THE CLUB

The workload began to drop off a bit as the moon began to wane, and I got back home just before eight o'clock to find the red light flashing on my answering machine and a message from Peter Hardy asking me to call him. I did, but he wasn't in, so I left a message on his machine. I was impatient to know what he'd managed to find out about Greig Turner and *Lilac Time*, but LA being LA I knew that it could be days before we actually got to speak person-to-person. I microwaved myself a frozen chicken dinner and was sitting at my desk going through some transcripts when the doorbell rang. It was after midnight and I wasn't expecting anyone, so I checked through the door viewer.

La-La Land isn't exactly what you'd call a safe haven after dark, even in my part of town, and being gang-raped by a group of bikers high on angel dust wasn't my idea of a fun way of spending a Wednesday evening. Paranoid, huh? You should try living here for a while.

There was nobody there, which didn't make me feel any better because that meant one of three things: they'd gone, they were hiding, or they'd gone round the back of the house and were breaking in as I stood with my eye pressed against the front door. Look, just because I'm paranoid doesn't mean there aren't a couple of guys out there with shotguns, okay? I went back to the study, and the doorbell rang again. I thought of calling the police right away but decided against it because if I was wrong and if I was overreacting I knew that it wouldn't be long before tales of Jamie Beaverbrook, the vampire hunter who was afraid of the dark, would be circulating among the boys in blue.

I went back and put my eye to the viewer. It was her. It was almost midnight, and she was standing outside my front door. What the hell was going on? I opened the door, and she smiled up at me.

"Hi," she said. She was wearing a black linen jacket with the sleeves pulled up to her elbows, a black T-shirt, black leather jeans, and wraparound sunglasses. She meant it when she said that black was her favorite color. God knows how she managed to cross the road without getting run over.

"Do you know what time it is?" I asked.

She grinned. "Late," she said. She looked at my clothes. "You weren't in bed were you?"

I wanted to ask her what she was doing, why she was there, how she'd got my address, and how come she looked so bloody attractive so late at night.

"Aren't you going to ask me in?" she said, almost petulantly.

A weird thought flashed through my mind, the bit in all the old Dracula movies where the count stands on the doorstep waiting to be admitted, because unless you invite the vampire over the threshold he can't get in.

She saw the look of hesitation on my face and shrugged. "Okay, fine. I just wanted to thank you, that's all."

She turned to go, and I stepped toward her and touched her shoulder. "I'm sorry, don't go," I said. "It's late, that's all. And I was surprised to see you."

She turned back to me, smiling. "You were so kind to me—you really seemed to care, you know. They were giving me such a hard time. I just came to say thanks."

I held the door open for her. "Come on in," I said. Her jacket brushed against me as she went inside. Somewhere up in the hills a dog howled like its balls had been trapped in a vise. I followed her inside and closed the door.

She walked through the house, checking it out like a prospective purchaser. "Neat," she said. "I like it."

"Turn left," I said. "We'll go into the study."

I watched her hips swing as she walked. God, she looked good. She stood in the middle of the study, looking around. She took off her sunglasses and turned to look at me. I'd forgotten how black her eyes were. There were no marks on the skin of her cheek, but I couldn't tell if they'd gone or if she'd hidden them with makeup.

"This is different," she said. "I never pictured you in a room like this. It's, I dunno, pretty severe. Not like the rest of the house at all."

"Yeah, this is the one room my wife let me call my own. She designed the rest."

She raised her eyebrows. "Your wife?"

"Ex-wife," I corrected.

"She has good taste, for sure. What was her name?"

"Deborah," I said, a bit miffed that she rated her taste above mine. I mean, I liked the wood-paneled, rugged intellectual look. I'd put a lot of thought into it.

"Divorced? Or did she, like, die?" The straightforward way she said it took me by surprise.

"Divorced. Take a good look at the place. It won't be long before I have to sell it."

"Alimony?"

"Alimony," I agreed.

She went over to the bookcase and scrutinized my diplomas. "These are pretty impressive," she said. "What does the D stand for?"

"Dean," I said.

"Jamie Dean?" she said, and then realization dawned. "James Dean? Your parents named you after James Dean? That's really cute."

"Yeah, my mother was a fan. I was born on the day he died."

"Friday, September thirtieth, nineteen fifty-five. Highway Forty-Six. Cholame Valley."

I was impressed. Most Californians knew where he'd died, but not many people would have known the exact date.

"You don't look like you were born in nineteen fifty-five."

I flashed her a sarcastic smile. She knew what I meant. "Day of the year," I said. "I was born on September thirtieth. And my mum was always a fan. Though I'm not sure how good an idea it was to saddle a kid with a movie star's name. Not a kid in the North of England, anyway. I got teased a bit at school."

"Is that why you call yourself Jamie and not James? And why you don't use Dean?"

"No, that's more for professional reasons. It'd be hard to be taken seriously as a psychologist with a name like James Dean."

"Sounds like the same reason to me, Jamie. It'd just be that the people who'd tease you would be older, that's all. Same teasing, different playground."

I couldn't believe it. The girl was barely out of her teens and she was trying to psychoanalyze me.

"That's not why at all. It's not a question of being teased. It's just that…"

73

"I know, you didn't want James Dean appearing on your office door. People might laugh."

"It's not a question of being laughed at; it's a question of being taken seriously."

She looked at me with an amused smile, her eyebrows raised. She didn't have to say anything. Maybe it was the same thing.

"Would you like a drink?" I asked.

"No thanks. I just came to thank you. And to take you out."

"Take me out?"

She laughed. "To show how much I appreciate your helping me. Get your car keys. Don't bother to change—you look interesting enough like that."

Interesting? An old pair of Levi's and a Billy Idol T-shirt is interesting? That's not how Deborah would have described it. It belonged to the "You're not going out in that, are you?" school of fashion.

"You got a jacket?" she asked. "Something leather?"

"I've got an old motorcycle jacket somewhere, but it's been years since I've worn it."

She laughed. "Great, go get it."

I was in the bedroom going through the closet when I realized that I was following her instructions like a little kid. It was strange. She wasn't putting me under any pressure, I just wanted to do as she said. I wanted to win her approval. To win her smile. I found the jacket, and to my amazement it still fit, and I went back to the study and stood there with my arms outstretched. "How's this?" I asked.

She put her head on one side and nodded thoughtfully. "Neat," she said. "But you should put the collar up."

"À la James Dean?"

"Try it."

I did, and she smiled. "It looks great."

"Where are we going?" I asked her.

"It's a surprise."

"Is it far?"

She laughed. "About an hour's ride on a good horse."

"What?"

She grinned at my confusion and shook her head. "It was a joke," she said. "Not far. Come on, let's get your car." She took me by the arm and half led, half pushed me to the hall. "Kitchen?" she said.

"What?"

"Kitchen. Where is it?"

I nodded to the left, and she took me into the kitchen. "Rice?" she said.

"Rice?"

"Rice. Do you have any rice, Jamie?" She spoke slowly, as if I were a retarded child, but she smiled to let me know that she was teasing me.

Yeah, I had rice. Deborah had some special Japanese stuff that she used for her sushi parties. "Cupboard by the fridge."

She knelt down and took out the large glass jar. "Neat. Garbage bags?" She looked over her shoulder. "Garbage bags?" she repeated. I pointed to the drawer. She stood up and pulled it open and took out two black plastic garbage bags. There was a brown paper bag on the work surface, and she poured three or four handfuls of rice into it, screwed the top closed, and put it into her jacket pocket. She rolled the garbage bags up and then waved them at me like a conductor winding up an orchestra. "Let's hit the road," she said.

"Terry, where are we going?"

"It's a surprise."

"I don't like surprises."

"You'll like this one. Trust me, Jamie."

She walked toward me, her black eyes seeming to swallow me up as she drew closer and put her arms around my neck. I could see the distorted reflection of my face in her pupils. I looked frightened. Her nose barely reached my chin, and she looked up at me. "I mean it. Trust me, Jamie."

I melted. "Okay."

"Yeah!" she said, and then she stood up on her toes and kissed me lightly on the cheek. "Come on." She grabbed my hand and took me through to the garage. It was only when we were driving through the city that I realized that she hadn't had to ask me the way to the garage, as if she already knew where it was.

She wouldn't tell me where we were going but gave me directions that took me to a part of LA that I hadn't been to before, dark streets, broken-down buildings and vacant lots, burnt-out cars, and littered sidewalks. Not my normal part of town, if you get my drift. I was sure that at one point we'd gone around in a circle, and for a wild moment I feared that she was setting me up for something. There was, when all was said and done, a corpse with a slashed throat that needed explaining, and as far as I knew De'Ath only had one name in the frame. Hers.

"There," she said, pointing.

"What?"

"There. Park there."

I drew the car off to the side and switched off the engine. It turned over for a few seconds before clunking to a halt. The timing was starting to go again. I made to go, but she put a restraining hand on my thigh.

"Wait," she said. Images flashed through my mind. A dark sidewalk. A figure in a long, black coat walking up to the car.

Bending down. A flash of bright steel. A red curtain. Her mouth. Her smile. Her teeth.

"Are you all right?"

"What?"

"Jeez, Jamie, I know it's way past your bedtime, but you're behaving like a total zombie. Wake up. I said, are you all right?"

"I'm fine."

Her hand was still on my thigh. I could feel her nails through the material of my jeans. I hadn't realized how sharp they were, like the claws of an animal. "Will you do something for me?" she asked.

I looked into her eyes. "Anything."

She slowly took her left hand out of her jacket pocket and dropped the rice-filled brown paper bag into my lap. "Put that down your trousers."

"What?"

"Jamie, will you stop saying what? Just do as I say, okay? Shove the bag of rice down the front of your pants. Trust me."

I did as she said, and then we both got out of the car. She walked round to my side and linked her arm through mine.

"Don't you ever lock it?" she asked.

"No point. They'd just cut through the soft top."

"They?"

"The bad guys. The forces of evil."

She laughed. "You're crazy."

"I'm a psychologist."

"They're not mutually exclusive, you know."

"Maybe you're right." I stopped walking and turned to look at her. "Terry, will you answer me one question?"

"Sure."

"Why am I walking around with a bag of rice down my trousers?"

She giggled and gently hit me on the head with the garbage bags. "That'd shitfire sure spoil the surprise," she said, and then she tugged at my arm. "Come on, we're nearly there."

We joined a line of people standing outside a movie theater. Even by Los Angeles standards they were a strange group. Everyone seemed young, at least ten years younger than me. Okay, maybe fifteen. Most of the men had makeup on, lots of mascara and eye shadow and black lipstick, and they were wearing long, shabby coats. The girls were in short black miniskirts and fishnet stockings and tops that showed off too much cleavage. Lots of makeup, too, just like the men. There were two big bouncers at the door, frisking everyone as they went in, but they were being friendly about it and there was a lot of laughing and joking. The line moved quickly, and when we got to the front the film was obviously close to starting because the body search was fairly cursory. They checked my pockets and looked at Terry's garbage bags, but that was about it. She had the tickets ready, and on the way through the foyer I saw a couple of posters advertising the film we were going to see. *The Rocky Horror Picture Show*. A British actor, Tim Curry, playing the part of a kinky transvestite scientist called Frank-N-Furter.

"Have you seen it before?" Terry asked as we went into the darkened theater.

"No," I answered. "You?"

"Only about a thousand times," she said. "Hurry up, it's starting!"

We were in the middle of the fifth row from the front, and we had to squeeze past a motley collection of freaks and weirdoes who were all singing the opening song in time with a huge pair of scarlet lips on the screen. Men were taking off their coats to reveal low-cut dresses and suspender belts.

"Get the rice out," Terry whispered as we sat down. I did as she said, and I could see a girl with spiky blonde hair and purple eye shadow a few seats along slipping a plastic bag of rice from under her leather miniskirt. She saw me looking at her and winked.

The lips disappeared from the screen, and Terry's right hand burrowed into the bag and came out with a handful of rice. She motioned to me to do the same. The audience seemed to have seen the film many times, judging by the way they were yelling out the dialogue and heckling, and then, when a wedding scene appeared, the air was filled with flying rice which showered down on us all to the sound of shrieks and catcalls.

"Neat, isn't it?" laughed Terry, her lips pressed against my ear.

"I've never seen anything like it," I agreed.

"It gets better," she said. "Believe me, it gets better."

An all-American couple called Brad and Janet were singing on the screen, and the audience was going wild. In the aisle a couple wearing outfits matching those of the actors jived and mimed to the soundtrack. Terry handed me one of the garbage bags. "Put this on your head," she whispered.

"What?"

"Put it on your head. Trust me."

There was a rustling around the theater, and it seemed that everyone was either holding a newspaper above their head or wearing a plastic bag. Terry put her bag on, and as I followed her example the film changed, Brad and Janet were sitting in a car in a rainstorm. Water began to pour down from above, splattering over the bag on my head and trickling down the back of my neck.

Terry giggled. "There's always someone who manages to smuggle water in," she whispered. "It's really neat, isn't it?"

"Yeah, neat," I said. "I just hope it's water they're throwing."

The rest of the film was just as chaotic, members of the audience dressed like the characters on screen, lip-synching the dialogue, others screaming out the punch lines, still others rushing up the screen and pointing at things, pretending to help to push buttons, pull levers, open curtains, close cupboards. It was unnerving. Audience participation in an asylum. Terry seemed to know the whole script by heart, and she sang along and yelled out punch lines with the rest of them, occasionally reaching over to squeeze my hand. She was having fun, and what the hell, so was I, sitting in a darkened cinema with enough crazies to fill a year's subscription of *Clinical Psychology*. The plot? I can't remember, something about building a man from spare parts, visitors from another planet, lots of men wearing stockings and suspenders, and Tim Curry murdering a lobotomized Meatloaf with an ice pick. But Terry, her I can picture vividly, her black eyes wide with pleasure, licking her lips and laughing, her hair swinging backwards and forwards, her laugh so cute that I just wanted to take her in my arms and crush her. I was falling in love with her; I knew that with a dread certainty. The realization brought with it a flurry of doubts, about how she felt, about the age difference, and above all the fact that I was working for the LAPD and she was a suspect in a homicide investigation.

The credits rolled and the lights came on, and she turned and caught me looking at her. She frowned and reached up and stroked my cheek. "Are you okay, Jamie D. Beaverbrook?"

I nodded and brought up my hand to hold hers. "I'm fine." I wanted to tell her how I felt, that she made my heart ache, but I held it back. Fear of rejection, I guess. Or ridicule.

"Do you want a drink? I know somewhere," she said.

"Sure."

We left the cinema arm in arm and walked back to the car.

"Is it far?" I asked.

"A few minutes, max," she said.

"On a good horse?"

She giggled. "I like the way you make me laugh, Jamie," she said.

She gave me directions, and five minutes later we pulled up across the road from a black-painted windowless building. Steps led up to double doors which had been opened, and above them was a neon sign which said "The Place." The door was being guarded by a broad-shouldered bald black man in a black suit. His impassive face broke into a grin when he saw Terry.

"Terry, my girl!" he boomed. "How's my favorite creature of the night?"

"Hanging in there, Toby," she said. She kissed him on the cheek. "This is my friend Jamie," she said as she breezed past him. Toby nodded at me, but I didn't get a grin. I followed Terry down a red hallway to another set of doors guarded by another black man, even bigger than Toby. He also greeted Terry by name and pushed open the doors for her, allowing the throbbing beat of heavy metal music to billow out. The dance floor was packed with pretty much the same sort of characters we'd seen in the cinema, lots of black, lots of leather, lots of skin and pierced ears and noses, and everywhere Terry was welcomed, a kiss on the cheek, a hug, a warm smile. She seemed to have an incredible number of friends, and I felt a surge of jealousy, especially when guys touched her, but she never spent more than a few minutes with any of them before moving off with me in her wake. The sound system was deafening, making conversation impossible, but by the look of it there was little if any interest in talking, just lots of body contact and flailing of limbs. I felt old. Hell, who am I kidding, I was old, it was just that my mind hadn't accepted it yet.

A bar ran the length of one side of the dance floor, shiny black wood and brass rails, with half a dozen barmen in matching black trousers and waistcoats doing their best to deal with the flow of orders. There was a crush at least three deep of people wanting to buy drinks, waving money and shouting to be heard above the brain-numbing music. Terry stopped and put her mouth up close against my right ear, so close I could feel her breath. I thought she was going to kiss me, but instead she asked me what I wanted to drink. I put my mouth against her ear and said I'd better get it, that she'd have no chance of getting through the crowds. She grinned and said that one of the barmen was a friend, so I asked her for a vodka and tonic.

She took me to a pillar and told me to stand there so that she could find me again, and then she made her way to the bar, for all the world like a black shark carving through a shoal of fish. She went to the far right of the bar where the crowd was thinner and where there was no barman serving, and she stood on the footrest to give herself an extra six inches of height, but even so she didn't stick out and I reckoned it would be some time before she got served.

To my left a young guy in a red and green Mohican haircut and a T-shirt slashed with a dozen cuts gyrated in front of a girl with waist-length blonde hair in a tight rubber dress that left little to the imagination. Behind them two brunettes in matching leather outfits were dancing slowly and kissing, oblivious to the pulsating beat, lost in their own bodies.

It was hot, and I could feel sweat on my face and in the small of my back. I looked back at Terry. She still hadn't been served. She wasn't shouting or waving or doing anything that would attract the attention of any of the men behind the bar. Instead, she seemed to be waiting and was staring intently at one of the barmen, a tall, thin guy with long black hair that was tied back in a feminine ponytail. He had long arms that seemed ungainly at first glance, jerkily moving from bottle to glass like a badly manipulated puppet, but he was fast and never seemed to make a mistake. He had deep-set eyes and a narrow face which always appeared to be set in a frown with deep furrows across his brow. He seemed a very intense guy, and when he was taking orders he stared the customer right in the face, almost glaring at them, and then he'd nod curtly and fill the order. He always seemed to hear them correctly first time, he never asked them to repeat, and unlike the rest of the serving staff, he wasn't constantly leaning over the bar to hear better. It didn't seem to matter where he stood or how quietly the customer spoke. It was as if the music just wasn't there, as if he was working in total silence. He never spoke either, just keyed in the orders into the cash register and pointed when the customers queried the amount. He was deaf, I realized. He was deaf and he was lip-reading. He was doing it well, too, by the look of it.

He finished serving two lagers to a couple of men wearing studded dog collars and leather vests and then scanned the bar, his eyes widening when he saw Terry. He headed toward her, smiling widely. He raised his open right hand and moved it back and forth, sign language for hello.

She mimicked the gesture, pointed to her right ear, and then made fists with both hands, moving them together then apart. The sign for noisy. She followed it by angling her fingers upright at right angles to her palms and then dropping both hands down. Then she put her left hand at chest height, palm down, and moved it in an arc over the right hand. The two movements together signified tonight. *Noisy tonight.*

He nodded, pointed with his right finger, and rotated it clockwise. Around the clock. *Always.* He pointed at her and then pointed his index finger directly up, palm in front of his face, and then rotated it anti-clockwise. *You alone?*

She waved her open right hand with the fingers together and the palm toward him made an S shape in the air. *Never.*

He laughed soundlessly.

She made two fists and brought the knuckles together, thumbs on top. With. She opened her fists and linked her hands together at the index fingers, separated them, switched positions, and linked again. Friend. *With friend.* She meant me.

He laughed again, placing his two fists together, knuckles meeting, and waggled his thumbs toward each other. The sign for lovers.

She shook her head and repeated the sign for friend. My heart fell.

He pointed to his own chest, patted his forehead, and pointed at her. *I know you.*

She pointed at her own head with her right index finger and moved it clockwise. *Crazy.*

He looked past her, scanning the crowds, and caught me looking at him. He smiled and then looked back at her. He made a sign at his forehead, as if gripping the brim of an imaginary hat, and then pointed. The sign for he. He made a V sign with the first two fingers of his right hand and pointed at his eyes, then swung the fingertips out and away from his body. Watch. *He watches.*

Terry turned from the bar and saw me. She frowned and tilted her head to one side. The barman was laughing and began to serve a girl with platinum hair who was well over six feet tall and who had a tattoo of a fire-breathing dragon on one shoulder. Terry's hands began to fly in front of her body. She pointed to me, then put her hand against her head and flicked up her index finger, then pointed the index fingers of both hands up and made rising circling motions in front of her face, then pressed her thumbs and first fingers together and joined her hands, and then moved them apart in a wavy motion. She had asked if I knew sign language. She did the movements quickly, as if testing me, and I had half a mind to pretend not to know what she was up to, but another part of me wanted to show off, to demonstrate that we had something in common.

Of course, I signed back. *You sign well.*

She grinned. *You too. How come you can do it?*

My sister is deaf, I signed.

Is she older or younger?

I put my fingertips on my chest and then moved them up to just above my shoulders, then repeated the action several times, the sign of spirits bubbling up. *Young. Deaf from birth,* I signed. *I learned with her.*

What's her name?

I signed her name letter by letter. *Patricia.* Terry frowned and signed back that she didn't understand. I realized my mistake; I'd used the British alphabet system, which was different from the American version. I knew both because Patricia had had some deaf friends from the States and I'd met them several times. I spelled the name out again, this time using the American system.

Unlike the UK system, it could be done with just the right hand.

This time Terry nodded and smiled.

I pointed to her, and then wiggled the fingertips of my right hand against my chin. *You're cute.* She grinned and pointed her right index finger parallel to her lips, moving it from right to left. *Liar.* Then she turned her back on me and caught the barman's eye again and ordered our drinks. She brought them over, weaving her way through the throngs of crazies without spilling a drop. I was impressed. She was still wearing her sunglasses, which I thought made her look kind of cute. She clinked her glass against mine and said something in what sounded like Russian.

"What did you say?"

"It's a Russian toast."

"Cheers then."

"You want to dance?"

I surveyed the heaving crowds and shuddered. "I don't think so. They look as if they'd eat me alive."

She laughed. "Well I do. Hold this for me."

I took her glass and watched as she squeezed onto the dance floor, found what passed for a space, and began to move. She danced well, well enough for some of the guys to stop looking at their partners and to watch her instead. She had a good sense of rhythm and used the floor and was soon lost in the music. A tall, black guy in too-tight trousers and a white silk shirt open to the waist eased toward her; she smiled at him, and they danced together as if they'd done it many times before. I was jealous, they looked good, and what they were doing was just about as sexual as you could get without touching. I envied him the way he seemed to know exactly what she was going to do next, and he knew how to react to her. They'd be great in bed together, it was blindingly obvious, and I wanted to kill him. I looked away and saw the bar-man looking at me. He smiled, and I grimaced.

Don't worry, he signed. *They're just friends. They dance together, that's all.*

I smiled back and lifted up the glasses to show that I couldn't sign back to him. He waved and went back to serving drinks. She danced with the guy for the best part of half an hour, and then he delivered her back to me, kissed her on the cheek, and gave me a mock bow before disappearing back into the sweating throng.

"You dance well," I said to her.

"I'd shitfire sure rather have danced with you, Jamie," she said, taking her glass. She put it, untouched, on a side table. She looked at her watch. "Come on, let's go."

"Where?"

"Trust me, Jamie. Just trust me."

She led me back outside, saying a dozen goodbyes as we left. "You've a lot of friends," I said.

She shrugged. "I've been coming here a long time. It's a really neat place."

We walked back to the car, arm in arm, our footsteps echoing in the still night air. "Your namesake had a cat, you know?" she said.

"Who?"

"James Dean. A Siamese kitten. Elizabeth Taylor gave it to him. The night before he died he took it to a neighbor's house. Everyone reckons he was a real macho type, you know, but he loved that kitten."

"What made you think of that?" I asked.

"Oh, I guess I was thinking about the questions you were asking me in the precinct house. Remember? Do you prefer cats to dogs? Funny question, that."

"It's not the reply that's important, it's the fact that you can answer. Some psychotics can't make choices. It wasn't a trick question." Overhead hung the moon, pockmarked and accusing. The occasional car drove by, but it was almost three o'clock, so they were few and far between. We walked between two apartment buildings, and I held her closer.

"Does that program, that Beaverbrook Program, always work?" she asked.

"I like to think so."

"Because I still don't, like, understand why you need a computer program to tell if someone is right in the head, you know?"

"Yeah, I know. Let me tell you a story."

"I'd like that," she said, squeezing my hand.

"There was a guy called Rosenhan who did some research in the early seventies. He told the staff of a teaching hospital that a number of fake patients would try to gain admission by claiming that they had symptoms of various mental illnesses."

"To check if they could spot them or not?"

"That's right. Each member of staff was asked to rate each new admission as to whether they were an impostor or not. Over a three-week period, just under two hundred new patients were admitted, and at least one in five was reckoned to be faking it by at least one member of staff."

"So? That proves they knew what they were doing, right?"

"Wrong," I said. "They were all genuine patients. Rosenhan didn't send any impostors."

"Wow!"

"Yeah. He was making the point that often psychiatrists can't tell the difference between sane and insane people. Classification of mental disorders has always been pretty unreliable."

She turned her head to look behind us, and then I heard someone running, the slap-slap of training shoes on the sidewalk. It was a man, a big man with wild, untamed hair and the beginnings of a beard. He was wearing a stained leather bomber jacket and torn jeans, and he was heading right for us. I figured he was drunk maybe, so I pulled Terry to one side to give him room to pass, but as he drew closer it was clear from his staring eyes that we had a problem. We were the only three people on the street, and he stopped running when he reached us. I held Terry tighter, and she put her hand on my stomach as if seeking reassurance. The guy was breathing heavily, and he ran a huge, dirt-encrusted hand across his unshaven chin. The other hand appeared from inside his jacket with a switchblade that must have been at least a foot long. He pressed a chrome button on the side, and the blade sprang out with a metallic click. I felt Terry's hand tense on my stomach, and then her nails scraped my flesh.

"Your fucking wallet," he said and thrust the knife to within an inch of my nose. "Give me your fucking wallet, you mother, or I'll slice your nose off."

"Okay, okay, just don't hurt us," I said, keeping my voice low and my eyes averted. I'd been mugged twice before in LA, and I knew all the dos and don'ts. Don't give them an excuse to hurt you, don't pose a threat, don't piss them off, just do as they say and appear to be as meek as possible, give them what they want, and don't try to stop them from getting away. Just remember as many details as possible so that you can tell the police afterwards, even though they've almost no chance of ever catching the guy. After the first mugging I began carrying around a spare wallet containing a few dollars and a couple of out-of-date credit cards, but that was back home in my other jacket; I hadn't thought to bring it with me tonight. And the wallet in my back pocket had several hundred dollars in it and my gold AmEx card. Damn. But no matter how much cash it contained, I'd happily hand it over if it meant he wouldn't hurt me or Terry. Money I could always replace, even with my alimony payments. I reached into my back pocket and took out the wallet.

"Come on, come on, gimme the fucking wallet!" he hissed and touched the knife against the tip of my nose. I felt Terry's hand slide across my stomach as she stepped to the side, putting distance between the two of us. I didn't want that, it was better for him to regard us as a couple, as one entity, because if he saw her as an individual then he might start to get other ideas. I tried to reach for her hand, but she moved away.

The mugger kept the knife on me but looked across at her. "Stay where you are, bitch!" he said. A car drove along the street, a red pickup; it slowed as it went by but then accelerated as if the driver had seen what was going on and hadn't wanted to get involved.

Terry spoke to the man in what sounded like Spanish. She took off her sunglasses, and her eyes flashed. She was angry, and she sounded it. Bad idea, I thought. If she wasn't careful she was going to push him over the edge; he was nervous enough as it was.

He grinned evilly and said something to her, also in Spanish. The knife wavered but not enough to make it worth my while trying to grab it; besides, he looked a hell of a lot stronger than me, and I doubted that I'd be able to overpower him, with or without the knife. His grin changed into a leer, and he said something else to her, his voice softer this time, and she cursed him. He laughed and took the knife away from my face and moved toward her.

"Leave her alone!" I yelled, and I grabbed for the knife. He swore and pulled it away and then slashed it across my arm. It was razor sharp, and it sliced through the leather sleeve. I felt it cut into my flesh. As he pulled the knife away, pain seared through my arm. I cried out, and he drew back and then plunged the knife forward toward my chest. I thought I was going to die. I really did. But when the knife was an inch from my chest, there was a blur, and before I knew what had happened his arm had stopped moving and Terry had hold of his wrist. It was weird. One moment she was standing there, her arms by her side, and the next she was reaching across my chest and gripping his wrist, her eyes fixed on his. She seemed calm and relaxed; there was even a hint of a smile on her lips. He grunted and cursed, and the veins on his neck stuck out as he pushed against her, but the knife moved no closer. I looked down and saw her nails digging deep into his flesh. She spoke to him, quietly this time, still in Spanish, but I could feel the menace in her voice. I was as hypnotized as he was, and I stood there immobile, no longer feeling the pain in my arm.

He pushed harder but made no progress, and then she moved, so quickly that later I couldn't remember how she'd done it, but one moment his arm was outstretched, the next it was bent back into an unnatural angle and there was a splintering crack that made my blood run cold. He didn't scream; he passed out almost immediately and slumped to the ground as the knife clattered onto the sidewalk.

"Come on, Jamie," she said, taking me by the arm. "I don't want us to have to explain this to the cops. We're, like, not on the best of terms at the moment."

We ran to the car, and she insisted that I drive a mile or so before I checked the damage to my arm. When she was satisfied that we were far enough away from the would-be mugger, she told me to pull to the side and take off my jacket. It was only a small cut—the thick leather had saved me from serious harm—and I doubted that it would even need a stitch. Terry took my hand and drew my arm up to her lips. She slowly licked along the skin until she came to the cut and then licked the blood away. I could feel her tongue testing the edges of the wound, then a gentle sucking sensation.

"Hey, what are you doing?" I asked her.

She stopped sucking and lifted her head. There was blood on her lips, and I was reminded of the first time I'd seen her, at the police station. "You don't know what he'd been doing with that blade," she said. "I'm cleaning the wound."

"What about AIDS?"

"Jamie, I hardly think you'll catch AIDS from a switchblade."

"Not me, you. You should be careful with blood."

She looked at me sternly. "Dr. Beaverbrook, are you telling me that you're HIV-positive?"

"No, of course not, it's just…"

She went back to licking the wound, her eyes on mine. It didn't hurt—far from it, it was soothing and, to be honest, downright sexy. I could see from her eyes that she was smiling, and I reached over with my other arm and stroked her hair.

"You should be careful," I said.

"What do you mean?"

"Tackling that guy. God, he could have so easily killed you."

She snorted contemptuously. "Huh, in your dreams," she said. "There's nothing someone like him can do to hurt me. There's nothing anyone can do to hurt me, Jamie. Trust me."

"Everyone feels like that when they're young, Terry. You feel like you can live forever, that nothing can damage you. I used to feel the same—we all did. You feel that you'll walk away from any car crash, that a plane can explode and you'll be the only survivor, that you'll never get seriously sick, that you'll live forever. You feel like you're immortal."

She nodded, her eyes wide, and I put the back of my hand against her cheek. She felt cool and dry, like bone china, but soft.

"It's an illusion, Terry—take it from someone who's been there. As you get older, you realize how short a time we have and how precious life is. You've got to learn not to take risks. All it takes is some nutter with a switchblade and it's all over."

She shook her head firmly. "No, I don't believe that, Jamie."

"The morgues are full of youngsters who didn't believe it. Trust me on this one," I said. "You'll change. Everyone does."

She put her head up close to mine, our noses almost touching. "Nothing can hurt me, Jamie. And as long as you're with me, nothing will be able to hurt you either."

I tried to lift up my arm to show her the cut, but she pushed it away and pressed her lips against mine, kissing me hard and watching me at the same time. I tried to tell her that she was wrong, that you grew out of the immortality complex, that when you hit thirty you became all too well aware of the body's failings and then you can't sleep at night for the sound of your heart ticking off the seconds, but then I lost myself in the kiss, and when I raised my hand it was to caress the back of her neck and not to show her the blood. Eventually she broke away and asked me to drive back to my house. While I drove she asked me about my work, about my time at university, my research. She didn't ask about Deborah, and I didn't explain.

When I opened the front door, I was hit by a wave of guilt as if Deborah were waiting there with an arsenal of sarcasm and bitterness, but of course there was nothing, and maybe that was worse.

Terry was the first girl I'd taken back since Deborah had left. I reached for the light switch, but Terry's hand covered mine and she whispered, "No, leave it," and then she put her arms around me and kicked the door shut with her heel as she kissed me. I put my arms around her waist and lifted her off her feet so that her head was level with mine. I couldn't see because it was pitch-dark in the hall, but I felt that she still had her eyes open, watching me. How old was she? Twenty-five, she'd said. Or thereabouts. God, I could barely remember what it felt liked to be twenty-five years old and to feel that I'd live forever. When I was twenty-five she'd have been fourteen with nothing more to worry about than which boy she had a crush on and whether or not she'd make the cheerleading team.

"You're drifting," she said.

"I'm what?"

"Drifting. Your mind has gone walkabout, and I want you to concentrate on me, Jamie. Okay?"

"Okay," I said, and then I kissed her again.

"Bedroom," she said.

"Bedroom?"

"Carry me to the bedroom," she said, lifting her legs and hooking them around my waist. She felt light, hardly any weight at all, though I could feel the tight strength of her young thighs.

"I can't see where I'm going," I complained.

"It's not that dark," she said. It was pitch-black. I stumbled toward the bedroom, hitting the walls a few times and once banging my shins against a coffee table, which made her laugh out loud.

I reached the bedroom in one piece, just about, and put her on the bed. The blinds were open, so for the first time I could actually see her in the light of the big, white moon that hung in the middle of the California night sky. She threw off her jacket, kicked up her legs, and undid the belt of her trousers, wriggling to slip them off. "Come on, Jamie," she giggled. "Get naked."

The zip on the motorcycle jacket made a ripping sound as I took it off, and I pulled the T-shirt over my head. Then I took off my jeans to the pitter-patter of hundreds of grains of rice raining down onto the carpet.

THE STAR

She was gone when I woke up, and I didn't remember her leaving in the night. I felt as if every bone in my body had been broken and then reset. There were bruises on my thighs and bite marks on my shoulders—not deep enough to draw blood, but I could see where her teeth had marked me. She'd been like an animal at times, screaming and biting and scratching, but she'd been gentle too, soft and imaginative, doing things to me that no one had ever done to me before. Part of me wanted to ask her how she knew how to give so much pleasure, how she knew just what to do and how long to do it, but I knew that I didn't really want to know the answer because the things she did in bed weren't the things you learn from books—they came only from experience. No one had ever made love to me the way she'd done, and I doubted that anyone else ever would. I'd asked her if she wanted to use anything, but she laughed and said no, there was no way she'd get pregnant, and I wondered if the flippant attitude came along with the immortality complex. But when I asked her if she was on the pill, she just kissed me and flipped me over onto my back, and I didn't ask her again.

She used the phone once during the night, I think, because I sort of remembered waking up to find her sitting on the edge of the bed whispering in a language which I didn't recognize but which sounded Slavic, Polish, or Russian maybe. I reached out for her in half-sleep, and she ruffled my hair and put the phone back and then made love to me again. I don't know, maybe I imagined that bit.

There was an indentation in the pillow, and I rolled over to her side of the bed and lay there, facedown, breathing in the smell of her. I went to shower and saw that she'd used the bathroom; the shower stall was wet, two of the towels were damp, and there were a few of her hairs in one of my brushes. I picked up one of them and ran it through my fingers, stretching it out to see how long it was. It was perfectly straight, no kinks or bends.

I love straight hair. I got so pissed off when Deborah went out and got hers permed, without even asking me whether or not I thought it was a good idea. I hated the way it looked, but even worse I hated the burnt smell that lingered for days afterwards. Terry's hair smelled fresh and clean, but as I ran the individual strand over my skin I could feel that it was strong too. I held it up to where I imagined the top of her head would be if she were standing next to me, and I dropped one end and allowed it to swing free. I imagined she was there, looking up at me, teeth parting as she smiled, standing up on tiptoe to kiss me. I caught my reflection in the mirror and realized how dumb I looked, so I put the hair back on the shelf above the sink. There were several others in the brush, and one of them was pure white. I pulled it out of the bristles and wound it around my left index finger. It had the same feel as the black hair but was totally devoid of pigment.

I showered and put on a white toweling robe and went into the kitchen to make myself coffee. There was no note from her anywhere, but the red light was flashing on the answering machine. I thought that she'd left a message for me on it, but it was Peter Hardy, asking me to call him again. I dialed his number, half expecting to end up speaking to his machine, but he picked it up on the third ring.

"We speak at last," I said.

"Hiya, Jamie. I tried to call just after midnight. You out with the crazies?"

"Just one," I laughed.

"How was she?"

"I'll tell you about it sometime. But not yet, okay?"

"Sure. Hey, that film, *Lilac Time*. Do you want to see it?"

"You've got a copy?"

"I haven't, but I know a man who does, and he says he'll lend it to me. Snag is, it's not on video, so we're going to have to go a viewing room."

"Is that a problem?"

"In LA? Of course not. It's only the likes of poor working folks like you and me that have to live without pools, Jacuzzis, and viewing rooms."

"Er, I've got a pool, Peter. And a Jacuzzi." Deborah had insisted that we have both when we were looking for houses. They weren't something I'd miss.

"Yeah, I know that, mate. You want to see the film or not?"

"Of course. The sooner the better."

"Okay, I've been on to a friend of mine, an agent who owes me a favor. He said he'll let us use his house. This afternoon. That suit you?"

"Shouldn't be a problem. I don't usually get really busy until the evening. I'll ask one of my colleagues to hold the fort. What's the address?"

He gave me the details and said he'd meet me there at three o'clock.

I spent the morning lying under my car trying to work out why I was getting a grinding noise from the near side whenever I had the steering on full lock. The springs looked okay, and I finally figured it was just a case of the shock absorber starting to go. I wasn't planning to do anything over the weekend, so I reckoned I'd probably have a go at doing it myself. That was one of the pleasures of owning an old car that was put together with nuts and bolts rather than a spot-welded, built-by-numbers Japanese model. I stripped off my coverall and washed the grease and dirt from my hands. There were times when I wished that I could repair my own body as easily as I took care of the car. If it needed new brakes or bulbs or the bodywork got dented, then you just ordered the parts and did the work and it was as good as new. Even almost fifty years after it had rolled off the production line it was virtually perfect. And if ever the engine wore out, it would be reasonably easy to replace; there were still plenty of specialist suppliers back in the UK who could ship one over. But my body, the organs that were beginning to show signs of wearing out, well, that's a whole different ball game. There was no replacement for the skin that was beginning to lose its elasticity and was becoming speckled with brown moles and wrinkled around my eyes. I could remember being young and playing in the fields around the family farm, playing football for hours and running with the dog and never getting tired. Now walking up a couple of flights of stairs left me out of breath.

I ate reasonably well, health-wise, but at times I could feel my veins and arteries silting up with cholesterol and fat globules, and at night the sound of my beating heart seemed less powerful than it used to back when I was a teenager and had most of my life ahead of me. I wished I could go back. There was a small cut by the thumb on my right hand, not much more than a nick, but I smeared antiseptic ointment over it. That's something else I'd noticed as I got older—cuts and abrasions took longer to heal, and it took weeks rather than days to shrug off colds and the like. It was as if my body was starting to get tired, and I wondered how long it would be before it gave up trying to repair itself and I was left to lie alone on some urine-stained bed, riddled with bed sores and waiting to die. I shook my head and tried to think of something else.

I went to the kitchen and microwaved myself a frozen lasagna and boosted my caffeine intake with two steaming cups of strong coffee. I always felt better after coffee.

The agent's house was in Beverly Hills, and the guy was obviously doing well because it was above the smog line. Just. It was a single-story ranch house affair, lots of cartwheels and exposed beams and cactus murals on the walls, and it had all the charm of a takeaway taco restaurant. I parked the Alpine between a white Corvette and Hardy's orange MGB. Hardy, like me, preferred old British cars to any of the American stuff, and we often used to help each other out with the hunt for spare parts. At any given time there was a good chance that one of our cars would have something mechanically adrift, and it was a rare occurrence for them both to be on the road together. I made a mental note to ask him if he fancied giving me a hand to fit the new shock absorbers.

The door opened before I could press the doorbell, and Hardy was there looking disgustingly healthy in a red and green track suit and brand new Reeboks. He became something of a health nut a couple of years back and worked out every day at one of LA's more serious gyms, where you actually went to work up a sweat rather than hit on out-of-work actresses.

With him was a balding man with blue-tinted glasses who was as wide as Hardy was tall. He had an expensive-looking Italian suit that looked as if it had been bought for the price tag rather than the style, and he was wearing shoes made from the hide of some animal that Greenpeace was probably fighting to save from extinction. He flashed me a gleaming smile and pumped my arm up and down enthusiastically when Hardy introduced us. His name was Archie Hemmings, and from what Hardy had told me earlier he represented some real heavy-hitters.

"You're the first vampire hunter I've ever met, Jamie. It's a pleasure, a real pleasure." I gave Hardy a pained look, and he shrugged. "Pete tells me you're on a case right now," Archie continued, unabashed. "So where's the stake and the holy water?" He punched me on the shoulder, and I thought about suing for whiplash. "Just kidding, Jamie. You wanna drink?"

"Bit early for me," I said.

We walked together into Archie's viewing room, the size of a small cinema but containing only a couple of dozen chairs, each as big as a seat in the first-class cabin of a 747 jet, complete with footrests and a place to put your drink, and upholstered in the skin of another endangered species. The seats were facing a screen, and there were noises from a small hole behind us where the projector was. Archie waited until Hardy and I had sat down before he killed the lights.

"You mind if I watch, Pete?" he asked.

"Of course not, Archie. Make yourself at home."

Archie laughed. "Right. Make myself at home. You guys." He took a large cigar out of the inside pocket of his suit, bit off the end, and spat it into a wastepaper basket by his seat. His cigarette lighter flared, and a few seconds later the air was filled with cloying smoke. The screen flickered, and the titles came up. *Lilac Time*.

It was black-and-white, and the sound quality was really bad—half the time I couldn't make out what was being said. The story was simple enough: a country doctor, played by Greig Turner, was blamed for a murder he didn't commit, and the only witness was a small girl who was so shocked by what she'd seen that she retreated into herself. The doctor was only saved by a schoolteacher who got the child to open up after a nail-biting courtroom scheme. It was quite gripping, I had to admit, though the poor sound quality was a nuisance. There was no doubt about the fact that Turner had charisma. The camera really loved him. There was something about the girl who played the schoolteacher, too, something I couldn't place until about halfway through the film. And then it suddenly hit me. She was the spitting image of Terry, facially anyway. She had the same mouth, the same dark eyes and long lashes, and the body was similar, too. This girl, though, was a blonde. I watched her closely for the rest of the film, and by the time the film flickered to a close and the doctor hugged the teacher and the jury stood and cheered and the judge banged his gavel, I was pretty sure that she must be related to Terry in some way.

I stood up as the film ended and walked closer to the screen so that I could get a good look at the credits. The girl who'd played the schoolteacher was called Lisa Sinopoli. I wrote it down on a scrap of paper.

"What's up?" Hardy asked.

"The girl looks familiar. Lisa Sinopoli. You ever heard of her?"

He shook his head. "Sounds Italian," he said.

"Thanks, Peter. You're a big help. What about Greig Turner? You turn up anything about him?"

Archie pulled himself out of his chair and switched on the lights.

"He was a minor star during the forties. He made four or five films, and then he just vanished," said Hardy.

"What happened?" I asked.

Hardy shrugged and pulled a face that said he didn't know. Archie lit another cigar, took a deep pull, and then jabbed it in my direction.

"He had a drinking problem. He was a bottle-a-day man, and we're talking whiskey not beer." He took another pull on the cigar.

"You knew him?" asked Hardy, obviously surprised.

Archie practically glowed with pride. "I know everybody in this town," he drawled.

"Yeah, but Archie, that film was made in 1952. You weren't even a twinkle in your father's eye when it was being made."

"You guys," said Archie, waving his cigar. Ash spilled over his trousers, and he brushed it away with a hand studded with gold rings. "He made a minor comeback in the late eighties. Character parts in made-for-TV movies. Nothing spectacular, but he was in work for a few years."

"Did you manage him?" I asked.

"Give me a break, Jamie," said Archie, almost savagely. "He was strictly minor league. I think he was handled by one of the smaller agencies. If a talent isn't getting seven figures a throw, it's not worth my while getting out of bed. You hear what I'm saying?"

"Yeah, Archie. I get your drift. Do you think you could do me a favor? Do you think you could find out who his last agents were?"

"Sure, no problem. Hey, how often does a guy get to help out a vampire hunter? Come on, let's go get a drink."

I had a vodka and tonic, and while I drank it I asked Hardy if he knew that James Dean had a cat.

"I didn't know that," he said, which surprised me because he devoured movie trivia like a vacuum cleaner sucks in dust, partly because it helped him when it came to writing showbiz features, but mainly because he'd been a movie buff since he was a kid. You'd be hard-pressed to name a movie he hadn't seen or a star he hadn't written about, and he had a near-photographic memory.

"A Siamese cat," I said.

"News to me," he said.

"Elizabeth Taylor gave it to him. He took it round to his neighbor's house the day before he died," I said.

Hardy frowned. "I thought I knew everything about James Dean," he mused. "Where did you read that?"

"I didn't read it, someone told me."

"Somebody who knew him?"

"Hardly. She's far too young for that."

"You been cradle-snatching again?"

"I'm not sure who's being snatched at the moment," I said.

Archie and Hardy asked me if I fancied going out for a meal with them to a new Thai place, but I said no, I had work to do.

I drove to the police station via my house so that I could change into a suit and pick up the laptop. I'd promised Rivron the night off for covering me during the day, so I had my hands full.

There was an old guy, seventy-four he said he was, who'd been brought in for smashing a row of shop windows on Rodeo Drive. He hadn't stolen anything, just walked from boutique to boutique smashing the glass frontages with a tire iron until a cruiser had turned up, and then he'd hit two officers over the head before they'd subdued him with their nightsticks. The man sat in front of me with a bandage across his head and a plaster holding his nose together while he moved and pressed the mouse. According to the program, he was suffering from Korsakoff's syndrome, probably induced by chronic alcoholism, so I recommended that they take him straight to a mental institution and don't even bother charging him. He was just old and sick and would be better off in a geriatric ward than in a holding cell.

I went back to my office and started writing up my report on the old man when the phone rang and I was called down to the interview rooms again, this time to run two black teenagers through the program. They were both cocky and aggressive, swearing at me and demanding their lawyers. They were wearing black and silver jackets with the logo of the LA Raiders, and according to De'Ath they were both members of the Bloods, one of LA's more homicidal adolescent street gangs, and were well known as crack dealers. They'd raped and beaten up a teenage girl on her way back home after cheerleading practice, taking it in turns to hold a knife to her throat. The girl was in intensive care, De'Ath told me, and it would be some time before she was cheering for the high school football team again. Before they left her they'd stuck the knife up inside her, just for the hell of it. The surgeon reckoned she'd live, but she wouldn't ever have children. Sick world, isn't it? One of the black kids asked me if I had any games he could play on the computer, and I wanted to smash it into his leering face and take a knife and stick it inside him the way he'd abused the girl. I put it out of my mind, ran him and his unsavory pal through the program, and told De'Ath that there was nothing clinically wrong with either of them. Nothing a lethal injection wouldn't cure, anyway.

Later I sat at my desk with my head in my hands and tears in my eyes, grieving for a girl whom I didn't even know. The phone rang and it was Terry, asking me how I was and why I was in the office so late. I lied and said I was fine and that I was just writing a few reports. She asked me if I wanted to go out for a late-night snack, and I looked at my watch and was surprised to see it was already one o'clock in the morning. The blinds were down, and I'd lost all sense of time. I said okay, and she asked me if I had my car and said she'd meet me outside in half an hour.

I finished the report on the old man and then went and told De'Ath I was calling it a night. Extra help had arrived in the form of one of the junior psychologists from a local hospital. He was in doing a shift, and he'd been well trained in the use of my program; I told De'Ath to call my cell phone if the shit really hit the fan.

"You going out for a bite?" he said, gnashing his teeth together and imitating a vampire's bite.

"Don't you ever give up, Samuel?" I asked dejectedly.

Two patrolmen walked by, and one of them crossed himself and laughed. His friend slapped him on his back.

"And another thing, Samuel. Can you ask your men to stop putting rubber bats and garlic on my car? It's just not funny."

"Hey man, no problem, I'll just put a note on the bulletin board. 'Vampire Hunter Demands Truce.' How does that sound?"

"Just fine, Samuel. Thanks a bunch."

He laughed uproariously as I walked down the corridor.

Terry was waiting for me in the precinct car park, leaning against the bonnet of my Alpine. She stepped forward to hug me and kissed me on the cheek. "Who's the comedian?" she asked, nodding toward the windscreen. Someone had put a plastic crucifix under the windscreen wiper on the passenger side. I grabbed it. It was a gory example of religious art, painted blood on its cheek, side, and hands, a grimace of agony on the tortured face. It wasn't pretty. I threw it into the gutter.

"You shouldn't do that, not, like, with a cross," she said.

"I didn't know you were religious," I said, opening the driver's door.

"I'm not," she said, getting in beside me. "Do you like Japanese food?"

"Raw fish? I love it. But at this time of the morning?"

"Night," she said. "It's still night. Trust me." She took me to a restaurant which was indeed open, and doing well by the look of it. It was close to Hollywood Boulevard and seemed to serve the same sort of clientele that went to the club Terry had taken me to. It was a combination of high-tech noise and neon and Japanese simplicity, with wall-mounted television sets showing Japanese game shows with the sound turned down, while a Japanese DJ behind a white metal console played deafening pop songs and jumped up and down a lot. The waitresses all seemed to be Japanese but wore white T-shirts and jeans instead of kimonos. A girl with waist-length hair and scarlet lipstick showed us to a corner table and handed us two menus. Terry asked me what I wanted and proceeded to order in Japanese.

The waitress expressed no surprise at being spoken to in her native language, so I guessed that Terry had been there before.

"How many languages do you speak?" I asked Terry as the waitress went over to the sushi bar.

"I dunno, I just kinda pick them up, you know," she said. "I've never found them difficult. I guess I've got an ear for them. So, how was your day?"

"Same as usual. Quieter now that the full moon is over."

"You believe that?"

"Sure." We chatted about the moon, and whether or not it affected people, while we waited for our food to arrive. I felt sort of guilty about not asking her about Greig Turner, but I wanted to get my thoughts straight before broaching the subject. Also, I had a feeling that it might drive some sort of a wedge between us, and I didn't want to risk spoiling it. Whatever "it" was I wasn't sure, but I knew that I wanted it to develop further, and showing her that I'd been rifling through her apartment would show a distinct lack of trust. And without trust, so they say, there is nothing.

The sushi arrived along with a Japanese beer for me. She mixed the green mustard stuff into a small saucer of brown soy sauce and watched as I ate. She only picked at her food, a small piece of cooked shrimp, some fatty tuna, a strip of yellowtail, and she did most of the talking. So what did we talk about? It was strange, really strange, but afterwards I had a hard job remembering what it was she said. I can remember the way she said it, the way she looked, the way she made me laugh, the way I felt, but I can't recall the topics. I can be more specific about what happened afterwards, when I'd driven her back to my house and undressed her and she'd kissed me all over, but I'd kind of like to keep that between the two of us, you know? Suffice it to say that I went to sleep with a big sloppy smile on my face and her curled up in the crook of my arm.

She was gone when I woke up. I showered and dressed and made coffee, and I was just thinking about plowing through some back issues of *Psychological Medicine* when the phone rang. It was a jubilant Archie Hemmings.

"Found him, Jamie!" he said.

"What, you found his agent?"

"Better than that, Jamie. Much better than that. I found the man himself!" I could picture him standing in his cactus-muraled lounge, stabbing at the air with his big cigar.

"You found Greig Turner? But he must be a hundred years old!"

"But he's still alive, Jamie. Maybe not exactly alive and kicking, but definitely alive. You want the address or what?"

"Way to go, Archie!" I said. Shit, I was as pleased as he was. He told me that Greig Turner was now in an old folks' home in Big Sur, about six hours' drive from Los Angeles on the way to San Francisco.

Six hours in a 1966 Sunbeam Alpine is not the most pleasant way to spend a day, but as soon as I'd thanked Archie from the bottom of my heart, I grabbed the photograph of Terry Ferriman and drove up to Big Sur. I had to stop for directions when I saw the first giant redwoods, and by five o'clock in the afternoon I was driving up to a large white stone house, the sort of place that very rich city-slickers head to on weekends for a spot of hunting, shooting, and fishing. It was composed of a main block and two wings, and behind were the rugged mountains of Los Padres National Forest. It was a good place to retire to, I thought as I climbed out of the car. The air was fresh and good, the place had a tranquil aura, and it looked as if it would take a fair amount of money to buy your way in.

I went in through the main entrance and found the administration office and introduced myself to the resident physician, a white-haired guy in his fifties called Dr. Gerard Lyttelton. He wore a starched white coat with three pens neatly lined up in the breast pocket, and with his swept-back hair and steel-rimmed spectacles he looked a bit like Einstein. I thought I was going to have problems convincing him to allow me to speak to Greig Turner, but it turned out that he was a fan. Of mine, that is, not of Greig Turner. He'd read a couple of papers I'd written on the Beaverbrook Program and was keen to talk to me about it. I hadn't brought my laptop with me, unfortunately, but I discussed a few case histories with him over a cup of weak tea before I turned the subject around to Turner.

"What is your interest in him?" he asked.

"I'm trying to trace a friend of mine," I said. "Somebody he used to know."

"Ah," said Dr. Lyttelton thoughtfully, replacing his cup in its white saucer. "Dr. Beaverbrook, you must realize that he is a very old man," he said.

"Jamie," I said. "Please call me Jamie. He's in his nineties, yes?"

"He is, but chronological age is not the most crucial factor. There are some people who live to be more than a hundred and never lose their faculties. Others can be virtually senile in their sixties."

"And what exactly is Mr. Turner's state of mind?"

He sighed and walked over to a tall, gray filing cabinet. "He has senile dementia of the Alzheimer type, but that is really to be expected in a man of his age." He pulled out a pale blue file and walked back to his desk. He didn't open it but toyed with it as he sat down. "You know about Alzheimer's disease, of course."

I nodded. "Memory disorders, delusions, dementia," I said.

"Then you know that as the patient's memory lapses become more marked, there is a tendency to fill in the gaps with guesswork. Or fantasy. But Mr. Turner's case is made more complex by late paraphrenia, a form of schizophrenia in which the most obvious manifestation is the delusion of persecution. He periodically hallucinates, he hears voices, he feels that forces are out to kill him. At times he can appear quite lucid, and he is quite capable of taking real conversations and events and slotting them into the most complicated fantasies. If you are planning to ask him for information, I'm afraid you are going to have your work cut out."

That wasn't what I wanted to hear, but nonetheless, I wasn't going to leave without speaking to Turner, ga-ga or not. "I'd still like to try, if that's all right with you."

He drummed his fingers on the file. "Of course, of course. I'll take you to him."

He took me out of the office, along a green-carpeted corridor, and into a pleasant conservatory full of lush green plants and cane furniture. A group of residents, two men and two women, were engrossed in a game of poker, and a young girl in a white uniform was serving them what looked like cocktails. The place was more like a high-class health farm than an old folks' home. We went through French windows, over a stone-flagged patio, and onto a beautifully manicured lawn where a game of croquet was underway. We skirted the edge of the game and then walked through a clump of willow trees. I heard the gentle burble of a stream and then saw a wheelchair in the shade of one of the trees. A pretty blonde nurse was sitting nearby reading a paperback book, and she looked up as Dr. Lyttelton and I approached.

"Good afternoon, Jean. How is Mr. Turner today?"

"We're fine, Dr. Lyttelton. We had a good lunch, and later we're going to watch some television." She was an attractive girl, her hair tied back in a neat bun, big blue eyes, and high cheekbones. She looked at me curiously, but the doctor didn't introduce me, just led me by her so that we stood in front of the wheelchair.

The figure sitting there bore little or no resemblance to the smiling movie star in the photograph in Terry's apartment. He looked for all the world like a turtle out of its shell, wrapped in a thick wool blanket despite warmth of the afternoon sun. All that remained of his black hair, so immaculately groomed in the photograph, were a few wisps of white, and his scalp was pockmarked with dark brown moles and liver spots. His forehead was furrowed, and there were deep lines around his pinkish, watery eyes. There were huge bags under his eyes which gave the impression of being full of a bluish liquid, and his nose appeared to have grown more bulbous. The skin of his face was drooping as if it had been made of wax and he'd been sitting in front of a hot blazing fire, and it had lost most of its color. His mouth was slack and slightly skewed, as if he'd had a small stroke some years earlier, and there was a trickle of saliva running down his chin. His eyes were blank, and he showed no signs of noticing either the doctor or myself.

"Jean," said Dr. Lyttelton, and he raised his eyebrows.

She put the book down on her chair and came over. "Oh, Mr. Turner, we're dribbling again," she cooed and took a white handkerchief from her pocket and dabbed his chin. When he was dry, she went back to her book. Turner didn't appear to react at all.

"So, how are you today, Mr. Turner?" the doctor asked.

For the first time Turner seemed to become aware of us. Something flickered in his eyes, and he forced a smile. His voice, when it came, was as dry as his ancient skin.

"Dr. Lyttelton?" It was a question, and the doctor nodded. "Life goes on," said Turner. I thought he was making a joke, and I smiled. "And on. And on. And on," said Turner. He was definitely joking.

"Have you had any visitors today?" the doctor asked.

Turner shook his head. One of his hands came out from behind the blanket and rested on the side of the wheelchair. It looked like a mummified claw. "No visitors," said the cracking voice. "No one left. Just me." He seemed to be making sense, though I didn't doubt Lyttelton's diagnosis. He obviously knew his stuff, and he'd cleverly picked my brains about the profiling program in his office. He'd given me a few good ideas for further research, too, and suggested a few papers that would be worth reading. So if the good doctor said that Turner sometimes went a bit loopy, I believed him.

Lyttelton put his hand on my shoulder. "Mr. Turner, this is Dr. Beaverbrook. He would like to talk to you for a while." Turner looked at me and smiled. He dribbled again.

Lyttelton turned to me. "I'll leave you alone with Mr. Turner," he said. "Nurse Orlowski will be close by if you should need her. Just bear in mind what I said earlier." He patted me on the back and then walked through the trees toward the house. The nurse looked at me, smiled, and then resumed her reading.

I squatted down in front of the old man so that my head was at his level and he didn't have to look up at me. I smiled at him, but there appeared to be nothing behind the vacant eyes. My mouth felt dry, and I had difficulty swallowing, not because I was nervous but because I knew I was looking at myself in fifty or sixty years' time, assuming that I lived that long. Great choice, don't you think—sitting in a chair with a brain like scrambled eggs, or death. That's all there is, there is no other choice, and Turner was a reminder of what lay ahead. I wanted to run away and drink and blot him out of my mind, but there were things I had to know.

"I saw one of your films, Mr. Turner," I said, speaking slowly. "*Lilac Time*. Do you remember it? *Lilac Time*?"

His eyes seemed to focus on my face, and he inhaled, the sound of his breath like a wind blowing through a derelict chimney.

"*Lilac Time*," he repeated.

"*Lilac Time*. You were the star. You made it in 1952. Do you remember?"

His thin lips curved up into a smile. "Lousy movie," he said. "Shot the whole thing in under six days. Can you believe it?"

The words came slowly, almost painfully, from the slit of a mouth. He had a slight lisp, and whenever his mouth opened up enough for me to see inside, I was looking into a pink hole devoid of teeth. I wondered what the former movie star had eaten for lunch, and I guessed it had been put through a liquidizer first. We begin with baby food, and we end with it. We start out helpless, and that's how we end our days.

I was surprised how quickly he'd remembered the film which he'd made sixty years earlier, but Alzheimer's disease can be like that, wiping out whole chunks of recent memories but leaving others, more distant ones, untouched. Maybe I'd be lucky.

"I enjoyed it," I lied, smiling.

"Bullshit," he said.

"It was a good story."

"What are you, a critic?" he wheezed. "Two thumbs up, huh?" His chest shuddered, and I thought for a second that he was having some sort of attack, and then I realized that the old man was laughing. The only sound coming from his mouth was a rasping wheeze, but his eyes had crinkled up and the furrows on either side of his mouth had curved into a smile.

Nurse Orlowski came over and dabbed at Turner's face with her handkerchief. "Please don't get us too excited," she said to me.

I looked at her tight-fitting uniform which did nothing to conceal her figure underneath. If anything was likely to excite the old man it would be her; she had enough sex appeal to arouse the dead. I wondered what it must be like, to be old and confined to a wheelchair and to have a sexy young blonde like Nurse Orlowski ministering to your needs. Wiping your face, feeding you, bathing you, taking you to the toilet. When Turner was in his prime, I bet he had girls like her queuing up to sleep with him. I bet he'd had to fight them off. He'd been so good-looking then, and rich, and famous. And now, what good had any of it been? He was just a dried-out husk, a shell, and the blonde with the ball-busting figure treated him like a baby and waited for him to die.

"I'll be careful," I said as she went back to her book.

Turner's eyes slowly closed, and then he jerked awake. The claw-hand twitched, and his eyelids fluttered, and then he went still, but his eyes were open and focused on me while he waited for me to speak. I wanted to ask him what it was like to be so old, to be so close to death. I knew the statistics, knew that there was a fair chance that I'd end up like Greig Turner, if I lived that long.

Alzheimer's hits one out of four people by the time they reach eighty-five years old, and it's the fourth biggest cause of death in the Western world, after heart disease, cancer, and strokes. There's no cure, it may be genetic, it may be an illness, but if you get it there's nothing that can be done; the brain cells die in the millions, and that's all there is. Doctors used to reckon that it was a normal part of aging and that it happened to everyone in varying degrees, but a Swiss psychiatrist, Dr. Alois Alzheimer, all the way back in 1901, did an autopsy on a woman who'd gone ga-ga in her fifties, and he discovered the lesions in her brain that identified the disease that was named after him. The one blessing is that by the time you've got Alzheimer's, you've forgotten you had it, if you see what I mean. It's like the old joke. Doctor to patient: "I've got good news and bad news. The bad news is that you've got AIDS. The good news is that you've got Alzheimer's disease so you'll be able to forget all about it." Ha-ha. Looking at Greig Turner and the dribble on his chin, Alzheimer's didn't strike me as a laughing matter. It wasn't a prospect I relished. Maybe death would be better. Maybe. I wanted to ask Turner whether there were any advantages at all in having lived so long, whether the memories made up for the awfulness of being alive in such a decrepit old body. But more than that I wanted to know about Terry Ferriman.

"Mr. Turner, do you know a girl called Terry Ferriman?"

"Never heard of her," he said.

"Terry Ferriman," I repeated. "Long black hair, about five-four, five-five. Bright girl."

"So many girls," he wheezed. "You think I'd remember them all?" Yes, I thought. This one you'd remember. No matter how many opened their legs for you, this one you'd never forget.

"You are sure?" I pressed, wondering if I'd strayed into one of the blanks in his memory.

"When? Back when I was a star? Jesus, I can't remember the movies, never mind the dames."

"No, this would be recent. Within the last few years. She had your photograph in her room."

"I don't know anyone called Terry. She had my picture? A fan, huh? I thought all my fans had died long ago."

"This girl is young. I thought she might have been related. Do you have any children, Mr. Turner? Or grandchildren?"

"Not that I know about," he cackled. He screwed his eyes up at me. "What are you suggesting, that I can't remember if I have a relative called Terry? What was your name again?"

"My name? Jamie Beaverbrook."

"I might be old, Mr. Beaverbrook, but I'm not stupid."

"I'm sorry," I said. I realized I'd fallen into the trap of treating him like a child, of behaving like Nurse Orlowski. "But this is very important to me. The picture she had of you was taken on the set of *Lilac Time*. There was a girl in the movie, a girl called Lisa Sinopoli."

"My wife," Turner said.

"No, Lisa Sinopoli. She played the schoolteacher."

"Yes, I know. She was my wife. We married after we'd finished the film."

"I didn't know. She was very pretty. You made a good team. In the movie."

Turner snorted.

"What happened to her?" I asked.

He fell silent for a while, and I listened to his uneven breathing. He dribbled, and the claw of a hand made as if he wanted to wipe away the saliva, but it fell back. "She left me," he said eventually.

A thought struck me. "Did you have any children?" I asked.

He looked at me and frowned. "Children? No, no children. Lisa could never have children."

"Is that why she left?" I asked, knowing that I had no right to ask the question but knowing also that Lisa Sinopoli could be the clue I was looking for. Her resemblance was so close to Terry that I was sure they were related. And if Terry was Lisa's daughter, or granddaughter, or even cousin, then that might explain the photograph of Turner being in her room. A family heirloom, maybe.

"No, that's not why she left," Turner said. He thrust his head forward, the folds of skin around his neck hanging loose like badly fitting drapes. "You from the agency?"

"What?" I said, confused.

"What did you say your name was?"

"Beaverbrook. Jamie Beaverbrook."

"You a detective?"

"No, I'm a psychologist," I said. He'd started rambling, so I tried to steer him back to the movie business where at least I appeared to be on safer ground.

"Did the two of you appear in other movies together?"

"Just the one. She didn't even want to do *Lilac Time*, but I talked her into it. Have you found her?"

"Found who?"

"Lisa. Isn't that why you're here? Because I paid you to look for her?"

Shit, he'd started rambling again. "No, I'm not looking for Lisa. I'm trying to get information about Terry Ferriman."

"Never heard of her."

I took the black-and-white photograph out of my inside pocket and held it out to him. His hand twitched, and I realized it would be too much of an effort for him to hold it, so I stood upright and walked to the side of the wheelchair where I could hold it in front of his face.

He stared at the picture, breathing heavily through his nose. "That's her," he wheezed.

"Yes, that's Terry," I said.

"No. That's her. That's Lisa."

"No, this is a new photograph. This is Terry Ferriman."

"No. That's Lisa. You think I don't know my own wife?"

"Lisa had blonde hair," I said. Now he wasn't making any sense at all.

He shook his head adamantly. "She insisted on wearing a wig for the movie. Wouldn't do it otherwise." He sounded suddenly stronger, more coherent, as if his anger was revitalizing the fatigued neurons in his weary brain.

I moved around in front of him and showed him the picture again. The day seemed to have gone suddenly cold. The nurse was watching me with a concerned look on her face.

"Are you sure?" I asked.

"Of course I'm sure." He looked up with pleading in his eyes. "You've found her?" he said, and the hope in his voice was pitiful.

"I'm not looking for her," I said.

"Then what are you doing here?" he shouted. "Why are you doing this to me? Why are you torturing me like this?"

Nurse Orlowski got to her feet and came up to me. "I think you should go—you're disturbing us," she said.

Turner was trembling, and there was a dry rattle coming from his throat. His claw seemed to have gone into a spasm.

"I just want to ask him a few more questions."

"No," she said, and there was steel in her voice. "This man is my patient. You must leave. Now."

I could see she was serious, but I could also see that there was little chance of getting any more sense out of Turner. I left the nurse kneeling next to the wheelchair and went back to the main building in search of Dr. Lyttelton. He was in his office, and he stood up to greet me.

"How did it go?" he asked.

"He seemed fairly lucid to me," I said. "Most of the time, any-way."

"He comes and goes," he agreed.

I showed the photograph to the doctor. "Has this girl ever been here to visit Mr. Turner?"

He studied it and then pushed his spectacles up his nose. "Can't say I've ever seen her."

"Terry Ferriman's her name," I said.

He shook his head. "Easy enough to check, though. We keep a note of all the visitors." He picked up Turner's file, which was still lying on the desk, and flicked through it. He scrutinized one page and shook his head again. "No. No Terry Ferriman has ever vis-ited him. In fact, he's had only one visitor in the past three years." He looked up from the file. "That's to be expected when they get to his age, of course. Relatives—even children—and friends tend to fall off with time. Eventually they're totally alone. I guess about half the residents here have no..."

I interrupted his depressing chain of thought. "The visitor," I said. "Who was it?"

He looked at the file again. "A Mr. Blumenthal. Matt Blumenthal. Ah, yes, I remember. He was a private detective."

"A detective?"

"Yes. At first we thought it was just one of his delusions. I remember, the first time he turned up we sent him away after explaining about Mr. Turner's illness. Mr. Turner ended up contacting a lawyer, and the next time Mr. Blumenthal spent almost an hour with him."

"When was this?"

He read from the file. "A year ago. And again about two months ago."

"Could you do me a big favor, Dr. Lyttelton? Could you give me the name of his company? I'd really like to talk to Mr. Blumenthal."

The doctor gave me the details, and I thanked him and left. It was just after six o'clock, and I didn't fancy the drive back to Los Angeles, so I checked into a motel a few miles away from the home. I rang Rivron. He wasn't in the office, but I left a message explaining that I couldn't get in that night and asking if he would hold the fort for me again. I didn't sleep well, but at least I didn't have any nightmares.

THE SUICIDE

I woke up just after dawn and rang Rivron again. He was sleeping, so I gave him a few seconds to clear his head before I explained that I was still out of town and wouldn't be able to get to the office before the afternoon. He said he'd cover for me and mumbled goodbye and hung up. It was too early for breakfast, and I didn't feel hungry, so I got into the car and drove back to LA. I was keen to call Blumenthal, but I figured his office wouldn't open until nine o'clock, and by then I was almost halfway there. I was driving on autopilot, hands gripping the vibrating wooden steering wheel, eyes fixed on the road, ears filled with the roaring of the engine. I don't like driving long distances, especially in the Alpine; I always worry that I'm pushing the old car too hard.

At just before eleven I stopped for brunch at a roadside restaurant, and I pulled up in front of my house at about two o'clock. There was a message on the machine from Terry saying that she'd call me later that night and one from Chuck Harrison asking if I'd phone him. I rang the phone company and got the number of Blumenthal's company. The switchboard girl seemed confused when I told her who I wanted to speak to, and then I was put through to a secretary who said she was very sorry but Mr. Blumenthal wasn't with the company anymore. I asked where he was working, and there was an embarrassed silence before the girl said that actually Mr. Blumenthal was dead. It was obvious from the way she'd said it that there was something she wasn't telling me, so I told her I was attached to the LAPD and asked to speak the president of the company.

He was a nice enough guy, and once I'd told him who I was he was more than happy to tell me the circumstances surrounding the demise of Mr. Matt Blumenthal. The detective had been murdered. He'd been found in an alley with his throat cut. My blood ran cold. I didn't ask for any more details because I didn't want to make waves, but I did ask him if he could tell me what case he had been working on. He said he'd have to get back to me with that information, and he rang off. I telephoned Filbin in the precinct, and luckily he was at his desk. I made polite conversation about a couple of cases and then asked him if they'd managed to identify the body in the Ferriman case. Yeah, he said. The corpse was a private dick, he said. One Matt Blumenthal. I went and poured myself a vodka and tonic, a big one, and nursed it on the couch. Ten minutes later Blumenthal's boss called to say he'd been hired to track down one Lisa Sinopoli. The client, surprise, surprise, was Greig Turner.

My hand shook as I replaced the receiver. I tried to fit the facts into a coherent shape, some sort of pattern that I could deal with. Terry Ferriman had been discovered crouching over the body of a man who had been drained of blood. That man was Matt Blumenthal, a private detective. In Terry Ferriman's apartment was a photograph of a 1950s movie star, Greig Turner. Greig Turner had been married to a girl, Lisa Sinopoli, who was the spitting image of Terry. And he had hired Matt Blumenthal to track down Lisa Sinopoli, who must have been in her late seventies at the very least.

It was almost a perfect circle, yet it made no sense. I drained the glass and poured myself another vodka, and after I'd drunk it I went to the bathroom. I held the brush in my hand and pulled out the black and white hairs that were there. An idea was forming in my mind, an idea so weird that I didn't want to put it into words. I took the hairs to my desk and slid them into a brown envelope, and then I called a friend of mine, a scientist at UCLA, and arranged to meet him in a bar later that evening.

I put on a clean shirt and suit and slipped the envelope and Terry's photograph into the inside pocket and drove to the precinct. On the way I had a sudden urge to see Terry, so I took a detour past North Alta Vista. I parked outside the building and rang the bell for her apartment, but she wasn't there—or if she was she wasn't answering. A young woman with two children came out of the main entrance and smiled as she walked by.

"I don't suppose you know Terry Ferriman?" I asked.

She shook her head. I described her, and the woman said yes, she knew who I meant, and that yes she was probably in because wasn't that her car I'd parked behind. It was a black top-of-the-range Porsche squatting at the curb like a huge metal beetle.

"That's Terry's car?" I said, surprised.

"Are you a friend?" she said suspiciously.

"Yes, but I never realized she drove a Porsche," I said. The woman still didn't look convinced, and the last thing I wanted was for her to phone the cops and report me as a suspicious character, so I showed her my LAPD identification and she relaxed.

"I'm not getting any answer," I said, pushing the bell again.

She looked at the console of buttons and squinted. "I thought she lived in the basement," she said. One of her children, a young girl, three years old at most, began crying. I reached down and tousled her hair. She cried all the louder. Children didn't seem to like me much these days. Maybe they knew something.

"Oh no, she's got a small apartment. Upstairs. I've been there."

"I'm sure she lives in the basement," the woman insisted.

I wondered if perhaps we were talking about different girls, so I showed her the black-and-white photograph. "That's her, for sure," she said. "And I've seen her going into the basement." She pointed at the console on the wall. "Try that bell," she said, watching as I did. I guess she was convinced by now that I was planning to break in.

There was still no answer, so I told her that I'd give up and get her on the phone. As I turned to go I had another thought, and I asked her for the name of the firm who looked after the building, handled rentals and that sort of thing. She gave me the name and a telephone number, and I wrote them down on the back of the envelope containing the strands of her hair. I could feel her eyes on me as I walked back to the car, so I didn't look through the windows of the black Porsche, much as I wanted to. Terry and I hadn't discussed cars to any great extent, just a few passing remarks about my love affair with the Alpine, but I would have expected her to have told me that she had a Porsche. Porsche owners aren't exactly renowned for modesty, if you know what I mean. I wondered too how a young girl who lived in a cramped one-bedroom apartment in a not particularly affluent part of the city could afford a car like that and the sky-high insurance premiums that went with it.

When I got to the office it was deserted. On my desk was a message from Rivron saying that Chuck Harrison had called, so I rang the lawyer first. He wanted to tell me that he'd drawn up the settlement papers and that I could go to his office anytime and sign them. He sounded disappointed that I was so willing to settle, but Deborah had taken all the fight out of me.

My next call was to the firm who managed the building where Terry lived. I got the boss on the line and told him who I was, checked that the North Alta Vista address was one of his properties, and asked him which apartment she rented.

The man, a slow-talking guy with a baritone voice, coughed and said that actually Ms. Ferriman didn't rent any of the apartments in the building. I interrupted him before he'd finished speaking and told him that I'd already been there along with a couple of homicide detectives, so I knew that she lived there.

He coughed again. "What I mean to say, Dr. Beaverbrook," he said patiently, "is that Ms. Ferriman doesn't rent any of the apartments there, she owns them."

"Owns which?" I asked.

"Ms. Ferriman owns them all," he said. "The whole building. We act as her agent, finding suitable tenants and such, collecting rents, making repairs."

I was staggered. At a conservative estimate the building must have been worth about ten million dollars. How on earth did a young girl come to own a piece of expensive real estate like that? Thoughts of the car flashed into my mind again.

"For how long have you been acting for Ms. Ferriman?" I asked.

Another dry cough. "For the last six years, to the best of my knowledge." Since she was a teenager. That didn't make sense.

"And are all the apartments occupied?" I asked.

"They are."

"But the one-bedroom apartment is used by Ms. Ferriman?"

"That is correct. And she also uses the basement. For storage, I understand. It is a substantial size, taking up as it does virtually all the basement area with the exception of the laundry facilities and the furnace."

"I don't want to sound as if I don't believe you, but I'm sure that I got the impression that she rented the apartment. The one-bedroom apartment."

"Oh no, I can assure you most definitely that she owns it. What made you think she rented?"

For a moment I wasn't sure, and then suddenly it came back to me. "There was a list," I said. "In the apartment. There was an inventory, a list of what the apartment contained, the sort of thing that a landlord would have, so that when the tenant moves out he can check if there was anything missing." Like a knife, I thought.

"Ah, I see your confusion, Mr. Beaverbrook. Yes, we ran an inventory on all the apartments some time ago at the request of Ms. Ferriman. And we did the one-bedroom apartment at the time, I remember, as she suggested that at some time in the future she might decide to rent it."

"And the basement?"

"No, no, the basement was to be kept for storage, I seem to remember. No, I don't think anyone from our office has ever been there. No need to, you see."

"Yes, I see. One more thing—when were you asked to do the inventory?"

There was a hesitation and an intake of breath as he thought. "I would think it would have been about six months ago," he said. "Several tenants had moved out, and Ms. Ferriman had redecorated, so she thought it would be an opportune moment to compile new inventories for the various apartments in the building."

I thanked him for his help and asked him for one more piece of information. The name of the bank to which his company passed on the rent from the various tenants in the building.

He said he was always happy to assist the LAPD in its inquiries. He seemed like a nice guy. I wondered about the knife. De'Ath thought it wasn't an issue anymore because the landlord's inventory showed that there was no knife missing. I wondered how he'd react when he found that Terry was effectively her own landlord and that the inventory had been her idea.

Rivron came back as I was replacing the receiver, and he dropped his laptop onto his desk. "You're back, then?" he said, and you didn't have to be psychic to tell that he was mightily pissed off at me.

"Yeah, I'm sorry about that," I said. "Are we busy?"

"Are we ever!" he said. He threw himself into his chair and scooted it backwards so that he could swing his feet on top the desk. "A loony with a grudge against women who's been spraying acid onto the legs of women with long blonde hair. A teenage girl who's been crucifying cats in her bedroom. Two armed robbers who claim to be hearing voices from beyond the grave. And a Bible salesman who said God spoke to him through his car radio and told him to drive through a crowd of tourists on Hollywood Boulevard. How's your day been?"

Yeah, he was definitely pissed off at me.

"I'm sorry about last night," I said. "I was on a case, and it took me longer than I thought to get there. How's it been so far this afternoon?"

"Those are the cases from this afternoon," he said. "There were another dozen or so last night. I didn't get home until dawn, and then De'Ath called me just before noon and hauled me back in."

"Good old Black De'Ath," I said. "He thinks that because he works twenty hours a day, everybody else should."

"Yeah, well at least you're here now," said Rivron. "There's a wolfman down in room C that you'd love to get your teeth into. Or vice versa."

I looked at my watch. "Hell, I can't. I've got a meeting." Rivron looked as if he was going to throw his computer at me, so I held up my hands in a gesture of surrender. "I won't be long—I swear to God I won't be long. I've got to see a guy from UCLA, that's all."

"About a case?" he asked.

"About a case," I said emphatically. "I'll be back in two hours, and then you can clear off home."

He didn't appear any happier, but there was nothing he could do because, when it came down to it, I was his boss. Not that I'd ever pull rank, but with Rivron I knew I wouldn't have to. I patted him on the shoulder on the way out.

The bar in which I'd arranged to meet Rick Muir was a fake Olde English pub, lots of plastic beams, a dartboard, warm beer, and chicken in a basket. It was run by a couple of homosexual expatriates whose camp act seemed to be every bit as fake as the decor.

Rick was an expatriate too, but his libido was heavily on the side of heterosexuality, which I always reckoned was his main reason for moving to the West Coast. He spent more time prowling the beaches for babes than he did in his lab, but he put out enough papers to justify his grants and was climbing pretty quickly through the academic hierarchy. He had the look of a Californian beach bum, blond hair that he tied back in a ponytail while in the lab, clear blue eyes, broad shoulders, and a film star tan. He was sitting at a table with a pint of something brown from the North of England in a tall glass in front of him. "Jamie, how goes it?" he asked, getting to his feet and shaking my hand.

A waitress hovered at my shoulder hoping to catch Rick's eye. He gave her one of his come-to-bed smiles, and I practically heard her whimper as he ordered a beer for me. Oh yes, did I mention that he's a good ten years younger than I am? About Terry's age, I guess.

"It's going well," I said as we both watched the waitress strut to the bar.

"Nice," he said.

"Very," I said.

We chatted for a while about the weather, about the relative merits of Californian and English women, about my divorce, and about his sex life, and then I finally got around to what I wanted Rick Muir, PhD, to do for me. I handed him the envelope. "Can you run that through your carbon dating equipment?" I asked.

"Sure," he said. "What is it?"

"Hair," I said.

He raised a quizzical eyebrow. "Human hair?"

"Yup."

He pulled a face. "How old do you think it is?" he asked. "I mean, is it fossilized or something? You know as well as I do that carbon dating is no good for recent samples. Even for something five hundred years old it's only really accurate to plus or minus a century. And even to get that degree of accuracy you've got to be shit hot with the technology."

"Which you are," I said, and ordered us two more beers from the waitress who looked only at Rick while I spoke to her.

"Which I am," he agreed, smiling at the girl and giving her a boyish wink. "What I'm saying, Jamie, is that there's no point in giving me a lock of a girl's hair and asking me to find out how old she is. That's not how it works. I can tell you if something is ten

128

thousand years old, or five thousand, but I can't tell you whether human hair is five weeks or five years old."

"But you would know if it was recent or not?"

"Well, yes," he said hesitantly, "but you could do pretty much the same by looking at it through a microscope. Or stroking it. Hair dries out pretty quickly once it's been cut. An easier way would be to do a chemical analysis, probably."

"What do you mean?"

"Check it for pollutants and the like. A lot of the shit in the air and in the water wasn't around fifty years ago, so their presence in animal or plant tissue can give a pretty good indication of its age. That can be a darn site more accurate than carbon dating."

I nodded and called for the check. "Just humor me, okay. Run it through your equipment, and if it doesn't work I'll try something else."

"And you won't tell me what it's all about?"

The check arrived, and I paid. The waitress thanked Rick. "It's crazy," I said. "Just humor me. If you find something, I'll tell you everything. And believe me, there'll be one hell of a paper in it for you." That seemed to satisfy him, and he put the envelope into his blazer pocket. I left him talking to the waitress and, by the look of it, getting her phone number.

Rivron was in one of the interview rooms when I got back to the precinct, so I left a message for him on his desk saying that he should call it a night, and I phoned down to the desk sergeant to see what else there was to do. I was told there was an arsonist in room E who'd killed a family of four by throwing a homemade Molotov cocktail through a bedroom window. He was claiming that they were Satanists who'd been casting spells on him. I ran him through the program, and it showed that he was perfectly sane. I told the investigating officers, and they went back for another chat with him. I was in the office typing out a report when De'Ath rolled in like a tank in top gear.

"My man," he said, a big smile on his face. "Are you winning the battle against the dark forces which are plaguing our city?"

"Who wants to know?" I said. I didn't trust him when he was in such a good mood. It usually meant he had bad news for me.

"Only I, your loyal ally in the everlasting struggle between good and evil." His grin widened, and he sat on the edge of Rivron's desk, his legs crossed at the ankles.

"Okay, I give in, Samuel. What's happened? Has my car been towed away? Or burst into flames? Or have immigration finally decided that I've overstayed my welcome?"

He removed a file from under his arm and waved it triumphantly in the air. "Terry Ferriman," he said. "The vampire."

"Alleged vampire," I said.

"She isn't," he said.

"Isn't a vampire? Or isn't Terry Ferriman?"

"The latter, my old friend. Whatever she may be, she ain't Ferriman, Terry. Not unless she's one of the undead. Or living dead. Or whatever it is you call them."

"What the hell are you talking about, Samuel?"

"Alan and Claire Ferriman died when she was eleven years old. In Utah. Car accident."

"I know that, Samuel. She told me, remember? She said she was an orphan."

He grinned. "Yeah, but what she didn't tell you was that Terry Ferriman died in the same car crash!"

"Are you sure?"

"Man, what do you take me for? The birth certificate she used to get a passport and driver's license belonged to the original Terry Ferriman. The kid was born in Los Angeles, but because she died out of state there was no cross-referencing done. Once our lady, whoever she is, got the birth certificate, the rest was easy. All the credit cards are genuine, and so is the social security number, but it's all based on a lie. There's a warrant out for her arrest right now. You will call if you see her, won't you?" His eyes narrowed, though he had the same easy smile on his face. Like the cat that had got the cream.

"Yeah, Samuel. I'll call you."

"Be sure you do," he said

"Any more evidence on the murder thing? Anything that'll tie her in to it?"

"Nothing. Yet. But that girl is sure as shit up to something." He waved the file under my nose. "You don't go to all this trouble unless you've got something to hide. We're trawling through as many computer databases as we can looking for people with her characteristics. And we're waiting for a rundown on her fingerprints."

On his way out he told me that there was a child-murderer waiting for me in room B. Terrific. I spent an hour or so probing the mind of the middle-aged woman in room B. She kept winking at me as she spoke. She was insane, but I guess that would be no comfort to the parents of the three young boys that she'd mutilated and killed. Yeah, according to the medical examiner that's the way it happened. She cut off their testicles and forced them into their mouths, and then she throttled them with a leather belt. It was unusual to find a female child-killer, especially one who preyed on children other than her own. I mean, women sometimes kill their own kids, but almost never do they go out and hunt others. She blamed the murders on an alter ego called Emma Wilson whom she spoke to all the time, even when she was running through the program, asking for her advice on which answer to give.

She had denied any involvement in the killings, even when confronted with the bodies in her basement, and as evidence of her innocence she produced notebooks full of scribblings which she said were messages from Emma. According to her file, the notes were all in her handwriting. Her eyes were almost blank, and she kept licking her lips as she spoke to me. According to the flashing cursor on the Beaverbrook Program, she was severely schizophrenic and needed help. She showed most of the primary symptoms of schizophrenia: thought-controlled disturbances and auditory hallucinations (Emma Wilson's voice in her head) and primary delusions (she kept on claiming that the officer who arrested her had been following her for nine months). The wink was a psychomotor disorder often exhibited by schizoid patients, and the program picked up another four factors indicative of the illness and pinned it down as hebephrenic schizophrenia. Given sensitive enough therapy coupled with medical treatment, she'd be able to live a normal enough life. That was unlikely to happen in view of the brutality of the murders, but at least I could tell De'Ath that there was no point in interrogating her; he'd have far more success if he let the shrinks loose on her. She'd open up if handled the right way. De'Ath suspected she might hold the key to another half a dozen missing-children cases. I hated child-killers. I really did.

I was alone in the office eating a turkey breast sandwich and pecking at the typewriter when De'Ath burst into the room. At first I thought he was pissed at the report on the woman, but it soon became clear that he had something else on his mind. He slammed the door behind him hard enough to rattle the glass and jabbed a black finger at me in time with his words.

"Why the fuck didn't you tell me about this guy Turner?" he shouted.

"Turner?" I said, confused, still thinking he was talking about the woman.

"Greig Turner. Old folks' home in Big Sur? You were there yesterday, remember?"

"What's happened?" I said. Something was wrong, I was sure. If it was just a matter of Lyttelton or his nurse making a complaint, De'Ath wouldn't be as angry as he was.

"He's dead," said De'Ath, pacing up and down. "He's dead, and according to his nurse you were his last visitor."

"Some dish, that nurse," I said. Male bonding, it never failed to win De'Ath over.

"I never saw her. I've just had my counterpart from Big Sur on the phone chewing me out and wanting to know what sort of investigation we're running on his turf."

Well, it almost never failed. De'Ath was clearly not going to be mollified by male bonding.

"I didn't know they had someone as high as you over in Big Sur," I said. Flattery often worked, too.

"Don't fuck around with me, Beaverbrook," spat De'Ath. But sometimes flattery didn't work, right? "You're in deep shit. You've been passing yourself off as an LAPD detective, and that's a criminal offense. Now what the fuck are you up to?"

I tried to remember what I'd told Dr. Lyttelton about the reason for my visit. I was pretty sure I hadn't mentioned Terry Ferriman to him, but he'd told me about Matt Blumenthal. De'Ath would almost certainly have checked up with Blumenthal's agency, which means they'd have told him the same as they told me, that the client was Greig Turner and that the subject of the inquiry was one Lisa Sinopoli. Was there any way De'Ath could connect Lisa Sinopoli with Terry Ferriman? I doubted it.

"Talk to me, Beaverbrook," De'Ath growled.

I couldn't think of a lie that would justify my visit to Turner. I racked my brain, but I simply couldn't think of anything. If I'd had more time then maybe I could have come up with a halfway convincing story, but De'Ath was prowling backwards and forwards like a bear with a sore head, and every train of thought I had ran straight back to Terry.

"It was the Ferriman thing," I said.

He stopped pacing and glared at me. "Fuck, I know that," he said. "You showed Lyttelton her photograph, don't you remember?"

Shit, I'd forgotten. I'd shown him the picture and asked if she'd ever visited Turner. And I'd told him her name. God, it was lucky I hadn't tried to lie because then De'Ath really would have given me a roasting. "Turner's picture was in her apartment. In the bedroom. Remember? Antique gilt frame. Movie star in a director's chair?"

De'Ath shook his head. "I knew it was a mistake letting you into the apartment. I knew it. Shit, shit, shit, Beaverbrook. Don't you ever fucking listen to me?"

"Of course I do, Samuel. You just said shit. Three times." He didn't laugh, but I felt him loosen up a little. "I saw the picture, and a friend of mine, an agent, said he knew where he was. I thought that if I spoke to Turner I might get more of an insight into her character. And Samuel, I don't remember trying to pass myself off as a detective, I really don't. I told Dr. Lyttelton that I was a psychologist, and he knew who I was anyway. He'd read some of my papers, and he was interested in my research."

He held up a hand. It was big and square, the sort of hand that belonged to a heavyweight boxer, which is exactly what De'Ath had been during his army days. "Okay, okay," he said. "What did you talk about? Whatever you said, it must have upset him."

"What makes you say that?"

"Why else would he kill himself?" said De'Ath. "Didn't I tell you that? Must have slipped my mind."

Killed himself? When De'Ath had told me that Turner was dead, I'd assumed that he'd just died naturally. It was obvious from what I'd seen that he didn't have much time left. "How could he have killed himself?" I asked. "The man I saw could barely move. He was in a wheelchair, and a nurse had to do everything for him."

De'Ath leaned against my desk and folded his arms across his chest. "It looks as if Turner tied a scarf around his neck and then looped it around his bedpost and rolled himself out of bed. It doesn't take much to strangle yourself. I've seen people do it from door handles. It just depends on how determined you are. But you're getting away from the point again, Beaverbrook. What did you two talk about?"

"I asked him if he knew Terry Ferriman. He said he didn't."

"The nurse says you showed him a photograph."

"Yeah, the same one I showed Lyttelton. It was a photograph of Ferriman."

"The nurse said Turner seemed upset by the picture. Or by something you said."

I shrugged. "He was tired, that's all. His mind was wandering, and a lot of the time he rambled. He's practically senile, according to Dr. Lyttelton."

De'Ath rubbed his chin thoughtfully. "A picture of Ferriman, huh? Where did you get it from?"

I had been hoping he wouldn't ask that because I'd stolen it from his desk. I shrugged. "God, I can't remember, Samuel. Somewhere, I don't know."

"Don't suppose you've got the picture on you now, have you?" he asked.

It was in my inside jacket pocket. "No," I lied.

"Just as well, I suppose," he said, looking me steadily in the eyes. He stood up and stretched his arms behind his back, interlocked the fingers of his massive hands, and squeezed until his shoulders cracked. He sighed. "That's better," he said. "So, you went all the way to Big Sur, spent almost half an hour with this guy Turner, and got nothing from it. Is that right?"

"That's about it."

"You ever heard of a Lisa Sinopoli?" he asked. I recognized the technique, the curveball question trying to catch me off guard, so I kept my face straight and looked him in the eye and said no, never heard of her. He didn't appear to be convinced by my "What, me?" act.

"Why do you ask?" I said.

"Seems Turner hired a detective to track down someone called Sinopoli. That and whoever was paying the nursing home bills."

"Bills? I don't follow."

"Most of Turner's money ran out long ago, according to Dr. Lyttelton. Seems the studios didn't pay their movie stars as much then as they do these days. But his bills have been paid by a bank in LA for the last ten years or so. A private eye named Matt Blumenthal had been hired to find out whose account was paying his bills."

"Maybe he thought it was this, what was her name, Sinopaul, who was keeping him. Maybe he wanted to thank her."

"Sinopoli," said De'Ath. "Her name was Sinopoli. No, I don't think so, Beaverbrook. I think you should stick to messing with their psyches and let me get on with the detective work. By the way, Filbin tells me you were asking about Blumenthal earlier?"

Another curveball. "Not specifically. I was just wondering how the case was going, that's all."

"You don't seem surprised, Beaverbrook," he said.

"I don't follow you."

"Filbin told you the victim in the Ferriman case had been identified and that his name was Blumenthal. I just told you that Blumenthal was hired by Turner. And you didn't seem surprised."

Shit. I'd dropped myself right in it. I'd been too busy working out what his next trick question was going to be. I let my mouth fall open. "You mean it's the same guy?" I said, faking astonishment as best I could while mentally kicking myself.

De'Ath looked at me with hard eyes, and I knew he was weighing me up. He shook his head. "Christ, man, this city sure is lucky that you weren't hired as a detective, that's for sure. Yeah, it's the same guy. There's obviously some connection between Ferriman and this guy Turner. I just wish I could find out what it is. Then maybe we'd be able to find out why she killed Blumenthal."

"Come on, Samuel. You still don't have any proof."

"Not yet I don't," he admitted. "But it's just a matter of time."

He seemed a lot less angry now. "What are you planning to do?" I asked.

He shrugged. "Visit the bank, I guess. The one that pays Turner's bills. It's one of those small ones, handles a lot of private accounts." He told me the name. "Ever heard of it?" he asked.

Yeah, I'd heard of it, but I didn't let on to De'Ath, and he left the office. I toyed with a gold pen that Deborah had given me for our third wedding anniversary while I figured out what to do next.

At the rate he was going, it wouldn't take Black De'Ath too long to figure out that Lisa Sinopoli and Terry Ferriman were one and the same because the bank that was helping to keep Greig

Turner in the style to which he'd become accustomed was the same one that had been collecting the rents for the building she owned on North Alta Vista. If De'Ath asked the bank manager about Terry, chances were that he'd find the link, though whether or not he'd realize that Sinopoli should now be in her eighties was another matter completely.

I'd really wanted to ask De'Ath if I could go with him to speak to the manager myself, but I knew that there was no way I could do that without telling him everything I knew, and I wasn't prepared to do that, not until I'd had a chance to speak to Terry. I watched from the window of my office until I saw De'Ath get into a car with Filbin and drive off. I gave it ten minutes and then drove downtown to the bank, parking some distance away from it because a bright red 1966 Sunbeam Alpine is fairly conspicuous, even in LA.

They were in the building for about half an hour, and when they came out De'Ath seemed a hell of a lot more relaxed than when he'd left my office. Filbin drove away with De'Ath talking animatedly in the passenger seat.

I waited until they were out of sight before walking into the bank and asking the girl if Lieutenant De'Ath was still in with the manager. When she said no, I'd just missed them, I pulled a face and asked her for the manager's name, and then I asked if she'd call through and see if he could spare me a few minutes.

He was waiting at the door of his office, a dapper man in his fifties in a black suit with a thin gray pinstripe, a crisp white shirt, and a small gold tiepin in the shape of a horseshoe in a dark blue tie with small white dots. He had the flabby handshake of an undertaker at the end of a long day and a worried frown on his face.

"You've just missed your colleagues, Mr....?" he said.

"Beaverbrook," I said. I'd already decided it wasn't worth the risk of lying to him because if De'Ath heard that someone had been asking questions about Terry Ferriman, he'd know right away it was me. "Jamie Beaverbrook. I work with Lieutenant De'Ath." Which, of course, was true, strictly speaking, and I hadn't actually said that I was a policeman, so if De'Ath threw me up against a wall and grabbed me by the throat and asked me what the hell I was doing pretending to be a cop, then I could put my hand on my heart and tell him that there had been some misunderstanding, Samuel.

"Come in, come in," he said and stepped aside to usher me into the office. As I walked by him, he patted me in the small of the back as if checking for a hidden transmitter, the sort of gesture which could have got him summoned for sexual misconduct if he'd done it to a woman.

His name was Piers Whitbeck, and his office was plush enough to soothe the egos of the bank's wealthy private clients, but not so luxurious that they'd worry about whose money was paying for it. Deep-pile carpet, rosewood furniture, comfortable black leather seats, and a few tasteful watercolors on the walls. A computer terminal sat discreetly on a table in a corner as if silently apologizing for its presence in the room. He shuffled behind his desk like a ballroom dancer, sat down, raised his eyebrows, looked over the top of his gold-rimmed half-moon spectacles, and asked how he could help me. I wished my own bank manager could have been half as accommodating, but I didn't think it worth asking him if he'd consider taking on my overdraft. Not with Deborah and her rottweiler breathing down my neck.

"I was hoping to catch Lieutenant De'Ath before he went," I lied. "I'm working on the case with him and Detective Filbin, but I came across some new information shortly after they left the precinct house." I made a show of taking a notebook out of my jacket pocket and flicking through its pages. There was nothing written on them, but he couldn't see that from across the desk. "Lieutenant De'Ath was here to ask you about a Lisa Sinopoli and payments made from an account to a retirement home in Big Sur?"

Whitbeck nodded. "That's correct."

"Well, just after he left the station, we received another name, and we believe that another account at this bank may well be involved." I looked down at the blank page in front of me. "A lady by the name of Terry Ferriman." I spelled the surname out for him. "I wonder, Mr. Whitbeck, if you could confirm that Ms. Ferriman has an account at this branch?"

He pushed the spectacles up his nose with the index finger of his right hand. "That is so, yes. In fact, Ms. Ferriman has several accounts at this bank."

I was impressed that he knew the names of his customers without having to consult his sullen computer. "Would she be a major client?"

He looked at me curiously. "All our clients are equally important to us, Mr. Beaverbrook. We pride ourselves on our standard of personal service."

"I suppose what I'm asking, Mr. Whitbeck, is how big a customer is she? Would you be able to give me an idea of the assets she has with the bank?"

He shook his head emphatically. "Not without a court order. We have to abide by client confidentiality, I'm afraid, much as I'd like to help."

"A court order is certainly a possibility, but it'll involve us both in quite a bit of time and trouble, and to be honest I don't think Ms. Ferriman's case actually merits it," I said. "Look, if you could give me a ballpark figure of her assets, nothing too specific, then hopefully I'll be able to eliminate her from our inquiries. You needn't tell me how many accounts, or how much is in each one, or even exact numbers. Just a ballpark figure which I won't even write down."

He looked over at his computer terminal and back at me, and I smiled ingratiatingly and nodded. "Well…" he said.

"Just a ballpark figure," I pressed. I put the notebook away and sat back in the chair.

He nodded as if he'd made up his mind. "Very well," he said, "but I'll deny that you ever got the information from this office. If you want a figure you can use, you'll have to come back with a court order. Understood?"

"Understood," I said.

"If you went on a figure of sixty, you wouldn't be too far out," he said quietly, as if he were a Russian agent giving me details of the Kremlin's nuclear capability.

"Sixty thousand dollars?" I said.

He looked up at the ceiling and shook his head, sighing mournfully as if dismayed at my stupidity. "Come, come, Mr. Beaverbrook, we are not some down-at-the-heels savings and loan, you know. Sixty million dollars. Or thereabouts."

THE BASEMENT

One of the perks of being a police psychologist is that you get to meet a wide range of people. Sure, a fair number of them are murders, rapists, and perverts, but every now and again I'd come across a pearl among the swine. Dave Burwash was a case in point. You might even say that he was one of my successes, seeing as how he wasn't doing life in a state penitentiary and he hadn't gone out and raped and killed a group of underage cheerleaders. Dave was one of the first criminals, make that *alleged* criminals because he got off on a technicality, that I came across. He'd been pulled in on a charge of breaking into a broker's office while wearing a Mickey Mouse mask, and I ran him through the program to see if the mask was a symptom of an underlying mental problem. He was fine. He was better than fine—he had an IQ of 156, which put him in the top half of one percent of the population, and I ran him through a few other tests that showed he had a particular aptitude for numbers. Yes, he'd told me, he'd always been good at adding up figures in his head. He'd worked in a bar for a while, and no matter how busy it got he'd beaten the electronic cash register hands down every time, and at school he'd amused his friends by multiplying numbers, big numbers, in his head. The sort of school he went to was the sort where the teachers were just glad if they got through the day without a shooting in the corridor, so they weren't exactly on the lookout for hidden talents of the type that Dave possessed. His father had run off soon after he was born, and his mother was often ill, so Dave took a succession of jobs. But then she got worse, and he turned to crime. He had a particular knack for lock-picking, I guess because of the mathematical side of it, the combinations and the tumblers; it was physical but required a keen mind, and he was, he told me proudly, having no problems getting to grips with electronic alarm systems. He was a criminal, there was no doubt about it, but there was a problem with missing evidence—the Mickey Mouse mask, believe it or not—when the case came to court, and Dave walked.

I took an immediate liking to the guy. He was five years or so younger than me and had a sarcastic approach to life. I helped get him into a computer programming course, and within a year he was running his own consultancy and earning five times what I was paid by the good old LAPD. He was a natural, better even than suggested by the program. I wasn't sure how he'd react to being asked to resume his old habits for one night, but he jumped at the chance.

He arrived at my house in a shiny new two-seater Mercedes, but I made him leave it outside my house and I drove him to North Alta Vista in the Alpine. We parked some distance away, and I carried the brown leather wallet containing the tools of his former trade and insisted that he walk a dozen or so paces behind me just in case, God forbid, we should attract the attention of an overzealous member of the local constabulary. Dave thought it was all great fun, but there was no way I was going to risk his future. We walked down an alley at the side of Terry's building, and when we were sure that we were alone in the darkness,

I tiptoed toward him and whispered in his ear. "This is it. Can you see a way in?"

"There's always a way in," he whispered back.

"As soon as you've got me in, get the hell out of here," I said. "I don't want you anywhere near the building if anything goes wrong. Walk up to the boulevard and catch a taxi from there. And leave the picks with me. And wear gloves. And..."

"Jamie," he said, interrupting, "you're making me nervous."

"Right," I said, handing over the soft leather wallet. "Right. Okay. I'll keep quiet. Are you sure you..."

He held up his hand to silence me and took the wallet. "Watch," he said. "And learn." In the distance we heard a siren wail, and somewhere in the dark a bottle smashed. "Relax," he whispered. "It's probably just a cat."

The windows were protected by metal grilles that appeared to have been locked from the inside, and after Dave had checked them out he shrugged disappointedly. Steps led down to a door, and he ran his hands over it and tapped it cautiously. "Metal," he whispered.

"Can you do it?" I asked.

There were three locks, evenly spaced down the left-hand side of the door, and he examined each one. "I can, but it'll take time," he said. "Let's see if there's an easier way." We walked farther down the alley and took a right turn, walking by a pile of fetid cardboard boxes and a cat that was chewing on something unsavory. It mewed as we went by, warning us not to tamper with whatever it had between its sharp teeth.

By now our eyes were used to the gloom. The moon was still out, but there were tall walls on either side of the alley and the moonlight couldn't penetrate down to where we were. Just starlight. It was enough. The windows there were also shuttered and covered with grilles. At the end of the alley was the yellow glow of streetlights, and I hung back to let him go out first. He turned to the right and then stopped to examine the doors of the double garage there before walking on and back to the main road. I caught up with him about fifty yards from the building. "Let's go get a drink," he said. I took the wallet back from him and put it into my jacket pocket.

He waited until we were in a bar on Sunset Boulevard with a couple of bottles of lager in front of us before leaning over conspiratorially. "It's just like the old days, Jamie," he said with a wink. In his dark sweatshirt and blue jeans he looked a lot more like the burglar of old than the successful and highly paid computer programmer which he'd become.

"Don't get to like it, Dave," I warned. I knew all too well the adrenaline kick that comes with breaking the law; I'd seen it many times in the interrogation rooms in precinct houses all over Los Angeles. I didn't want to turn Dave back to his old ways, and not for the first time I regretted asking him along. I had no right to jeopardize his new life, even if I had been the catalyst who caused it. It was as if I was playing God, and the way he was reveling in it and treating it like an adventure just made me feel worse.

He raised his bottle in salute and drank from it, then wiped his lips with the back of his hand, realizing as he did that he was still wearing his black leather gloves. He slid them off and put them into his back pocket.

"The windows are too difficult," he said. "We'd have to cut our way in. That in itself isn't a problem—a good pair of bolt-cutters will do the job—but we don't have a good pair of bolt-cutters. And there's a chance that they're wired, though I wasn't able to see anything. The door would be easier, but as I said, if you want them picked it'll take time. In a perfect world I'd drill them out, but that would make noise, even with a muffled drill. And again…"

"We don't have a drill," I finished for him. "Or a muffler."

"Ain't that the truth," he laughed.

"Okay, so you saw the door to the garage—one of those up-and-over jobs it was?"

I nodded.

"That I can have open in two minutes. It's operated by remote control, but there's a lock too, and I can pick that with no trouble at all. The one snag is, it's pretty exposed. Streetlights, cars going by."

"Dave, I don't want you taking any risks, okay? It's just not worth it."

He put a hand on my shoulder. "If it wasn't important, you wouldn't have asked, I know that. It'll be okay, but I'm going to need you to keep a lookout for me. We'll walk back, and when we get to the building, you hang back thirty feet or so and start whistling as soon as I reach the door. I'll make it look as if I'm using a key. If I don't get it open in a minute or so, I'll leave it and we'll try later. If you see anything that might give us problems, you stop whistling. That's all. No shouting, no waving, just stop whistling. We'll move on and try later. Clear?"

"Clear," I said, though I was far from happy about what he planned to do.

He picked up his bottle of lager and clinked it against mine. "Jamie, we'll make a criminal out of you yet," he laughed.

"What do we do when the door's open?" I asked.

"I guess there'll be another door inside leading to the basement itself. I'll have to pick that for you too."

"Dave, I don't want you inside that house. You get me in, and then you get the hell away."

He shook his head. "Just getting you into the garage won't be enough. I'll have to go inside and deal with the rest of the locks before you can get into the house. And what will you do if there's an alarm inside?" He saw that I was about to argue, and he held up his hand to silence me. "Jamie, no arguments. Besides, as soon as we're in the garage we'll close the door. We'll be safer there than in the alley."

"I suppose you're right," I agreed reluctantly. I think the urge to see inside Terry's mysterious basement had got the better of my judgment.

We finished our lagers and went back to the house. As we'd agreed, I held back and whistled as best I could as Dave knelt down by the lock and inserted one of the metal picks from the wallet. He tried a second, and a third, then a fourth, and then he straightened his back and lifted the door with a grating sound that set my teeth on edge. He slipped inside, and I followed him. As I shut the door a pickup truck drove by, but I doubted that the driver would have seen anything.

A fluorescent light had flickered on as soon as he'd swung the door open, and it bathed the concrete floor in a stark white light that was almost blinding after the soft yellow streetlights outside. It was musty-smelling as if it hadn't been used, though there was a small patch of oil on one side of the garage as if a car had been there recently. Terry's Porsche, maybe? There were metal racks against one of the walls and a selection of tools, but they were dust-covered and festooned with cobwebs, so she obviously wasn't much of a mechanic. Or, more probably, the Porsche never needed any work done on it, Teutonic engineering and all that.

"Jamie, you can stop whistling now," said Dave with a grin.

To the left was a white-painted wooden door with a brass lock. Dave carefully ran his fingers around the doorframe, peered through the cracks at either side and at the top and bottom, and then went to work with his picks. It took him three minutes, and then I heard a metallic click and the door slowly opened inwards. Dave made as if to go through the door, but I stepped forward and pulled him back.

"No," I hissed. "I'm on my own from here on in. Thanks for everything, Dave, but you must go now."

He looked as if he was about to refuse, but he could see that I was serious. "Okay," he said. "Close the door after me."

He told me to switch off the light, and as I did he swung the door halfway up, ducked under it, and was away. I closed it behind him and stood waiting for my eyes to get accustomed to the dark. They didn't. I waited for a full five minutes, but I still couldn't see my hand when I held it in front of my eyes. The garage was completely lightproof. I couldn't even remember where the light switch was in relation to where I was standing. I groped against the wall but couldn't find it, then took a step to the left and banged against something wooden. Had there been a crate there before? Or a box? I couldn't remember. I felt a cold breeze on my left cheek, and I turned my head that way but couldn't see anything. Was that the direction of the door leading inside the house? I squinted a little and it seemed as if there was a gray rectangle in the blackness, but it could have been my eyes playing tricks.

I remembered I had a miniature Mag flashlight on my key ring, a present from Deborah in the days when she used to buy me presents. Way back when. I pulled it out of my pocket, the keys jangling like a wind chime, and twisted the light on. I ran the circle of light around the walls of the garage and allowed it to settle on the white door. There was a cool breeze coming from that direction, but I couldn't understand how that could be because all the windows Dave and I had seen had been shuttered and locked.

I decided against switching on the light and walked carefully across the garage floor to the door. It made no sound when

I pushed it, and I stepped over the threshold, holding my breath. Beyond the doorway was a red-carpeted hallway. There was a rough mat on the floor, and I wiped my feet on it and then stepped onto the plush pile. It made a quiet brushing noise as I walked, the sound of a cat being stroked. As I swung the flashlight around, I saw another beam of light and a figure in the shadows. I jumped back, my heart thudding, and it jumped back simultaneously, and I realized I'd been frightened by a mirror.

"Calm down, Jamie," I muttered to myself. The mirror was old, very old, obviously an expensive antique. It was as tall as a man, and the frame was painted gold. I looked at it closely. No, gold leaf more likely. Real gold. It must have been worth a fortune. The door from the garage had opened into the middle of the hall, facing the mirror, and it stretched out to the right and left. There were two doors leading off the hall, one at either end, and I decided to head for the right, hoping that there weren't any more locks and wondering what I'd do if there were. I worried too about alarms and thought that maybe it hadn't been such a good idea to send Dave away. It would also have made me feel a lot better wandering around in the dark if I'd had someone with me, but I knew that was childish. There was nothing to be frightened of in the dark. That's what I told myself, anyway.

There was a brass knob on the door, and I turned it slowly and pushed. It opened, and there was no sound from the hinges, just the swishing of the bottom of the door against the thick carpet. Beyond was another hall off which led at least eight doors. There were probably more, but the thin beam of light couldn't penetrate any farther through the darkness. I was starting to feel like I was in a game of Dungeons and Dragons, the fantasy game I used to play at university, where you go through a maze fighting imaginary demons and monsters, but you've no idea of where you're going or where the monsters are—the only one who knows is the guy controlling the game, the Dungeon Master. All you are told about is the tiny bit you're in, be it a cave or a room or a corridor with a thick red carpet.

I opened one of the doors and entered a room which must have been about twenty feet square with high ceilings and no windows. There was a glittering chandelier hanging from the center of the ceiling and a brass light switch by the door, and there were paintings on all of the walls. I couldn't see much detail of the paintings because the flashlight didn't throw enough light to illuminate them entirely, so I could only examine them a little at a time. They were big and obviously old. Some of them were sea scenes, big galleons engaged in bloody battles with cannons firing and sails flapping in the wind, while others were landscapes, images of farming practices that had long gone.

I looked for signatures in the corners of the paintings but couldn't find any, though I was pretty sure one of them was a Turner. I'd been around the Turner collection at the Tate in London, and the one on the wall was definitely similar. If it was a Turner, Christ, what would it have been worth? Millions, I guess.

I left the gallery, checked up and down the corridor, and went into the next room. The door felt much heavier, and I really had to push to open it—and once inside I could see why. The back of the door was faked up to look as if it were covered in shelves of leather-bound books. When I closed the door it formed part of a bookcase, and it was difficult to see where the join was, to make out which were real books and which were the fakes. I opened the door and left it ajar because I was sure that otherwise I'd have trouble finding my way out of the room again. It was about twice as long as the first room and lined from floor to ceiling with books. The ceiling was high, at least twelve feet, and there were several small stepladders so that you could reach the books on the top shelves. There must have been several thousand books in the library, and I walked around, reading the titles in the light of the flashlight. One wall was composed entirely of fiction, and it looked as if most of them were first editions. It was an eclectic mix—modern thrillers, detective stories from the forties, classics from the eighteenth and nineteenth centuries, poetry, romances, ghost stories. The rest of the books were nonfiction, a wide range of subjects, including geography, science, cooking, and a whole collection of textbooks on everything from anatomy to zoology. They were in many different languages, too; I spotted French, German, Russian, Italian, Spanish, Chinese, and some that I couldn't identify. I wondered where she had got all the books from; they all seemed in pristine condition, as if they'd been bought by the yard by some interior decorator.

I couldn't see any order to the collection, either; they weren't grouped in subjects, or languages, or alphabetically. I shone the torch around looking for a catalog system of some kind, a card index or a computer. There was nothing.

She either had an incredible memory or didn't care where the books were. Had they even been read? I took one of the books, a first edition of *For Whom the Bell Tolls*, and flicked through it. It was in beautiful condition, but two of the pages had been bent over as if to mark the place where she'd finished reading, so I guess that answered my question. I flicked the pages with my thumb, making a rippling noise, and I saw writing on one of the pages near the front, a scribble in blue ink.

I went back page by page until I got to the one that had been written on. I read the inscription, and it felt as if the temperature of the room had dropped by ten degrees. I looked up at the door, but it was still only slightly ajar and there was no breeze. I shuddered and reread the words on the page. "To the girl with the blackest eyes I've ever seen." He hadn't signed it, but his initials were there. E.H. There was no date, either. I examined the book, and it seemed genuine enough, though obviously I couldn't vouch for the handwriting. When had Hemingway died? Sometime in the sixties, I thought, but I wasn't sure. I slid the book back into its place and pulled out the one on its right. *The Maltese Falcon.* By Dashiell Hammett. One of my favorites. Hammett, I knew, had died in 1961. I couldn't remember when he'd written the book, but I reckoned it must have been about 1930. Maybe 1929. I didn't open the book because I was scared of what I might find. I held it in my hands and tapped it against my chin and breathed in the smell of a book that was more than sixty years old. I took a deep breath and opened it. There, on the title page, was a black-inked scrawl. "Lisa—I'll never forget you. Ever," it said, and there was a signature. Hammett's signature.

I had a friend once, his name was Gilbert Leighton. We were at university together, and then he set up a practice in partnership with a guy from Birmingham; soon after they were up and running he invited me around to his new Harley Street offices. To boast, I guess, to show me how well he was doing even though his marks were an average fifteen percent below mine all through our academic years. He wanted to take me down to his garage and show me his Rolls, too, but I passed on that. What did impress me wasn't the expensive leather couch or the wood-paneled walls or the gorgeous blonde receptionist with the top three buttons of her dress undone. No, what really impressed me was the collection of signed photographs on one wall, next to his academic and professional qualifications. There was Bill Clinton, and a message which said, "Gilbert—Thanks for everything, Bill," and there was a head-and-shoulders shot of a pouting Angelina Jolie with

"Love and thanks, Angelina" written in one corner with a flourish and three kisses. The collection included top politicians, singers, movie stars, and media personalities, all with personal messages to good old Gilbert.

I remember turning to look at him, wide-mouthed, and he was laughing soundlessly and shaking his head. "Your face," he said.

"How did you…?" I began asking.

"Gloria," he said.

"Gloria?"

He nodded toward the reception area. "Gloria. The blonde bombshell. She does them for me. She's a wizard with Photoshop. Pretty good, huh?"

"Pretty dishonest," I answered. He did all right, though. He lives with Gloria in the South of France now and makes a fortune listening to the problems of the super-rich.

Maybe that was it, I thought. Maybe Terry likes collecting fake signatures, fake goodwill messages from long-dead authors. It didn't seem likely though, and it would be an expensive joke to play, defacing first editions which would fetch thousands at auction. I put back *The Maltese Falcon* and chose another book at random. Robert Louis Stevenson. *Kidnapped.* I opened it quickly, and I was fumbling so much that I almost missed it, but it was there in almost pure copperplate writing. A signed first edition of *Kidnapped.* With a personal message. A message that referred to black eyes. The book fell from my nerveless fingers, and I backed away from it, my chest tight. A muscle in my right cheek began to spasm, and I put my hand against it and pressed hard, trying to stop the nervous tic. I swung the flashlight back and forth so that I could see the whole length of the library, fearful that there were monsters lurking in the dark corners, waiting to pounce and rip me apart as soon as the beam of light passed them by. It was as if the light was my protection—it was the only thing they feared. Something knocked against my shoulder blades, and I leapt forward and whirled around, only to see that it was the bookshelves. I'd backed right across the library. The copy of *Kidnapped* lay facedown. I couldn't bring myself to pick it up. For a moment or two I thought I'd lost the door, but then I saw the irregularity among the bookshelves and pulled it open and slipped once again into the hallway. I leaned against the wall and pulled the door shut behind me, knowing that I shouldn't have left the book on the floor but figuring that I could always go back later. When I'd calmed down.

I tried the door opposite and was surprised to find a modern office; it had the same plush carpet but chrome and glass furniture and several expensive-looking desktop computers. The air in the room was definitely colder than in the rest of the building, and I guessed there must have been some sort of air-conditioning for the computers, but it was discreetly hidden away. There were a line of matte black filing cabinets ranged against one of the walls, and they weren't locked. On the front of one of the cabinets were letters, A–E, F–K, and so on, stenciled on the front of the drawers. On an impulse I held the flashlight in my teeth with the keys banging against my chin while I pulled open the section that contained F, and sure enough there was a file for Ferriman, Terry. A birth certificate, photocopies of credit card application forms, social security number, academic qualifications, passport. And a death certificate. It was there. The death certificate for Terry Ferriman. Aged eleven. I put the file back and pulled out the one next to it. Granger, Helen. There was a birth certificate in the file, and a death certificate, along with death certificates and the marriage license of the girl's parents.

I put it back and went to the drawer containing the S files. There was no file for Sinopoli, Lisa, but as I pushed the drawer shut I saw that the one next to it had a label on it that said "Dead Files, H–K." I looked at the cabinets; there were six of them, and five contained dead files. Each cabinet had six drawers, which meant that there were thirty drawers full of dead files. When I pulled open the one labeled R–S, it was packed tight, and I had to struggle to get the Sinopoli file out. It was the paper trail of a life, the life of Lisa Sinopoli: her birth certificate, her exam results, her bank statements, paychecks from her time in Hollywood, receipts, deeds to property she'd owned, a marriage certificate confirming that she'd tied the knot with Greig Turner when she was twenty-two years old, and two death certificates. One, the real one, I suppose, showing that she'd died of TB at the age of six. The other, the one she'd have needed to kill off the identity when she moved on, was dated 1954.

If I read it right, the dead files were identities she'd already used. The other cabinet contained files of future possibilities.

Part of me held out a vague hope that maybe she was just involved in some complicated credit card scam or check-kiting or any other common-or-garden fraud. That I could cope with— that wouldn't have me waking up in the middle of the night in a cold sweat. But then I remembered the signed copy of *Kidnapped*, and I knew that there was no straightforward explanation for it. I wondered how far back the dead files went. I flicked through the ones in the R–S drawer and got back to 1847, a woman called Anne-Cecile Rullier, but I couldn't make sense of the documents, what with them being in French and all. It was also obvious that the more recent the file, the more documentation it contained, showing that it was getting progressively harder to maintain a new identity. That probably explained why there were computers in the room.

I went over to one of the machines, a top-of-the-range Sony laptop, and I managed to switch it on, but I couldn't get into its password-protected files.

I left the air-conditioned room and tiptoed along the hall to the next door and went in. It contained a display of Egyptian artifacts, and they were old, old, old. There were statues, a lot of gold jewelry, a gold cat that reared up on its back legs as if playing, and some stones with hieroglyphics on them. I wondered if they were recent acquisitions, and I hoped they were because I didn't like to think what the alternative possibility was. That was too much to even consider right then.

I pushed open the next door down the hall and shone my flashlight on the wall opposite. Terry's face looked back at me, the eyes glinting, the skin a pale white, and it took a second or so during which my heart stopped beating before I realized that it was a portrait, a life-size painting hanging on the wall. It was a good one, almost like a photograph. She was sitting in a straight-backed chair by the side of a Victorian fireplace, unsmiling and with her hair tied back, but it was definitely Terry. I played the beam of light along the wall, and it illuminated a second portrait, this one much older and not quite as good. The room was full of portraits; some of them were clearly very old, the varnish going brown and the colors fading, while others appeared fresh and new, as if they'd just been painted yesterday. They were all of Terry, with one possible exception, and that was a Picasso that may or may not have been her. It was difficult to say because there was an eye in one corner and a nose in the middle, but I figured there was a fair chance it was meant to be her because the eye was jet black. Picasso painted her, can you believe that? Robert Louis

Stevenson gave her a copy of his book, and Picasso painted her. There was a single statue in the room, a life-size sculpture of her in pure white marble.

Her voice, when she spoke, made me jump, and I dropped the torch. "I know it's vain, Jamie, but I get such pleasure looking at them," she said. I whirled round but couldn't see her, and the thought flashed through my mind that she must be able to see in absolute darkness.

"Terry," I said. "Is that you?" Of course it was her, and I know it was a stupid thing to say, but I couldn't see a thing, and for all I knew she could have been standing there with an axe in her hand. I knelt down and groped for the flashlight and shone it in the direction of her voice. She was sitting at the far end of the room in a leather wing chair, and when the beam of light hit her face she threw up her hands to shield her eyes, blinking and turning her head.

"Jamie, there's a light switch to your left. Why don't you just switch that on?"

I did as she said, and a series of recessed lights snapped on. She sat demurely in the chair, her hands back on her knees, her head to one side as she looked at me. She was wearing a black dress that I vaguely recognized, and then I remembered that I'd never seen her in a proper dress before. I turned and looked at the portrait, the big one that had startled me when I first entered the room. It was the same dress.

I looked back at her, and she'd got to her feet and was walking toward me. I hadn't heard her move. "Do you think it's vain?" she asked.

I shrugged. "They're beautiful pictures," I said. "I can see why you'd want to keep them." She held out her hand, and I looked at it.

"The flashlight," she said. "Give me the flashlight."

I gave it to her, and she switched it off and handed it back to me, the keys jingling in the silence. "What are you doing here, Jamie?" she asked, brushing her hair behind her ears as she spoke.

I thought of lying, I thought of saying that I'd come round to see her and found the garage door open, that I was hoping to give her a scare, but I knew there was no point because she'd caught me prowling around her apartment in the dark like some amateur burglar. No, I couldn't lie, but I couldn't bring myself to tell her the truth, that I believed that Terry Ferriman wasn't her real name and that whoever she was she'd been on the earth for at least two centuries and probably a hell of a lot longer than that. The Egyptian artifacts worried me. I could just about cope with the concept that a girl could live for a couple of hundred years, but the possibility of thousands of years sent my mind reeling.

"Well?" she said. She was standing less than an arm's length from me, her head tilted up and a hint of a smile on her lips.

"Who are you?" I said, which wasn't exactly original, but it was all I could come up with.

"Who do you want me to be?" she replied, almost whispering.

"You're not Terry Ferriman," I said, the words catching in my throat. "The real Terry Ferriman is dead."

"Do the police know?" she asked, not denying the accusation.

"Yes," I said. "They're looking for you now. I'm surprised they haven't been here already."

"They know about the basement?" she said, frowning, and I realized that of course they didn't.

De'Ath would have sent men around to her small apartment upstairs. Unless they were lucky like me, they wouldn't discover that she owned the whole building.

"No, you're right. I don't think they do."

"How did you find out?" she asked, and I told her about her neighbor and my conversation with the real estate agent.

"And how did you get in?" I explained about Dave Burwash, and she laughed and reached up to touch my cheek.

"Clever boy," she whispered softly. "So clever."

"What's going on, Terry?" I said. "Who are you?"

She dropped her hand from my cheek and took me gently by the arm, leading me to the door. She didn't speak as she took me along the hall and opened another door. She went in first and switched on the lights, and I followed her. It was a long room with no windows, but tapestries on the walls stopped it from feeling claustrophobic. The furniture was comfortable and obviously antique; there were wooden chairs with red velvet cushions, a chaise longue, and two overstuffed sofas on either side of a marble fireplace. The fire wasn't lit, and there was a screen in front of it depicting a castle with a knight on horseback riding up to the portcullis. On a low oak sideboard there was a collection of photographs in silver and gold frames, and as she guided me to one of the sofas I saw that she was in some of the pictures and that most of them were black-and-white.

"Do you want a drink, Jamie?" she asked as she sat me down. "You look as if you need one." I nodded. I think I must have been in a state of shock. I felt as if I'd been hypnotized.

She walked over to the sideboard where there was a group of bottles and decanters on a silver tray. "Brandy?" she said over her shoulder, and I said that would be fine. At least I tried to—I'm not sure if the words came out or not. I watched her as she poured brandy from a decanter into a crystal glass. There was something different about her, and it wasn't the fact that she was wearing a dress for the first time. It was more the way she held herself; she was carrying herself like a woman and not like a gauche girl the way she'd been when I first met her. And there was something else.

"I think you'll like this," she said as she carried the glass over to me. I realized then what it was, what it was that had changed. Her voice. Or rather the way she was speaking. Gone was the "gee whiz" breathless Valley Girl voice, and in its place was the soft but confident tones of a woman who knew exactly what she wanted and how to get it. She'd dropped an act, and I knew with a cold certainty that I was about to have the real Terry Ferriman revealed to me. It wasn't knowing the truth that frightened me, though, it was not knowing what she planned to do after she'd told me. I'd fallen in love with Terry Ferriman, not the person who sat gracefully on the sofa next to me with her hands folded in her lap and watched me sip the brandy in the way that a cat watches a mouse it has cornered.

"Good?" she asked.

"Very good," I said, though if the truth were told I couldn't taste a thing as a warm glow spread down through my chest.

She smiled. "That brandy was laid down in eighteen hundred and two, Jamie," she said. "Three years after Napoleon took power in France."

"Really?" I said, eyebrows raised. I took another sip, but I still couldn't taste it. The glow was spreading to my stomach, though, and I felt a little light-headed.

"It was," she continued, "a very good year."

"For brandy?" I said.

"For many things," she said. "It was a glorious summer."

My head swam, and I shook it to try and clear it. I panicked, wondering if maybe she'd drugged me. I remembered the dream, her crouching over a body, blood on her mouth, and I remembered the feel of her warm lips against the skin of my neck.

"Drink your brandy and relax, Jamie," she said. "And don't worry. I'm not going to hurt you. Trust me." Her voice was as soothing and as warming as the brandy, but part of me felt that she was talking to me like a doctor talks to a patient. How could I trust someone who'd lied to me in the way that she'd done? Hell, nothing I knew about Terry Ferriman appeared to be the truth. I swallowed the rest of the brandy in one gulp.

"What were you looking for, Jamie?" she said, taking the empty glass from my hands. She rubbed it between her palms as she watched me.

"I don't know. The truth, I suppose. I guess I wanted to know the truth. Does that sound banal?"

"And did you find it?" she asked, ignoring my question.

"I saw the files," I said. "I saw the dead files, the identities you've used. And I saw the ones that you'll be using in the future. How old are you, Terry? Who are you?"

"You really want to know?" she asked. "Do you really think you could deal with it, Jamie? You say you came here to discover the truth. But is that what you really want? Think about it, Jamie. Think about what the truth means."

Greig Turner flashed into my mind, the shriveled husk of a human being, decaying while the girl he loved stayed the same. What was worse, knowing that he was dying, knowing that he'd lost her, or knowing that she would still be around long after he'd been buried or cremated or whatever they did with the bodies of faded-out movie stars? Would he be happier if he thought she had died, or that she too was living out her final years in a wheelchair in some hidden-away nursing home? I remembered the look of horror on his face when I'd told him that the photograph of Terry Ferriman was a recent one and not an old picture of Lisa Sinopoli, the girl he'd married and lost.

"Greig Turner," I said. "Did he know what you are?"

"No," she said emphatically. "Not then he didn't. But eventually he suspected. That's why he hired a detective to track me down."

"Matt Blumenthal."

"Matt Blumenthal," she repeated.

"You killed him here, didn't you?" I said. "In this basement."

"He died here. But I didn't kill him."

"Who did?"

"That's part of knowing the truth, Jamie. First you've got to decide if you want to know everything."

"Why did you have Turner's photograph in your apartment upstairs?"

"He was my husband. I always felt close to him. I wanted his picture around." She went over to the sideboard to refill my glass.

"So why didn't you stay in touch with him? Why did you leave him?"

"You saw him. Doesn't that answer your question?"

"You left him because he was old? You wouldn't see him because he was dying and you're still young?"

She shook her head. "No, that's not it at all. It was for his sake—it was his feelings I was trying to protect. How do you think he'd feel knowing that I'm the way I am and he's the way he is? I thought it was better that he thought I was dead. And if he hadn't hired that detective, and if you hadn't gone to see him, then maybe he'd have died a lot happier than he did." She came back with the glass and held it down to me. My right hand was shaking as I took it, and I used both hands to hold it to my lips.

"You know he's dead, then?" I asked after I'd swallowed.

"Yes, I know he's dead." She sat down next to me and put her hand on my knee.

"What do you want from me?" I asked.

"To spend time with you," she said. "To be with you."

"For how long?"

"Forever," she said, looking at me steadily. I could feel myself beginning to drown in her bottomless black eyes, and I had to pull myself back.

"That's not possible and you know it," I replied.

"It's possible," she said.

"How?"

"That's part of knowing the full truth, Jamie. First you've got to decide if you can handle it. If you really want it."

"Didn't Greig Turner want it? Didn't he want to stay with you forever?"

Her hand clenched on my leg, and I felt the nails bite into the cloth of my trousers and pinch the skin underneath. "I didn't leave Greig because he was getting old. He left me. He was the one who betrayed me; he's the one who couldn't keep out of other women's beds. I loved him, I begged him not to do it, but he wouldn't listen. He threw it away. And by the time he realized what he'd lost, it was too late. He wasn't trying to get me back; that's not why he hired Blumenthal. He found out that I'd been paying his bills at his nursing home in Big Sur. I think he suspected then that something was wrong. He didn't want me back, Jamie. He just didn't want to die."

"Nobody does, Terry. Shit, do I still call you Terry, or what? What name do you use?"

"Terry is fine."

"What was your original name?"

"The first?"

"Yeah, the first."

She laughed. "It was such a long time ago," she said, and then she said something that sounded like "Malinkila." I asked her to repeat it, but I still couldn't make my mouth form the sounds.

"Egyptian?" I said, and she nodded, and we both knew then that I'd reached the point of no turning back.

"You're ready?" she asked.

"Yes."

"You're sure?"

"Yes."

"Then ask." She settled back in the sofa and waited while I tried to get my thoughts in order. There was so much I wanted to know. I wanted to know who she was, how old she was, who had killed Matt Blumenthal, why she had been found with his body, and what she meant when she said she wanted to be with me forever.

"How old are you? What are you?" I asked.

"I'm not quite sure; that's the answer to both questions, Jamie. I think it's been between four and five thousand years, but for a long time I wasn't counting, if you know what I mean. Time didn't have the same meaning back then. I was just living, surviving. Moving from place to place, from country to country."

"But you were born in Egypt?"

"Yes."

"Four thousand years ago?"

"Or thereabouts. I remember the Great Pyramids being built at Giza, and the Sphinx, and I guess that was about two thousand five hundred BC. It took me a long time to get my head straight too. You can imagine what it was like, when all those around me were getting older and I stayed the same, exactly as you see me today. For centuries I lived as an outcast, scared to live near people for too long because they always turned against me in the end."

She said it the way I once told a nephew that I remembered the days before flat-screen televisions and mobile phones. That piece of news was greeted with an eight-year-old's gasp of amazement, but that was nothing to how I felt at her matter-of-fact revelation. "As to what I am, I'm not sure how to describe it."

"Vampire?" I said, and she threw back her head and laughed. Her neck was long and pale white, unlined and unmarked. The neck of a child.

"Jamie, do I look like a vampire?" she asked.

I looked at her flowing black dress, her black eyes, the white, perfect teeth, and the glistening hair, and a small voice inside said yes, that's exactly what you do look like, and what else do you call someone who's as old as the pyramids and who was found over a corpse in an alley with blood on her full, red lips?

"Well?" she pressed.

"I guess not," I said.

"There are gaps in what I remember," she said. "That's why I'm a bit vague about actually how old I am."

"You remember your parents?"

"Sort of. I remember that they'd have nothing to do with me after my twenty-third summer. People had shorter life spans then, and they aged faster. I never got sick, and I showed no signs of aging. They made me leave. I don't remember what they looked like, but I remember how it felt to be rejected by them. I've never forgotten."

I shook my head in bewilderment. "Four thousand years," I said. "It doesn't seem possible. How did it happen? How many more like you are there?"

She shrugged. "I don't know how it happened. Genes, I suppose. It's a mutation. As to how many more there are—just a handful, I think. I know of six. It's not hereditary, if that's what you're getting at. My mother and father and my four brothers were all normal. They all died before they were forty."

"The others, are you all in contact?" I was aware that the questions I was asking weren't following any logical progression; I was asking things at random. If I was going to get anywhere close to understanding her and what she was, I was going to have to take a more scientific approach. God, I wished I had a digital recorder with me, or at least a notebook and pen.

"Not all the time. You have to remember that it's not easy for us to live in normal society, Jamie. We have to keep on moving; we can never stay in one place for more than ten years in case we are discovered. And once we've moved on, we have to wait at least fifty years before we move back. But yes, we do meet, we do help each other whenever we can. We have to. We're all we've got."

"You say you had to keep moving. Where have you lived?"

"God, Jamie, you'd be better off asking me where I haven't lived. My first memories are of Egypt, then when Egypt went into decline I moved to Greece and then to Rome. When Rome was sacked, and that was what, four seventy-six AD, then I moved to Byzantium. I was in what's now called the Middle East round about eight hundred AD, then went to China and on to Kiev when it was the cultural center of the Slavic empire. I moved out when Genghis Kahn moved in; I was in Constantinople when it fell to the Ottoman Turks in fourteen fifty-three. I was in Florence during the Renaissance, in London when the Great Plague swept through Europe, in Paris during the Revolution, in Switzerland during the First World War, and I've been in the States since the nineteen twenties."

"And how many identities have you used?" The questions still had no logic, and I knew that I was asking them just to keep talking while I tried to get my mind around the basic premise that she'd laid before me—namely that Terry Ferriman was immortal. By asking questions, no matter how banal, I was at least helping to convince myself that she was telling the truth. But still the question that lurked uncomfortably at the back of my mind was what the hell did she plan to do with me, and was I going to end up like Matt Blumenthal, lying flat on my back in an alley somewhere, drained of my lifeblood?

She laughed and shook my shoulders. "Jamie, for God's sake, how should I know? It's only in the last few centuries that I've had to keep records, and you saw how much space they took up in the filing cabinets. Hundreds, thousands maybe. In the old days, in the real old days, all I had to do was to move to another country or even just another town and change my name. This business with assuming new identities and applying for passports and driver's licenses and social security numbers and bank accounts is relatively recent."

"And you've never been sick?"

"Not even during the Great Plague. Never. But you saw how I'm allergic to sunlight. We all are. And we do have another what you might call a weakness."

"A weakness?"

"We think it's connected to the gene that makes us immortal. We are missing the enzymes in a couple of crucial biochemical pathways, which means we must periodically ingest certain proteins which we are lacking."

Realization broke over me like a tropical cloudburst. "Blood," I said. "You have to have blood. Human blood."

"Not necessarily blood, but that's just about the most efficient way of ingesting them, yes."

I stood up and felt my knees buckle slightly. I didn't know if it was the fear or the brandy, but I locked my legs and fought to keep my balance. "And you say you're not vampires? What else would you call it? You live forever and you drink human blood? Oh God, I don't believe this, I really don't…"

I guess I must have passed out then because when I woke up I was lying on my back on a black leather couch and looking up at a white-tiled ceiling. I raised my head and saw that I was in some sort of laboratory, gray-speckled linoleum and lots of white Formica working surfaces, and I recognized some of the equipment there—a centrifuge, what looked like a scintillation counter, and a pair of electronic scales. There was a whole lot of stuff I didn't recognize, though. When I lifted my arms I half expected to meet resistance, but there were no thick leather straps holding me down. She was standing by a sink, and as I sat up she came over with a glass of water.

"I'm sorry, Jamie," she said. "I guess it was a mistake giving you the brandy."

"Even though it was a good year," I said and took the water from her and drank it. It felt cold and refreshing and went some way to clearing my head.

"Even though it was a good year," she repeated and smiled. "Are you okay?"

I laughed ruefully because okay didn't exactly sum up the state of my mind just then. Poleaxed maybe. Stunned, possibly. But not okay. Definitely not okay.

"How did I get here?" I asked, looking around the lab. There was no way of telling if I was even still in the same building, or how long I'd been out. I checked my watch. Two thirty in the morning.

"I carried you," she said. She carried me. Just like that. I must weigh almost half as much again as she does, and she carried me. And if she carried me, then she could just as easily have carried

Matt Blumenthal, with or without the eight pints of blood that should have been in his body.

"You were asking about the blood," she said, as if she'd been reading my mind.

"The blood?"

"You wanted to know how we got the proteins we need, the ones our own bodies can't synthesize." She went over to a large refrigerator that was big enough to walk in. She pulled at its big, chrome handle, and it made a hissing noise as it opened. She held it open wide so that I could see its contents. Plastic sachets of blood, all neatly racked and labeled. "We don't go around biting the necks of young virgins, Jamie. Not anymore, anyway. There's no need. It's not the blood we need—it's just a small fraction of the proteins in it. We buy the stuff in bulk through a couple of medical supply companies we own, and we extract the proteins here."

"We?" I asked.

"A friend of mine helped me set up the lab, a guy called Neil Hamshire. Lately he's really got into science in a big way. He's the one who identified the proteins we're missing and worked out the extraction procedures using collection tubes containing silica gel polymers."

"Where is he?" I asked. I held out the empty glass for her to take.

"I wish I knew," she said. "He disappeared about six months ago. I think the government has got him. They've been on our trail for at least ten years. Possibly longer."

"I don't understand. Why would the government be after you?"

"Think about it, Jamie. We're a threat to them. Not because we mean them harm, but because of the way we are. We are outside any of their controls, financially and legally. We are in a position to amass any sort of knowledge we want; we have the ability to acquire any skills we want just by applying ourselves over a long period of time. Neil has spent more than fifty years in various laboratories around the world. If he were to ever publish some of the stuff he's discovered, he'd have a dozen Nobel prizes. There are no secrets in the world that we can't get to, eventually. We just have to keep trying, and eventually we get what we want, because we outlast everyone else."

"So long as you aren't discovered?"

"That's right. We have to keep moving, and we have to keep changing identities, and that's getting harder and harder because more and more records are stored on computers and cross-referenced. They've caught several of my friends over the years."

"Friends?"

"People like me. And the more they find out about us, the easier it becomes for them to track us down. It'll only be a matter of time before they find out that we buy blood, for instance. And I think they're already trying to track us down through bank records. It isn't as easy to hide money as it used to be. It used to be that you could put a thousand dollars in a bank account and leave it for fifty years or so at compound interest and go back and take it out. Not anymore. It's as hard now to transfer assets and property as it is to switch identities. Everything changed after nine-eleven. Now Homeland Security is on the case of every financial transaction over ten thousand dollars, and they are all over passport and driver's license applications. It's not as easy as it used to be to switch identities."

I thought of the millions she had in the bank downtown, and I wondered how much else she had squirreled away around the world. Fallback positions.

"Who in the government does this? Who is trying to catch you? Is it the FBI? The CIA? Homeland Security?"

"Worse. Much worse. They don't even have any of the restrictions on their actions that keep the CIA in check. It's like a witch hunt. No, it's not *like* a witch hunt. It *is* a witch hunt. That's exactly what it is, and if they get their way they'll be burning us at the stake."

"And you think they've got this friend of yours, this Neil… what was his surname?"

"Hamshire. Without the 'P'. Neil Hamshire. Yeah, he was on his way to the lab here one evening, and he just vanished. He wouldn't have gone voluntarily because he was in the middle of an experiment, something he'd been working on for over a year."

"What was that?"

"Genetics. He was trying to find a way of correcting the flaw in our genes so that we don't need to ingest the proteins. And he wanted to do something about the problem we have with sunlight. And some other stuff. He wouldn't have just walked away from it, I'm sure of that."

She put the empty glass down by the sink and walked over to me, the dress flowing behind her like a black sail. Her hands reached up to hold my head, a cool palm on each of my cheeks, and then her lips were against mine, the action so sudden that I didn't have time to draw breath, and when she took her lips away I was gasping, my heart racing and my pulse pounding in my ears.

"What do you want?" I asked. "What is it you want from me?"

"Haven't you guessed?" she said. "Isn't it obvious?" She paused and then tilted her head down a fraction so that she was looking at me from under hooded lids as if telling me a guilty secret. "Jamie, I love you. I have since I first saw you, even before you ran that ridiculous program by me."

"Ridiculous!" I snorted. "What do you mean?" Hell, she was dismissing my life's work as if it were no more than a child's crossword puzzle.

"I'm sorry," she said, reaching out and ruffling my hair. "It's just that when you've taken on so many personalities as I have, psychological tests like yours are, well, laughable. I'm sorry, but that's the way it is." She saw how crestfallen I looked. "Oh, come on, Jamie. Just accept that I'm in a different league than the normal psychos you come across in your line of work. Don't take it as a personal affront against your professionalism."

"Do you mean it?" I asked.

"About your professionalism?"

"About loving me."

"Totally."

I smiled and slid off the couch and took her in my arms, and her head came up and this time I remembered to take a deep breath first. Her tongue slipped in between my teeth while one of her hands gently massaged the back of my neck and the other moved down the front of my trousers, caressing and feeling for me. I tried to pull her down onto the couch, but she slipped out of my grasp and took me by the hand out of the laboratory and along the corridor to another room. She didn't turn on the main light but led me confidently through the pitch dark and switched on a small lamp on a side table next to a king-size four-poster bed. She pushed me back onto the bed and took off her dress before climbing on top of me and removing my clothes, and then she did all the things she'd done to me before in bed and a few other things too, and then I guess I must have passed out again because when I woke up I had a splitting headache and I was alone.

Terry's dress was lying on a chair, so she couldn't have been far away. My throat was dry, and I had trouble swallowing, so I pulled on my boxer shorts and went looking for a bathroom and a painkiller. I found the bathroom door on the second try and hit the light switch. I was getting used to rooms without windows. There was a glass by the sink, and I filled it with cold water and took a mouthful, swirled it around my mouth, spat it out, and then drank for real. I drained the glass and refilled it and then opened the mirrored cabinet on the wall looking for painkillers. There was mouthwash and antiseptic and a couple of sachets of herb hair shampoo, but nothing that would get rid of my headache. I closed the cabinet and pulled open a drawer under the sink. There were no painkillers there, but there was a black leather wallet. I took it out and flipped it open. There was a plastic window on the left-hand side containing a private investigator's license in the name of Matt Blumenthal. His driver's license was in a side pocket along with a green American Express card and a couple of hundred dollars in the section for notes.

When I looked up it was to find Terry's face looking back at me from the mirrored cabinet. I turned round quickly, and the wallet fell to the floor. She knelt down in front of me and picked it up and tapped it against her leg as she stood up. She had on a black silk robe with an orange and green dragon on the back that rippled as she moved, as if it were preparing to breathe fire.

"I didn't kill him, Jamie," she said quietly. "You must believe me."

"That's his wallet, though," I said, trembling. "And you were found over his body."

"He came around here one evening when I wasn't at home. But my friend was. He surprised my friend in the laboratory, and he reacted without thinking."

"There was no blood in the body when it was found."

She lifted her chin and tutted as if I'd said something irrelevant. "Christ, Jamie, my friend stabbed him in the chest. What else do you expect?"

"And you moved the body to the alley?"

"We both did. I mean, I could have managed on my own, either of us could, but we did it together. He was in his car when the police arrived, so he left. There was no point in both of us getting caught."

"He left you?" I said in disbelief.

"Like I said, there was no point in us both getting caught. We knew there was no murder weapon around, so there'd be no hard evidence. We'd removed all his identification. We thought he was a burglar; it was only afterwards that I discovered that Greig had hired him to track me down. Jamie, come back to bed." She hugged herself in the robe, the wallet still in her hand.

"There was blood on your face, Terry. On your lips."

"I don't know how that got there. I suppose I must have got it on my hands when I helped move the body and then maybe wiped it across my face. Let's go to bed, Jamie. Please."

"I want to sort this out first. This friend, this man. Who is he? A lover?"

She shook her head. "No, he's not a lover."

"Where is he now?"

"Around. He doesn't live here, if that's what you mean. I live here alone. In fact, most of the time I live in the apartment upstairs—it's cozier. This is more of a storage place and somewhere to work."

"Why do you keep all that stuff? The pictures, the portraits, the books?"

"Memories," she said, and there was genuine sadness in her voice. "They're all I have left. The people who gave me those things, most of them anyway, are long dead. I can't keep them, but I can keep what they gave me. I owe it to them. Can you understand that?"

I leaned back against the sink and felt the marble dig into my spine. "What are you planning to add to your collection that'll remind you of me in years to come?" I said bitterly.

She took a step forward and put a finger up against my lips, silencing me. "It won't come to that, Jamie."

I seized her hand and pushed it away. "How can you say that?" I shouted. "How can you possibly say that? How many others have you left? How many have you walked away from? Why do you think I'll be any different?"

"Because of the work Neil was doing," she said softly. "He had isolated the gene that gives us our longevity, and he was close to designing a way of incorporating it into normal human DNA. Jamie, he can make you one of us. If that's what you want." She held out her hand for mine, and I slowly reached out and took it. She squeezed gently. "You have to decide, Jamie. I want you with me for all time, and if you want it too it's yours for the taking. No bites on the neck, not like it is in the movies, just a straightforward scientific procedure."

"But this Hamshire guy is missing."

"We'll find him," she said. We, she said. Not I. That's what I remembered as she led me back along the hall to the bedroom. We.

THE DREAM

I knew I was dreaming, but I couldn't wake up. Couldn't or didn't want to—I'm not sure which it was or to what extent there was an element of free will, but no matter what the reason I just let what was happening flow over me. Terry was there, and maybe that was the reason I didn't want to wake up. She was dressed in black, a jacket that might have been my motorcycle jacket over a black T-shirt, black jeans, and black boots with what looked like silver tips on the toes. Her hair was tied back in a ponytail, and I remember thinking that I'd never seen her wearing her hair that way before and how good it looked.

We were in a wood, but not the normal sort of forest you find in real life. It was a caricature, the sort you'd see around the wicked witch's castle in a Walt Disney cartoon: deformed, gnarled trees with spindly branches that seemed to writhe and grasp as we moved close to them. It was a cold, dark, fearful place. The trees had no leaves or buds, and there was no grass on the floor of the forest, just damp, musty-smelling soil the color of coal.

It was night, but I had no trouble seeing Terry or the trees because overhead hung a full moon, the sky so clear that I could see the individual craters on its surface. Terry looked at me and smiled, and her teeth were as white as the moon and sharp, as sharp as a wolf's. She slowly put her head back so that I could see her whole throat exposed, and her ponytail hung backwards away from the upturned collar of her jacket. And then I heard the howl. I thought at first that it was coming from somewhere far in the distance because it was so quiet, but as it built and echoed around the forest it became obvious that it was her, howling at the moon. It was a terrible, mournful sound, the sound of a she-wolf in pain, howling for some great injustice that had been done to her. The howl trailed off, and she lowered her chin and looked at me again. She pointed her index finger at her throat and moved it down a short distance, to where the Adam's apple would be if she had one. The sign for thirsty.

I put my index fingers together at waist level, pointing forward, and then moved them to the left, separating and bringing them together as they moved. The sign for also. I was thirsty too. I knew too that it was important that we didn't speak, that whatever we were doing had to be done in silence.

She waved me behind a tree, and I hugged a large trunk, its bark cracked and creased into deep furrows filled with a pungent brown moss. Terry moved next to another twisted tree, but I could still see her clearly. It wasn't just the moonlight—something had happened to my eyes that allowed me to see clearly even though it was well past midnight and we were in the depths of the forest. And I knew that if I reached up to feel my teeth I'd find them long and sharp, like hers.

She made quick, stabbing motions with her pointed index finger, then pointed both index figures at each other and made a series of rolling motions. *They come.* She pressed her index finger against her pursed lips. *Be quiet.* I scowled. I knew that. Did she think I was stupid?

I crouched down and waited. My hearing was intensified, too. It was as if I could hear the slightest noise no matter how far away it was. High overhead I could hear the feathery flapping of an owl on the wing; to my right, a hundred yards or so, a small mouse scuffled along the ground, and if I really tried I could hear its tiny heart beating a hundred times a minute. I could hear the footsteps of men walking in the distance. Three men. No. I put my head on one side and focused on the sound. Two men and a child. A small child, its steps hesitant and clumsy. I listened carefully and realized that the two adults were holding the child by an arm each because occasionally the small steps would disappear as if the child was being swung in fun. I heard the swish of a skirt against smooth legs and knew for certain that it was a man, a woman, and a child. Almost half a mile away. So far away, and yet I knew everything. That was why I didn't try to escape from the dream, even though I knew I was asleep. I was enjoying the power.

Terry looked at me over her shoulder. No deaf and dumb sign language this time—she just raised one eyebrow. *Ready?* I nodded.

She moved, so quickly that I couldn't see the individual motions; it was just a black blur like a shadow cast by a curtain waving in the wind. A flicker. One moment she was crouched down at the base of the tree, the next she was in the air, her arms outstretched, her ponytail streaming behind her. I stood up and tried to follow, not sure what I should do. I ran, and then my foot caught in something, a tree root perhaps, but instead of falling I kept moving through the air, a few feet above the ground. And then I arched my back and began to move up, curving through the air, twigs brushing against my arms, my eyes stinging from the wind. There was no need to flap my arms or push or do anything. I kept moving faster and faster, and I seemed to be able to change direction just by moving my head. Terry was ahead of me, and she turned and smiled and beckoned for me to catch her up. I flew faster, not knowing how I was speeding up but doing it anyway, and then I drew level with her and she reached out and touched me lightly on the shoulder, congratulating me, making me feel good.

We flew up so that we were skimming the tops of the trees, and then she pointed and I saw the three figures in the distance, walking side by side down a narrow path that threaded its way through the forest. Terry grinned and licked her lips, and then she swooped down and I followed, the sudden descent pulling the wind from my lungs and making me gasp. They didn't see us until we were right on top of them. The man was in his early fifties, a strong, weather-beaten face, dark brown eyes, a firm chin, wearing a dark workman's jacket and dirt-streaked jeans, the woman a few years younger but still pretty, big blue eyes, a laughing mouth, her hair hidden by a colorful scarf, and she was wearing a dark green coat over a green and white checked dress. The girl was about four or five years old, curly blonde hair, giggling and tugging at her parents' arms, wanting to be lifted. What happened next came as a series of disparate images, like photographs shot with a time-lapse camera: the man looking up, his eyes widening with fear; the woman's left hand jumping up to her mouth to stifle her scream; Terry laughing; the child crying; Terry's hand reaching out, the fingers curled; the man's throat ripped clean open, blood spurting over his shoulder; the woman moving to scoop up the child; Terry laughing and rolling as she flew, her other hand curving to strike; the child falling to the ground, arms and legs scrabbling for something to hold on to; the woman's coat covered with blood as she crumpled to the ground. Then Terry and I were up in the air again, the cold breeze in our faces as we soared above the trees.

We circled, watching the girl kneel by her mother's side, taking her cold hand in her own and pushing it against her cheek, her tears mixing with the blood. Terry pointed at me and then at the girl. My turn. We dived down together, the ground rushing up, and again it came as a series of separate images: the girl, blood on her cheek; Terry laughing; the girl's eyes open and blue, misty with tears; Terry's teeth, sharp and white, making small biting motions; my hand forming a claw; the girl reaching up with a small hand as if trying to fend off the attack; the forest floor leaping up at me. Then I twisted and turned and veered away from the girl and the two bodies, and next I was standing behind them, my feet on the ground, my hand aching in its still-formed claw. I looked up and saw Terry whirling through the air, her eyes hard and menacing, and then she flowed down and landed next to the girl and picked her up around the waist. The woman groaned as she lay dying on the ground, but Terry ignored her. The girl cried out and struggled, but Terry put her mouth next to her ear and whispered something and the child went still as if drugged. Terry kept her eyes on me as she walked up with the child.

"She's yours, Jamie," she said as she got close.

"No," I said. "I don't want her."

"She's yours," she repeated, only this time her face was changing. She wasn't Terry anymore; she had blonde hair, blonde like the child's, and her eyes were the same blue. It wasn't Terry anymore, it was Deborah holding the child, only the child wasn't a child anymore, it was a baby.

"She's yours," said Deborah, and she held up the baby. It wasn't healthy and laughing anymore; it was crying and in pain, and its lower half was as deformed and twisted as the trees in the forest around us.

"No!" I yelled. "No! No!"

Deborah narrowed her eyes, and there was hate in them. "You can't kill a child!" she screamed.

"I don't want to kill her," I shouted back. "I don't! I don't!"

Then I woke up to find Terry looking down on me, her hair brushing against my face. "Jamie? What's wrong?" she asked as she put her hand up against my forehead. I was sweating.

"Bad dream," I said.

"I'll say. What about?"

I shook my head and swallowed. "Nothing," I said.

She smiled ruefully. "Jamie, if you don't want to tell me, that's one thing, but there's no need to lie. I've been lying here next to you for the last five minutes wondering whether or not to wake you up you looked so uncomfortable, so don't give me that 'nothing' crap."

I closed my eyes. "I'm sorry," I said. "It's my problem."

"Problem?" she repeated, frowning. She lay down by my side, her chin resting on her right palm as she played with my chest with her left hand. "Was I in it? The dream?"

"Yes," I said. It was easier to speak to her with my eyes closed. Strange patterns in red and orange danced around, spirals and circles, almost hypnotic. Her voice seemed very far away, as if she were speaking to me from the end of a very long tunnel.

"You shouted something about a baby?"

"A child. We were hunting a child."

"We?"

"You and me. We were in a wood, a terrifying, dark, cruel wood, blackened trees, tangles of brambles, a nightmare sort of place. We were flying."

"Flying?" She sounded amused.

"We were flying through the woods, above them, and then we were attacking a couple and their child." I felt pressure on my eyelids and realized that Terry was kissing them softly. "You killed them," I said. "You ripped out their throats."

"It was a bad dream, that's all," she said soothingly. "We don't fly through the air, Jamie. We don't rip out people's throats. We don't kill children. We don't kill babies."

I felt the tears go then, welling up and forcing their way through my closed eyelids. She gently brushed them away with the back of her hand.

"Who's April?" she asked. I tensed, flinched almost. She caressed my forehead again. "You called out her name. And Deborah, your wife's name. Who's April?"

"My daughter," I said. The two words sounded strange. I don't think I'd ever used them before.

"I didn't know you had a daughter," she said.

"I don't," I answered. "Not anymore."

"What happened?" she asked, her voice little more than a whisper.

"She died."

"Oh Jamie, I'm sorry. I'm so sorry." She lay next to me in silence for a while before she spoke again. "Do you want to talk about it?" she asked.

"No," I said. "Yes. I don't know."

"How did she die?"

"In hospital. A few days after she was born."

"She got sick?"

"She was born with spina bifida. She was all messed up, below the waist. God, it was so sad. She looked so perfect everywhere else—her little hands, her lips, big blue eyes like her mother's. She was so cute. But everything else just came out all screwed up. There was nothing we could do, nothing the doctors could do."

"When was this?" she asked.

"About a year ago. Last April. That's why we called her April."

"Is that why you got divorced?"

The tears were flooding out now, and I opened my eyes, letting them flow down my cheeks and wet the pillow. It wasn't the first time I'd cried for April, and I was sure it wouldn't be the last.

"Deborah divorced me about six months later."

"She blamed you?"

"Not for April being the way she was, no."

She said nothing, just put her head against my shoulder and held me. I closed my eyes again. I could picture April lying in the plastic bubble, her eyes open, looking right at me. Deborah was next to me, her hand on the plastic, trying to touch our child. She was crying, and so was I. There was a doctor there too. He wasn't crying, but then it wasn't his baby.

"Tell me, Jamie," said Terry.

"I can't."

She lapsed into silence again. Eventually I began to speak, to tell her. About the conversation Deborah and I had later, back in her hospital room. About what should happen to April. About quality of life, about how it wasn't fair for her, about how she'd never, ever, have a normal life, that maybe she'd be better off…

"Dead?" said Terry, finishing the sentence for me. "You said that?"

I opened my eyes. "I said it, but I don't think I meant it. I'm still not sure. I think I was playing devil's advocate, you know, testing her feelings. I remember telling her that the doctors could do it, they could just not try so hard to keep her alive and she'd just go, quietly, no pain. I wasn't saying they should, I just said they could. She went crazy; she accused me of all sorts of things and said I was in it with the doctors, that we all wanted April dead and that I didn't love her because she wasn't perfect, that I hated anything that wasn't one hundred percent right. She screamed and slapped me, and then she just went quiet and hardly spoke to me again. April died the day after. Deborah didn't say anything, but I knew she blamed me. She thought I'd spoken to the doctors and got them to do it. I didn't, Terry, I honestly didn't. I didn't kill her. I'd never kill a child."

She held me tightly. "I know, Jamie. I know you wouldn't."

"I tried to tell Deborah that, but she wouldn't listen. She never went home. She went to stay with a friend instead, and a few months later she filed for divorce. Now she's using her lawyers to punish me."

"She needs someone to blame, Jamie, that's all. If she can blame you, then it takes the guilt off her own shoulders. The more she can punish you, the better she feels about herself."

"God, you think I don't know that?" I said, unable to keep the bitterness out of my voice even though it wasn't Terry that I was angry about. "I'm the psychologist, remember?"

"I remember," she said. "But sometimes perhaps you can't see the woods for the trees, you know?"

"Yeah, I know. I'm sorry."

"There's nothing to be sorry about, Jamie. And there's no need to feel guilty. You didn't do anything wrong."

"I know," I said, but inside I wasn't so sure. What really made me feel bad was that, deep down, I wasn't sure whether or not I really had wanted April to die. My conscious mind, that was sure that I really had been playing devil's advocate with Deborah, preparing her for the time when April would die as the doctors had said she would, but below that, in the black depths of my mind, there lurked the thought that maybe, just maybe, I'd wanted her to be taken away because she wasn't perfect—she was a reminder that things went wrong that couldn't be fixed and that the time would come when my own body would be beyond repair. Deborah knew how I felt about growing old. She threw that in my face toward the end. The car, she'd said, that's why I spent so much time working on the car, because that was something that I could stop from getting older just by spending time and money on it. But it wouldn't do any good, she said, the car would still be around long after I'd gone. I was the problem, not the car. I was the one who was getting older, and I was the one who was going to die, so why the hell didn't I just grow up and accept it. Not everything in life was perfect, and not everything stayed perfect. Part of me wanted to explain that to Terry, but I didn't—I just ran it through my mind, round and round like a child's merry-go-round, the golden horses with gaping mouths and staring eyes galloping faster and faster but getting nowhere.

"Easy, Jamie," said Terry, smoothing my brow. "Take it easy. You're breathing like a train." She kept nuzzling my neck and kissing me softly, murmuring words in a language that I didn't recognize but which were soothing nonetheless, until waves of blackness enfolded me and I dropped back into sleep.

THE VISITORS

When I woke up she was still holding me, and I felt a lot more stable. Telling her about April had helped; there had been no more nightmares, and when I awoke I felt refreshed, almost new, as if a load had been lifted from my shoulders even though I was all too well aware that nothing had changed. If anything, I had more to worry about after what Terry had revealed. I left the basement before it got light. I'd wanted to stay with Terry, but she said she had things to do and it would be easier if I was out from under her feet. She explained that since Blumenthal had discovered the basement, she'd decided that she would have to move on, to shed the identity of Terry Ferriman the way a snake loses its old skin. That took time, she said, money had to be moved, assets reallocated, and documents prepared. Once that was out the way, she said, she'd be back in touch and we'd go on to the next stage. If I wanted to. After I'd thought about it. I told her that I already knew the answer and that I loved her as much as she said she loved me, maybe more so, and that I was quite prepared to do whatever was required. She kissed me and told me that I had to think about it because once it was done there was no turning back, and the next thing I knew I was standing outside in the street.

There was a message on the answering machine from Chuck Harrison and one from Rick Muir. Rick said he had good news and bad news for me. The bad news was that there was nothing untoward about the hair at all. The good news? Yeah, he'd pulled the waitress. Frankly, neither piece of news surprised me. I felt wrecked, the result of making love to Terry and the mental stress of coming to terms with what she'd told me.

I rang Chuck Harrison's office and got his answering machine. I left a message, telling him to hang fire on any settlement and that I'd be in later in the day. I'd had enough of lying down and allowing Deborah and her lawyer to walk all over me, tired of taking the blame for what had happened to April. I guess that talking to Terry about it, opening up for the first time, had helped me face up to the fact that it wasn't my fault, that nobody was to blame. I'd help Deborah start a new life, I'd give her all the financial and moral support she needed, but I wasn't going to let her punish me anymore. I didn't tell any of that to Chuck's answering machine, though.

I stripped off and fell into bed. I was drifting in and out of sleep when the doorbell rang. It was light outside, but only just, and at first I thought the phone had rung and I was groping for it when the doorbell rang again. I pulled on a white toweling robe and padded down the hall. I checked the door viewer and saw two uniformed cops looking bored. One was chewing gum, the other had his hand on the butt of his holstered gun, and I had a feeling that it wasn't a social call.

I opened the door. I didn't recognize either of them. The one with his hand on his gun moved to the side so that he could draw it quickly if I made a threatening move. Behind them, parked by the curb, was a police car.

"Hiya, guys, can I help you?" I said, trying to sound more cheerful than I felt.

"Jamie Beaverbrook?" asked the gum-chewer.

"Yes. Is there a problem?"

The gum-chewer shifted his shoulders in his jacket as if it was uncomfortable. "We'd like you to come with us, sir," he said.

"Where?"

"The precinct, sir."

"Is it a case?"

"All we know is that you are to come with us, sir." The "sir" always seemed to come as an afterthought.

"Hang on while I dress and get my laptop." I made to close the door, but he stabbed his foot against it.

"If you don't mind, we'd like to wait inside while you get dressed, sir. And you won't need the computer. Our orders are to get you downtown as quickly as possible."

Behind him the other officer's hand tightened on the butt of his gun. I didn't like this—I didn't like this one bit. For once I'd have been grateful if they'd cracked a vampire joke or made the sign of the cross, anything to break the tension. "And if I refuse?" I asked.

"Then we'll still come in, sir," he said.

Defeated, I turned my back on them and headed for the bedroom. The gum-chewer followed me and watched as I picked out a suit. I figured if it was trouble I might as well look the part. "Do I have time to shower and shave?" I asked him.

"You can do that down at the precinct, sir," he said. Oh yeah, I thought, happens all the time. The nice, kind police officers downtown always allow the poor, misunderstood felons a wash and brush up before they got down to the third degree. I dressed and knotted on a red power tie and then went with them to the car. They said not one word to me all the way to the precinct, not one lousy word. Other than a couple of speeding tickets, it was my first ever taste of the wrong side of the law, and I could appreciate why so many of the men and women I had to interview looked so nervous. It was the not knowing that was so worrying. The uncertainty. At least I knew what police procedure was and that I had an expensive lawyer to call on if I had to, but even so I was scared shitless. They took me in, walking on either side of me as if escorting a mass murderer, and led me through the reception area. There were several officers there that I recognized, but they all avoided looking at me. We went through Homicide, and I kept looking for De'Ath, but there was no sign of him. Captain Canonico was there, though, standing by the water cooler and filling a cone-shaped paper cup. He saw me as he straightened up and grinned evilly.

"Looks like you're up to your neck in shit this time, Beaverbrook," he said.

"What's going on, Captain?" I asked him.

"A couple of heavyweights from Washington want a word in your shell-like ear." He emptied the water into his mouth, wiped his lips with the back of his hand, and nodded at the gum-chewer. "They want you to see him in my office." Then he turned his back on me and refilled his cup. The fact that whoever it was had swung enough weight to commandeer Canonico's office made me feel even more nervous, and my stomach grumbled acidly as they took me to the room and knocked. A man in a gray suit opened it, looked at the uniformed officer, and then looked at me. He opened the door wider. I saw Rivron get up from a chair. He avoided my eyes as he walked by me. To my mind he looked guilty, but then I probably did too.

The door clicked closed. There were two men, and both of them were wearing gray suits, shiny black shoes, and crisp white shirts. There the resemblance ended. The one who'd opened the door was tall and thin and had a sallow, almost funereal complexion, pale lips, and eyes that were a surprising shade of green, totally out of character with the rest of his colorless features. The other was just as tall, a shade over six feet, but he had thick sandy hair and a rash of freckles across a snub nose and plump cheeks. He was broad-shouldered and had obviously been a football player in his college days but still had a few years to go yet before he went to seed. Both were in their early thirties but had eyes that seemed much older, as if they'd spent most of their working lives being bored. Neither of them offered to shake my hand, but they both introduced themselves. The thin one was called Sugar, and the football player was Hooper. That was it. No first names, no rank. I asked to see their identification, and they smiled the smile of predators scenting prey. "No ID," said Hooper.

"Not as such," said Sugar.

"What do you mean, not as such?" I asked.

"Well," said Sugar, "if you were to come up with a real fancy lawyer who could get the backing of a very important judge, then maybe, just maybe, we might come up with a Washington telephone number that he could call. And then the judge would speak to your lawyer, and your lawyer would speak to you, and then you'd be speaking to us again."

"At the moment it's just you and the good captain and a couple of members of the department here who know that we're involved," said Hooper.

"And frankly," said Sugar, "that's how we'd rather keep it, for the moment at least."

"The fewer people who know, the better," added Hooper.

"Know what?" I asked.

"That is, as they say, the sixty-four-thousand-dollar question," said Sugar.

"Why don't you sit down," said Hooper. He walked by me and rested his hand on the back of the chair in front of Canonico's desk.

"Then we can shoot the breeze," said Sugar, leaning back in Canonico's chair.

"Chew the fat," added Hooper.

"Have you two been working together long?" I asked.

They smiled. "A while," said Hooper.

"Does it show?" asked Sugar.

"A bit, yeah."

I sat down, and Hooper went around the desk and stood next to Sugar. He put his hands behind his back and looked for all the world like an undertaker paying his respects. He looked at me like a cat wondering whether to eat a mouse or toy with it for a while. "We, Mr. Sugar and I, work for an agency in Washington which is connected, you could say, with national security. And homeland security, or at least the security of the homeland. But we were around long before nine-eleven and the War on Terror. We also liaise closely with our counterparts in other countries. Our task is to spot individuals who may at some point pose a threat to national security."

"To nip them in the bud, as it were," said Sugar.

"We tend to use profiling techniques," said Hooper.

"Not racial, of course," said Sugar.

"Perish the thought," said Hooper.

"But we do know our enemy," said Sugar.

"Oh yes," agreed Hooper. "That we do."

"I still don't follow you," I said, but I had a pretty good idea where they were heading.

"Terry Ferriman," said Hooper.

"Terry Ferriman," repeated Sugar.

"Ah," I said.

The three of us said nothing for almost a full minute, and it was Sugar who eventually broke the silence.

"What can you tell us about her?" he asked.

"In what way?" I replied.

"You've been making a number of inquiries about the lady. About her background, finances, circumstances. We'd like to know what conclusion you've reached."

I nodded. "She was originally brought in as a suspect in a murder inquiry. She was bailed, and as far as I know there isn't much of a case against her," I lied. After last night's conversation with her, I knew exactly how much of a case there was against her and her friend. Had she told me his name? I couldn't remember; she'd given me far too much information to digest at one sitting. I needed to talk to her again.

"We know that," said Sugar patiently.

"You extended your own inquiry beyond a simple grading of her mental state?" asked Hooper.

"Yes, that's true."

"Would you mind telling us why?" said Sugar, smiling.

"She intrigued me."

"There was something unusual about her grading, something shown up by the Beaverbrook Program?" asked Hooper.

I tried not to show any reaction to the fact that they knew about my program. "No, it was personal," I said.

"Personal?" repeated Sugar.

I had the impression that the two men in suits knew exactly what my feelings for Terry were, and what I'd found out. They knew and they were testing me, probably to ascertain whether I was with them or against them. What I wanted to know was who the hell were these two men from Washington and how they knew that I'd been investigating Terry Ferriman. De'Ath maybe, or perhaps Rivron. Or maybe the databases De'Ath had been accessing had triggered something in Washington.

"You had a relationship with her?" said Hooper.

"You could say that, yes," I said.

"A sexual relationship?" asked Sugar.

I hesitated, but then nodded. I had a hunch that lying, at least obvious untruths, would do me more harm than good at this stage.

"Did she tell you much about herself?" asked Hooper.

"Pillow talk, as it were," added Sugar, grinning.

I ran my hand through my hair. "I'm very much in the dark here," I said. "I think I've only got a small part of a very big picture, and it's causing me some confusion. Could you give me some sort of briefing first, so I get a rough idea of what's going on?"

Sugar linked his hands together behind his head. "You mean we show your ours and you show us yours?"

"A sort of quid pro quo?" said Hooper dryly. "Is that what you're suggesting?"

"It would be a help," I said lamely.

Hooper and Sugar looked at each other, and then Sugar nod ded. From the body language I guessed that he was the higher ranking of the two.

"There are something like seven billion people on this planet," said Hooper slowly. "Thousands are born every hour. The vast majority are like you and me. We are born, we marry, have children, and eventually we die. The species moves on. That applies to ninety-nine point nine nine nine nine percent of the population. But every now and again, in something like one in a hundred million births, something happens. A mutation. An alteration at the DNA level, inside the chromosomes of the cells. The mutation can take several forms, but the end result is something which is not human. Something which can be less than human, or, in some cases, more than human."

"You're talking about monsters," I said.

Hooper shook his head slowly. "Not monsters," he said. "Mutants. Born of completely normal parents. In the old days they might have been called monsters, and many of them passed into folklore, tales told around the campfires."

"Folklore?" I said. "What do you mean specifically?"

"Vampires," said Sugar, and he wasn't smiling now. "Vampires and werewolves and shape-shifters. That was what they were called, and the definitions still work as labels, though they are not especially accurate."

"If you're saying such things exist, why isn't it common knowledge? Why are they still regarded as fiction?"

"Statistics," said Hooper. "Such mutations are a very rare occurrence. Even today with a population of four billion there are probably no more than one or two a year born around the world. A hundred years ago it would have been one every ten years or so. And it's only recently that we've had the capability of keeping track of people. Before they could move around and conceal their identities. Now everything is on computers. There's nowhere to hide."

What he said made sense. It also went some way to explaining how they knew I was involved. God knows how many computerized trip wires De'Ath had gone blundering through while he was chasing up Terry's background. "How many does your organization know of?" I asked.

Hooper looked at Sugar for guidance, and Sugar nodded.

"We know of seven what I suppose you'd call vampires. Four in the United States, two in the Soviet Union, one in Eastern

Europe. We suspect there are some in China, but the authorities in Beijing aren't especially forthcoming. There are no werewolves or shape-shifters in the States, but there are three in the Soviet Union, two in India, and one in Albania. Again we're in the dark about China."

"You don't really mean vampires and werewolves, do you?" I asked him.

Hooper shook his head. "Not as you'd see them in movies, no. The vampires we're trying to track down don't wear black cloaks and turn into bats. They can eat all the garlic they want, you can see them in mirrors, and they have no problems crossing running water. They don't have sharp incisors, either. But they are virtually immortal. The gene which causes aging is missing, and their cells continue to replicate ad infinitum. They usually have an allergy to bright sunlight. They are very strong, very intelligent, and they need blood. The gene mutation leaves them unable to synthesize certain essential amino acids, which they must therefore obtain by other means. Blood is the easiest source of supply, though blood-rich organs such as the heart or liver will also do."

"And they live forever? Is that what you're saying?"

Sugar shrugged. "There seems to be no limit on the number of times their cells divide. We know of one who is more than two thousand years old. You'd never know it to look at him. He's little more than a boy. Even carbon dating doesn't help date him. But under hypnosis, we've gone back with him to ancient Rome."

The mention of carbon dating made me wonder if they knew about my trip to UCLA, and if they'd been told about my inquiries. I had a nasty feeling that the men belonged to an organization whose tentacles were spread throughout the world's scientific community. No, tentacles weren't a good analogy. A spider's web, maybe, thin filaments running back to their headquarters waiting for the slight tremble that would suggest that somebody, somewhere, was asking the sort of questions you'd ask if you were on the track of a vampire.

"And the werewolves and, what did you call them, shapeshifters?" I asked.

"They're more complex, and even rarer than the vampires," said Sugar. "I've never seen one, though I've seen a video of one of the Russian examples undergoing transformation. Pretty heavy stuff, I can tell you."

"What's it like?"

"To be honest, it's not as impressive as the sort of special effects you see in movies like *The Howling* or even that Michael Jackson video, but it's a whole different ball game when you know it's the real thing."

"What if the film you saw was faked?"

Sugar snorted. "The sort of guys we liaise with don't play games like that, Dr. Beaverbrook. They're not exactly selected for their senses of humor, you know."

I shook my head in disbelief. Vampires. Werewolves. Things that go bump in the night. Part of me expected Canonico and his colleagues to come bursting in through the door with wooden stakes and mallets screaming, "You've been punked!" but the two men in gray suits were too serious for it to be a joke. This wasn't a setup. It was for real. It was for real, and I was frightened for Terry.

"So," said Sugar, stretching his arms above his head. "Enough about us. I think you've gathered by now that we suspect that this Terry Ferriman is one of these mutants."

"It's possible," I said. "I guess."

Sugar scowled and brought his arms down hard on top of the desk, making me jump with the ferocity of the movement.

Hooper didn't even flinch; he just kept looking at me with his cold, emerald eyes. "Don't fuck with us, Beaverbrook," said Sugar. "In terms of operational powers, we rank way above the country's law enforcement agencies and antiterrorist organizations. CIA, FBI, any group of initials you want to come up with, we're head and shoulders above the lot. We answer to only one man, and he reports directly to the president. We can make you disappear, Beaverbrook. We can take you to the sort of places you haven't even conceived in your worst nightmares, and we can talk to you there. But if we have to do that, you won't leave. Ever. You're either with us, or you're against us. And if you decide you're against us, you give up any rights that you might have. Am I making myself clear, Beaverbrook?"

"Yes," I said.

"I can't hear you."

"Yes," I said, louder this time.

"Good," said Sugar. "Now, you've been making inquiries about Ms. Ferriman. What conclusions have you drawn?"

"She isn't Terry Ferriman," I said slowly. "The real Terry Ferriman died more than twenty years ago. She took over her identity. She's rich, very, very rich. She seems to have access to tens of millions of dollars in a bank account with no real means of accounting for it. She owns a big apartment building but pretends to live in a tiny apartment there." I figured that De'Ath had probably already told them about the money in the bank, and it wasn't much of a step to have found out about the building. I didn't mention the basement because I hoped that they might have missed that. I told them about finding Greig Turner's picture and about my meeting with the former film star because De'Ath knew about that, too. It was important that I appeared to be cooperating.

"What about her personality?" Sugar asked. "How did she seem to you?"

"She was fine on the program, and that would show up if she was lying or being evasive. But she seemed to know a lot more than you'd expect for someone of her age."

"Her apparent age," corrected Hooper.

"Her apparent age," I agreed. "She could speak several languages, yet didn't really explain how she'd learnt them. She was amazingly confident, too. As if she knew exactly what she was doing. As if she was in control."

"What about physically?" asked Sugar.

"I guess the first time I met her I reckoned she looked younger than her age." I caught Hooper looking at me. "Than her apparent age. I'd have put her in her teens. And the way she spoke was often like a teenager. Yet she seemed to know so much. It was as if…"

"As if she was acting young. Pretending," Sugar interrupted. I nodded in agreement.

"What about her body?" asked Hooper.

"Like a teenager's," I said.

"Did you see much of it? Her body, I mean," asked Sugar.

"A fair bit," I said, unsure what he was getting at.

"You already admitted you were lovers," he said. "I'm assuming you left the lights on."

I was about to protest, but I saw Sugar's eyes harden, so I thought better of it. "Yes," I said. "At least, we went to bed once. Just once."

"Did you use any form of contraception?"

The surprise must have shown on my face because Sugar grinned at my discomfort. "I'll explain later," he said. "Just answer the question."

"No, we didn't. She said she wouldn't get pregnant. I assumed she meant she was on the pill or something."

Sugar and Hooper looked at each other, and something unspoken passed between them. Sugar looked back at me. "Did she bite you?" he asked.

"No," I answered, emphatically. I felt a sort of tremor of anticipation run along my spine because if she had asked me, I'd have let her. No doubt about it.

"Did she take blood from you in any way?"

"No," I said, equally emphatically. Then I suddenly remembered the night she'd taken me to The Place, how the mugger had cut me and how she'd licked the wound clean. Sugar must have seen something in my face because he asked me if I was sure. I told him what had happened.

"Did she tell you why she was doing it?"

"She just said she was cleaning it."

"Did she ask you to take blood from her?" Sugar asked.

I laughed out loud but could see that he was serious. "Why on earth would she do that?" I asked.

"Is that a yes or a no?" he pressed.

"No. Never," I said. He nodded as if he believed me.

"Did she ever ask you to do anything for her?" asked Hooper.

"Lots of stuff. Everyday things, you know. What do you mean? What do you think she might have asked me to do?"

Sugar got up out of his chair and walked over to the window. He stood and looked out, his hands clasped behind his back. "You have to understand, Dr. Beaverbrook, that these people usually want something from the people they get close to. They tend to keep to themselves, because the more people who know them, the more chance there is of them being discovered. They don't age, and after five years, perhaps as much as ten, it becomes noticeable. If they do get close to someone, it's because they want something."

"We met by accident," I said. "I was called in to examine her, that was all. We got on well together."

"You hit on her?" asked Hooper.

"No," I said angrily. "I'm a professional. It would have been totally unethical for me to have done that."

"So," said Sugar, still with his back to me. "She hit on you?"

I had to think about that one. She'd turned up at my house late at night, dragged me out, and yes, at the end of the night she'd seduced me. It had been all her doing. I hadn't realized at the time, it had felt so good, but I hadn't had to do anything. "Yeah. You could say that."

Sugar turned round and smiled. "And why do you think she did that?"

"What do you mean?" I asked, feeling defensive.

"Why do you think a pretty girl of her age—her apparent age—wanted to get involved with someone so much older?"

"I'm only thirty-five," I said, realizing how weak that sounded.

"You look older," said Hooper, unsympathetically.

"Thanks. But we're only talking about an age gap of ten years or so. That's not unusual."

"The girl is beautiful," said Sugar. "And very rich, as you say. She could have any man she wanted. So why did she choose you?"

"Maybe she wanted me," I said.

Hooper made a sort of snorting noise and put his hand over his mouth. I glared at him, but they were making me think.

"Did she ask you about your work?" asked Sugar, sitting down again.

"Of course."

"Did she ask about vampires, things like that?" he pressed.

"Never."

"She never asked if you knew where they were held?" he said.

"I don't follow."

"Is it possible that she was hoping that you would tell her where the rest of her kind are? The ones we know about."

"But I don't know where they are being held. Until I met you two, I had no idea that they even existed."

"Yes, but she wouldn't have known that," said Hooper.

"You think I was being set up?" I asked.

"Sounds like it," said Hooper.

Sugar drummed his fingers lightly on the desktop. There was no tune, no rhythm, just random tapping. "Dr. Beaverbrook, it's important that you understand something, that you don't allow yourself to get too attached to her." He spoke quietly, his head thrust forward to close the distance between us, as if he was drawing me into his confidence. "These people, these mutations, are different from us—they don't form emotional attachments. They are loners, complete and absolute loners. They only get close to other people when they need something—when they need blood, for instance. Or information. This might sound trite, but they don't fall in love. You must not imagine that it's possible for her to, how can I say this, have feelings for you. Do you hear what I'm saying?"

"Yes," I said, but I felt that he was lying. I knew the strength of her feelings. And I knew that I loved her with all my heart. With all my soul.

Sugar looked at me intently as if trying to peer into my mind, and for a brief moment it almost felt as if he were probing through my synapses like a burglar rooting through a bedroom closet. And the valuables he was looking for were my true feelings.

"They don't even form attachments with their own kind," Sugar continued. "They meet occasionally, they help each other, but generally they keep away from each other."

"For safety?" I said. "So they can't give each other away?"

"No. Because they prefer it that way. They can't help themselves. How good is your biochemistry, Dr. Beaverbrook?"

I shrugged. "A bit rusty."

"Ever heard of a hormone called oxytocin?"

"Sure," I answered.

"They call it the happiness hormone," Sugar continued. "It's a peptide secreted by the pituitary gland at the base of the brain."

Something surfaced at the back of my mind, a paper I'd read a year or so earlier. "It stimulates uterine contractions during childbirth, doesn't it?" I said.

Sugar looked impressed. "And starts milk production," he added. "It's long been known as a muscle contractor. But recent research has shown that it's much more than that. Researchers at Rockefeller University in New York gave doses of oxytocin to female mice and found that they were almost twice as keen to mate as control animals. Another experiment showed that female rats given the hormone make more of an effort to nuzzle their young, and male rats take more trouble to build a nest. If you block the effect of the hormone, you get the opposite effects. Sometimes the parents even go so far as to kill their offspring. The hormone is also thought to increase the sensations of sexual arousal."

As I listened to Sugar's explanation, I began to realize that he was more than just a cop in a gray suit. I got the impression that he was giving me an idiot's guide to the subject and that his knowledge ran much deeper.

"Scientists at the National Institute of Mental Health in Maryland discovered that brains of sociable mice are particularly turned on by oxytocin, and after extra shots of it they seem to enjoy physical contact even more. It's like they want to get inside each other, almost. But they also found that solitary mice were hardly affected at all."

"So you're saying that some mice are receptive to the hormone, and some aren't?"

"It's not just mice, Dr. Beaverbrook. It looks as if it does a similar job in humans. Oxytocin is the trigger for tactile contact between humans. It makes you want to hug, to hold hands, to stroke. Levels of the hormone jump four or five times during orgasm and ejaculation in humans. It either triggers orgasm or is triggered by it. We're not sure which comes first, if you forgive the pun."

I smiled, but I was still confused. "Where is this biochemistry lecture heading?" I asked him. Sugar linked his fingers on the desk and rubbed his thumbs together. He had big thumbs, the nails almost square. "The investigation we've done on the vampires we have suggests that at no point do they secrete the hormone. Nor is there any indication that they posses receptors which recognize oxytocin. In simple terms, the hormone has no effect. In vivo or in vitro. It does not exist in their bodies. Whatever genetic mutation it is which gives them their longevity also appears to do away with their need for oxytocin, and with it the desire to be sociable. They do not need company, Dr. Beaverbrook. Nor do they need sex. I doubt if either the males or the females get any enjoyment from the sexual act whatsoever."

I remembered how Terry had been in bed, how she'd screamed, how she'd held me, how she'd touched me. Had she been acting? Had she faked it? I realized Sugar was staring at me, and so I fought to control my feelings.

"So, how was she in bed?" asked Hooper. I'd forgotten he was there, so intent had I been on Sugar's speech. Hooper was openly leering at me, and I wanted to punch him in the mouth. I breathed deeply and evenly and tried to relax. I didn't answer his question and looked back at Sugar.

"What he asks is valid, even if it was tactlessly put," said Sugar. "I know that what I'm saying will annoy the shit out of you, but you have to understand quite clearly what I'm saying. They don't need contact with others. They don't need sex."

"Only with their own kind, you mean."

"No, that's not what I mean. They don't need sex, period. They don't reproduce. They can't. They're sterile. Men and women. Their sterility is at the gene level—it's nothing to do with sperm levels or blockages in fallopian tubes or any of that stuff. Their DNA just won't recombine. Everything looks normal, their chromosomes split just fine, but they don't combine again. The men ejaculate, the women ovulate, everything is just as it should be, but no matter what you do you can't make the DNA in the sperm and the egg combine."

I began to wonder what sorts of experiments Sugar and his colleagues had been carrying out on the mutants they already had. And what they planned to do with Terry. I heard a throbbing noise from outside the building, and the windows began to tremble like an approaching earthquake. Hooper walked behind Sugar and looked out.

"It makes sense, when you think about it," Sugar continued, seemingly oblivious to the noise outside. "Humans are born, they produce children, they die. The old makes way for the new. That's how the human race has progressed over the thousands of years we've been on the earth. If we didn't die, there wouldn't be enough room for everyone. But if your body isn't going to die, if the cells can reproduce themselves ad infinitum, it takes away the need to procreate. There is no need to replace the original. And without the need for procreation, there is no desire for the sex act."

An act, I thought. Is that what it was? An act?

"There's something else you need to know," said Hopper. "We have her in custody. We brought her in this morning. Not long after you left her."

He stared at me, trying to gauge my reaction. I tried to hide my confusion.

"What did you think? That we wouldn't have her under surveillance?"

"Can I see her?" I asked. The throbbing was louder now. Hooper's head was back as he looked up into the bright blue sky. He used both hands to shield his eyes from the sun.

"This could be your last chance," said Hooper, without turning around. Sugar stood up and motioned me over to the window. We stood on either side of Hooper. He was looking at a white helicopter hovering just above our building, its tail swinging from right to left as it moved down, its rotor a blur. Below most of the vehicles had been removed from the car park and a landing area cordoned off with thick yellow tape marked "Police Line—Do Not Cross." All around the perimeter were armed police, and on the tops of the buildings around us I could see SWAT units in place, their rifles trained on the car park. Drivers passing the precinct building stopped and wound down their windows to get a better look, and pedestrians craned their necks upwards. The helicopter hovered and then drifted slowly down until its skids touched the ground. The pilot kept the blades turning. The side door slid open, and two men in suits and dark glasses got out.

The police around the car park tensed and almost as one raised their weapons, seemingly toward us, but I realized they were covering somebody below us, coming out of the building. When they came into view a few seconds later all we could see were their backs, but I saw enough to know that it was Terry, surrounded by half a dozen guards. She was wearing white paper coveralls, and they'd also made her wear a restraining jacket, thick canvas with leather straps, the sort they use for controlling lunatics, and they'd shackled her legs together.

As the group reached the helicopter, two of the guards held her shoulders and moved her around, and for the first time I saw her face. Her hair was loose around her head, and her chin was up defiantly. Another man stepped forward with a black bag in his hand and moved as if to put it over her head. She twisted to avoid it, and for a wild moment I thought she saw me. Maybe she did, I don't know, but she stopped moving, and then they forced the bag over her head like it was a lynching and bundled her into the helicopter. Three of the guards piled in after her, followed by the two men in suits, then the engine noise picked up and the helicopter lifted off the ground and circled once around the car park, blowing off hats and sending litter whirling around before heading off east. Car drivers and pedestrians were standing bemused, not sure if they were watching the real thing or a movie being shot. I saw one of the drivers, a tall, thin man wearing a black Stetson, thump the roof of his red pickup and climb back into the driver's seat, and gradually the onlookers realized the fun was over and dispersed.

"Where are you taking her?" I asked. Hooper stayed by the window as I went back to my seat. I stood behind it, my hands gripping the backrest, while Sugar sat down behind the desk and looked up at me.

"Best you don't know," said Sugar quietly. "And anyway, we can't tell you. It's on a need-to-know basis like you've never seen before. And you don't even come close to needing to know. Classified to the nth degree."

"Why?"

"Because it's taken us a long time to track them down. We don't want to risk losing them, not until we've finished our research."

Research, he said, but from what he'd told me so far it seemed more like dissection. They were taking them apart piece by piece.

"What's the aim of this research?" I asked.

Sugar rubbed the back of his neck with his hand and then slid it round to scratch his jaw. "Genetic, mainly," he said. "We're trying to isolate the gene that gives them their longevity."

"And then what? I assume it's not just sheer scientific curiosity."

Sugar grinned. "No, it's more than that. We're getting to the stage where we can manipulate genes, cure genetic defects before they happen. We can introduce genes into chromosomes before conception. Genetic engineering."

"You want to make people live forever?"

"I just do the research, Dr. Beaverbrook. I just add to our scientific knowledge."

"I don't remember seeing anything about vampires in *Scientific American*," I said.

"I didn't say I published. I just do the research."

"But you don't share the research?"

"There's a lot of research done by the Defense Department which isn't shared," said Sugar.

"Need-to-know only," I said.

"You got it." He leaned back in his chair and studied me again. "Have you fallen for this girl?" he said.

"No," I lied.

He looked at me for a full ten seconds, saying nothing. I could hear the helicopter in the distance, faint like a buzzing insect trapped under a glass.

"I think there's a good chance she hoped you'd be able to tell her where we're holding the rest of her kind. I think that's why she got close to you. It's important that you believe that, Dr. Beaverbrook. It's important that you realize that you have to be with us on this, not against us."

I said nothing. The helicopter noise faded and died.

"Sometimes they promise people things," he continued. "They tell people they can join them. Become like them. Did she promise you that, Dr. Beaverbrook? Did she make you an offer you couldn't refuse?"

"No," I lied again.

"If she did, and I'm not saying I don't believe you, but if she did, then it's important that you understand something. It's not like in the movies. They don't bite you on the neck and turn you into one of the living dead. That's not how it works. The mechanism that stops them aging and dying isn't carried in the blood. It's not some sort of virus or infection that can be transmitted through the blood or any other secretions. They're the way they are because of their genetic makeup, because they carry genes we don't have. We're as different as wolves and sheep. A sheep doesn't turn into a wolf when it gets bitten. And the only time the wolf goes among the sheep is when it wants something. Usually to feed. You ever see that movie *The Hunger*? The one with David Bowie and Catherine Deneuve?"

"I saw it," I said, knowing what he was going to say. It's not like it is in the movies. No one could accuse Sugar of being subtle.

"Okay, so you'll remember that she's a four-thousand-year-old vampire living in New York who chooses companions and turns them into vampires. She bites them and they live for a few hundred years. Remember?"

I nodded. "I remember."

"It doesn't happen. Genes can't be transferred through blood, any more than you can get pregnant from a love-bite. Genetic engineering is possible, but only before conception. We can take a chromosome and alter it, we can breed new plants and animals already, we can create our own mutations, and eventually we'll be able to prevent most genetic disorders, but there's nothing we can do to alter the genetic makeup of an existing organism. Maybe in the future, once we've isolated the immortality gene, we can slot it into human DNA and create a human being who'll live forever, but that's for our children or grandchildren; it won't do anything for us. Long term it might be possible, I'll be honest. Scientists are working on using viruses to carry genes into the nucleus of existing cells, hoping to cure diseases like Parkinson's disease and Lesch-Nyhan syndrome, and there's similar work being done on nerve disorders like Alzheimer's and Huntington's diseases. It's starting to look as if we just might be able to modify a virus like herpes simplex so that it carries an enzyme-producing gene into the nuclei of nerve cells in a patient. If that proves to be possible, then the next step would be use the procedure to modify the nuclei of all the cells in the human body. We could, for instance, change a person's eyes from brown to blue. Or make them taller. Or more intelligent. Or live forever. But that's the equivalent of talking about a heart transplant during the Middle Ages. We are the way we are, and nothing is going to change that. We are born, we live, we die. That's the rules we play by, Dr. Beaverbrook. Whatever she might have said to you, whatever she might have promised, they can't change those rules."

"I hear what you're saying," I said. It was true. He'd finally got through to me. It wasn't just what he was saying, it was the way he was saying it. I believed him. But I needed time to think. He was like a life insurance salesman, smooth and slick and persuasive, holding out the pen and asking whether I wanted to make weekly or monthly payments. I wanted to see how I felt when I was on my own, when my head was clear. I had a lot to think about.

"There's something else you must know," said Sugar. "What has happened here has to remain a secret. You can understand that, I'm sure. We go to a great deal of trouble to ensure that our work remains confidential. Our organization will do everything it takes to maintain that confidentiality. I am a scientist, as you might have gathered. Mr. Hooper here is involved more on the, how should I say it, security side."

"Security," repeated Hooper, as if hearing the word for the first time. He smiled at me with the look of a tailor measuring me up for a suit.

"You are on the side of the angels, Dr. Beaverbrook. You're doing good work with the LAPD. We'd like you to stay on our side. I know the odds are against it, but maybe in the future you'll come up against another of her type. We'd like to think that you'd call us if that happens. What we wouldn't like to think is that you were on their side, that you were misguided enough to think that you should help them. If we were ever to think that, Mr. Hooper here or someone like him would pay you a visit."

"Is that a threat?" I said.

"An observation," said Sugar.

"A promise," said Hooper. He seemed to be savoring the thought.

That was it; the interview was at an end. I let myself out of the office. De'Ath was at his desk, and Captain Canonico was standing over him as if checking his homework. De'Ath raised his eyebrows but said nothing, and I had the feeling that his boss had warned him not to speak to me. I walked by them without a word. It was only when I'd left the building that I remembered that my car was back at home. I cursed. There was precious little chance of a cab cruising past, and it was too far to walk. I went back inside and asked the desk sergeant if there was any chance of a cruiser taking me home. I didn't know the guy. About as much chance as hell freezing over, he said, and nodded at a poster on the wall that had the number of a local taxi firm. I rang the number on my cell phone, and a taxi arrived within fifteen minutes.

I sank back in the seat and closed my eyes, rubbing my temples with the palms of my hand all the way back to the house, my thoughts in a whirl. I'd lost Terry, I'd been threatened by men in gray suits who didn't even carry ID, and I'd been told that the U.S. government was carrying out research on vampires and werewolves. My legs were trembling, and I felt as if I was going to throw up. I managed to keep the nausea under control until the cab dropped me outside my house, but by the time I'd unlocked the door and reached the bathroom my stomach lurched and I vomited again and again. I knelt down beside the toilet and rested my arms on its polished wooden seat, flushed it, and then threw up once more. When I had nothing left to vomit, I got to my feet and poured myself a glass of water to get the bitter taste out of my mouth. I was splashing cold water over my face when the doorbell rang.

There was nobody on the doorstep, and for a wild moment I thought that maybe Terry had escaped, but I quickly killed the idea. There was no way on earth she'd be able to get away from her captors. I looked up and down the street. It was deserted except for a few parked cars. I recognized most of the vehicles as belonging to my neighbors, with one exception. A red pickup. The hairs prickled on the back of my neck, and I slammed the door and double locked it. As I turned around I almost bumped into him. He was tall, almost a head taller than I was, but it was hard to judge it exactly because of the big black Stetson perched on his head. He used the index finger of his right hand to push the brim of the hat so that it slipped back, and he grinned. It was an aw-shucks sort of grin, and he looked like a typical redneck, blue and white checked shirt, Levi's jeans, a thick leather belt, and scuffed cowboy boots, broad shoulders and a tight waist, a squarish face with the beginnings of a beard, and piercing blue eyes. There were wrinkles around the eyes as if he'd spent too much time squinting under the sun. His face had a slight sheen to it as if he were sweating, but then I realized that he was wearing sunblock cream. He had big hands with thick fingers and neatly clipped nails. They appeared to be greasy too.

I stepped backwards and bumped into the door. One of the locks pressed into my shoulder, and I winced. "Who are you?" I shouted. "What are you doing in my home?"

His grin widened, showing the sort of teeth you normally see in toothpaste advertisements. He tucked his thumbs into the belt and let his hands hang on either side of a silver buckle in the shape of a flying eagle. It was as if he was daring me to hit him, but I could see how muscular he was under the shirt and knew that there would be no point. There was a time to fight and a time to be scared. I was scared. Shitless.

"What do you want?" I said, but I already knew what he wanted. He continued to look at me with amused eyes. "I don't know where they've taken her," I said in answer to his unspoken question. I pressed myself into the wooden door, trying to force it to absorb me. "They don't trust me."

"Well now, I can see why they wouldn't," he said quietly. He moved his right hand, quickly enough to make me jump, and my stomach muscles tensed involuntarily, expecting a blow, but he simply reached into the chest pocket of his work shirt and took out a toothpick. He began to wiggle it between his back teeth as he scrutinized my face. His silence and his smile were unnerving; I'd have preferred him to have been threatening, or abusive. I could easily imagine him smiling as he ripped my throat apart and gorged on my blood.

"They think I might try to help you," I whispered.

"And would they be right?" he asked, putting his left arm over my head and leaning against the door. He spoke with a slight Slavic accent that jarred with the redneck outfit. He pushed his head forward so that his face was just inches from mine. He let go of the toothpick, leaving it stuck between his back teeth, and put the other hand against the door, trapping me between his arms. Not that he needed to physically hold me there; I was as hypnotized as a rabbit in front of a snake. I looked down at the floor, unable to meet his gaze.

"Don't look away," he said quietly. I lifted my head, but after a few seconds I dropped it again. He took his right hand off the door and gripped my chin, not hard enough to hurt, but there was no doubting his strength as he raised my head. He was slowly chewing the toothpick and had the same amused look in his eyes. "Don't look away," he repeated. "Just take it easy and look at me. Where did they take Annabelle?"

"Annabelle?"

"Terry, then. Where did they take Terry?"

"I don't know. I honestly don't know." I tried to look away, but his grip tightened on my chin. He looked deep into my eyes. I don't know what he was looking for, whether he could see the veins pulse in my neck and was counting the beats, of if he was measuring my breathing rate, or if he was seeing how much sweat was oozing out of my pores, but whatever he was doing I knew without a shadow of a doubt that he was able to tell whether or not I was telling the truth as accurately as any mechanical lie detector.

"Did they tell you where they were holding my friends?" he asked, his voice steady, almost friendly.

"No. No, they didn't." It was hard to speak with his hand holding my chin. The words came out sort of slurred.

"Will they allow you to see her?"

"I don't think so. No, I'm sure they won't. They don't trust me."

"Why not? Why don't they trust you?"

"They think I'm in love with her."

He smiled and with a few chewing movements transferred the toothpick across his mouth. "And are you?"

I hesitated, but only for a second. There was no point in lying to him. I looked straight back at him. Right into his eyes, as blue as the desert sky. "Yes," I said. "I am."

"Did they mention a man called Hamshire?"

"The geneticist?"

He raised his eyebrows and stopped chewing. "So they did talk about him?"

I tried to shake my head, but his hand refused to move. "No, they didn't. But Terry talked about him. Before they got her."

"But the men who took her didn't speak of him?"

"No. No, they didn't." A sudden thought struck me. "They did say they were holding others like her."

"Did they say if they were being held together? Or separately?"

"They didn't say. But I got the impression they were at one place. The ones in the U.S., anyway."

"Did they say what they were doing with them?"

"Research."

"Sugar was one of them, yes?"

"Yes."

"Did he say exactly what his research was?"

"Genetic engineering," I said. "He's trying to isolate the longevity gene and slot it into human DNA."

The man snorted with disbelief. "That's what he told you, huh?" For a moment I felt the hand tighten as if he was about to squeeze my skull and burst it, and then just as suddenly he relaxed. "You think he wants everyone in the world to live forever, do you?" He laughed, and it was a cruel sound, loaded with irony. "Think what that would do for the economy, Dr. Beaverbrook. Imagine telling a garbage collector he was going to live forever. Or a secretary. Who'd do the menial tasks in a society where everyone lived forever? Wake up and smell the coffee. It would be used to keep a few key people alive forever. People with money. With power. But first, they'd get rid of us. Me and Annabelle and the rest of our kind."

"Annabelle? Is that Terry's name?"

"She has many names. We all do."

"I don't understand any of this."

"Sugar is working on a virus which will recognize the longevity gene. Hamshire had seen some of their research papers. He'd been hacking into a couple of government computers while doing research at Cal-Tech. We think that's how they got him. From what he read, it looks as if Sugar wants a virus that will enter the walls of all cells but only bind to the amino acids which make up the gene that allows us to live forever. And once it binds, it will change configuration and become toxic. Lethal. It will hone in on our DNA and kill us, without harming humans in any way. They plan to introduce it into the atmosphere or the water. Sugar's plan is to design a virus with a very short half-life, on the order of a few weeks. Within a year none of us will be left, and they can then begin consolidating the gene into their own cell nuclei. There will be a new order in the world. I don't think it would be a world that you would be comfortable in."

He stopped. "I shouldn't be telling you this," he said. He pushed himself away from the door and stood in front of me, his hands on his hips. "You know nothing, Dr. Beaverbrook. Nothing that can help me." He looked disappointed, and I realized then that Sugar had at least been partly telling the truth. The vampires had hoped that I would lead them to Terry. And to the rest of the captive mutants. And now that I had proved otherwise, I was obviously no use to them. His hand moved forward, and I flinched, but all he did was seize the door handle and twist it. He grinned at my discomfort. "No, that's not what I'm here for," he said. "If it was up to me, I'd probably do it, but she said no. She likes you, believe it or not. And she doesn't want you hurt. Crazy girl, huh?" I moved out of the way, and he opened the door and strode down the pathway. He didn't even bother to look back as he walked to the pickup truck and drove off.

THE PRISON

And that was the last time I saw her. Until today, that is. Ten years, that's how long it took, ten years of trying to convince them that I was on their side, that I regarded Terry Ferriman as nothing more than a laboratory animal to be studied. I knew that if I ever let on just how much she meant to me, then they'd never let me see her, so for the first eight years I didn't even try. I stayed with the LAPD but started to do some research work at UCLA, initially an extension of my criminal work, but I gradually moved into the effects of aging on intelligence and behavior and particularly comparisons between chronological, biological, functional, and subjective age. It was interesting research in its own right, notwithstanding that my main reason for doing it was to get to see Terry again. At any one time a person's age can be classed in four ways—how old he is in years, how old his body actually appears to be, the status level the person holds in society, and how old the person feels inside.

Take me, for instance, sitting at my military desk with Terry's picture in front of me, propped up against my laptop. Chronological age? No problem—forty-five.

Biological age? Well, if I'm brutally honest, I'd have to say my body is that of a man a good ten years older. I can't read or drive without glasses, four of my teeth are capped, and my hair is thinning. My hearing is nowhere as good as it used to be, especially with high-frequency sounds. I can't get through the night without getting up to go to the bathroom at least once. My skin is losing its elasticity fast, which accounts for the sagging around my jowls and the wrinkling.

Functional age? I guess I've done well and achieved quite a lot during my academic career. Even being modest I'd say I've achieved as much as most academics would have done by the time they were sixty. I was in a rush, I suppose.

Subjective age? I dunno. Inside I feel exactly the same as I did when I was sixteen. I know a few more tricks, I know how to handle situations because I've been through them so many times, but inside it's still the same teenager, the same insecurities, fears, and desires.

The lightning flashes behind me again, a double flash. How would I rate Terry's age? Chronological—more than four thousand years, she'd said. Biological—in her late teens. Functional—God, it would take a normal person, even a highly successful businessman, hundreds of years to acquire the assets she has. Subjective? That I don't know. I can't comprehend how it must feel to live so long. Maybe she too still felt as if she were sixteen.

Anyway, over the years I developed a program similar to the Beaverbrook Model which through question and answer could determine the four ages of a subject. Much of the work I did involved measurement of fluid intelligence, the ability to solve new and unusual problems. Fluid intelligence peaks at adolescence and then declines steadily, whereas crystallized intelligence, the knowledge and skills acquired in life, increases up until the start of adolescence and then increases only slowly until it plateaus in old age. I published a stack of papers in the best psychology journals, and though I kept working for the LAPD, I managed to travel overseas a lot to interview some of the oldest people in the world—in Ecuador, Russia, and India—incorporating the results into the computer model. I put in a few other features too, so that the program got into a person's psyche more thoroughly than ten years with an analyst.

Unlike Sugar and his researchers, I made sure I published as much as possible, and I knew it would be obvious to them that the work I was doing could be helpful in their hunt for immortals. Used properly, my new research could be used to identify members of the population whose functional and subjective ages were way out of kilter with their chronological and biological ages. I kept applying for access to Terry and the rest of the immortals—for research purposes, I said.

Eventually permission was granted by some agency or another, and a team of six agents came and picked me up at home in a limousine with darkened windows, darkened so that I couldn't see out. I told them I needed my laptop, and they allowed me to take it with me. One of the agents took a chrome gun-like thing out of an aluminum case, placed it against my upper arm, and pulled the trigger. Everything went hazy, and then black, and when I woke up they'd taken my watch and the laptop and I was in what could have passed for a Holiday Inn bedroom except for the fact that there were no windows. There was a TV, and the papers were delivered every day, and I could choose my own food from a leather-bound menu, but other than the food deliveries I didn't see or speak to another human being for two weeks. I was in quarantine. Before they'd allow me to see her, they had to be convinced that I wasn't being followed. No conversations, no phone calls, no letters. After two weeks a guy in a white coat unlocked the door and gave me another shot. When I awoke, I was lying on a bunk in a steel-lined room. The first thing I saw was a CCTV camera staring at me. I guess it was being monitored continuously because within seconds of my waking up the door was unlocked and two beefy men in gray coveralls came in. Someone had taken off my clothes while I was unconscious and had dressed me in a pale blue coverall with "VISITOR" stamped across the front in large white capital letters. One of the men handed me a Styrofoam cup of warm water, and I drank deeply to wash away the bitter taste that coated the inside of my mouth.

"You'll soon feel better; the effects disappear quite quickly," said a voice at the door. I looked up to see an elderly man with a pair of gold-rimmed spectacles perched on the end of his nose. He had a kindly face, topped with a mane of white hair, and he spoke with a vaguely French accent. He sat down on the bunk beside me and felt for my pulse. Satisfied, he shone a small torch into my eyes, nodded, and pronounced me fit.

He disappeared as quickly as he'd arrived, and another man arrived, this one younger and fitter and wearing a dark blue suit and carrying a clipboard. It was a checklist of things I was not to disclose during my conversation with Terry (though she was referred to throughout as "the inmate"), mainly news events, the date, time of day, location of the prison (not that I knew it), that sort of stuff. When he'd finished reading the list out to me, he handed me a pen and made me sign at the bottom before he too left the room. The two guards then escorted me along the corridor to an elevator. Both carried M-1 carbines, and the safeties were off, their fingers never leaving the trigger guards. They tapped a six-figure code into a small keypad to call the lift, and when it arrived, the doors hissed open to reveal another grim-faced guard, wearing a similar uniform but holding an assault rifle at the ready.

There was no way of telling how far down the lift went, but it fell quickly enough to make my stomach heave, and it was a full thirty seconds before it came to a halt and the door opened. Two more guards were waiting for me, almost doubles of the ones who'd led me to the lift God knows how many floors above, and they escorted me along another metal-lined corridor, their steel-tipped boots echoing as they walked. My bare feet slapped on the cold metal floor. The coverall was all I was wearing; I could feel that I was naked underneath the cotton material.

There were CCTV cameras at regular intervals along the corridor, and as we passed them I could hear the whirring of a servo-mechanism as they turned to watch us go. At the end of the corridor was what looked like another lift, but after one of the guards tapped in another six-digit code and pressed his thumb against a small square of illuminated Perspex, the doors opened to reveal a square room, about the size of a school classroom.

At the far right side of the room was a panel of booths, each with a plastic bucket chair facing a steel wall in which was set a pane of glass about a meter square. Through the glass I could see a matching row of seats, facing toward me. To the right of each window was a telephone, not the modern sort but the old-fashioned black Bakelite type, the sort you see in old movies. I heard the doors close behind me. The two guards stood at either side with their guns at the ready, their eyes watchful, almost fearful. They said nothing, but I guessed that I was supposed to sit in one of the booths. There was no indication which I was supposed to use, and as I approached the line of chairs I saw that there was nobody on the other side of the glass. I sat down and waited, the plastic cold against my backside through the thin material. Beyond the glass I saw a smaller room, also metal lined, and a single door with no handle or visible lock. The walls were also featureless, though there were what appeared to be ventilation grilles set into the ceiling.

After five minutes or so (there was no way of telling how long because they'd taken my watch), the door opened and a guard came in carrying an automatic rifle. He walked into the room, his eyes flicking from left to right, and then stood to one side. Behind him I saw Terry. She looked small and frail, pretty much the way I'd first seen her in De'Ath's interrogation room more than ten years earlier, her hair loose around her shoulders, her skin pale, and her eyes lowered. She was wearing a robe that looked as if it was made from the same material as my coveralls and which ended just below her knees. They'd given her a pair of brown plastic sandals for her feet, and she was having trouble walking, but that wasn't because of her footwear—it was because the bastards had chained her feet together. There were big chrome clasps above each ankle joined by a chrome chain which couldn't have been more than eighteen inches long, which meant that she had to shuffle rather than walk. My heart went out to her. Her arms weren't chained, which surprised me at first, but then I realized that they were more concerned about inhibiting her movements than preventing her from attacking anyone. They had assault rifles, and by the look of it she had nothing, just the robe and the sandals. If they were as thorough with her as they had been with me, then I knew that she'd never come within a million miles of anything that could conceivably be used as a weapon.

She walked into the middle of the room, and another guard followed her in. I saw a third guard close the door behind them, but even though it was made of steel several inches thick, I could hear no slamming or grating sound. The glass was obviously completely soundproof and, for all I knew, probably bulletproof as well. Terry was in her own sterile world, completely insulated, and almost certainly had been for the last ten years. The guards in her room took up positions on either side of the door, their fingers on the triggers of their rifles. Both of them were wearing miniature headphones I noticed, small black earpieces with wires running round their necks and disappearing into their coveralls. Were they constantly receiving instructions from some central command point, or were they using music or white noise to blot out anything she might say to them? I had no way of knowing.

Terry raised her eyes and saw me for the first time. Her face broke into a smile, and then it quickly disappeared, as if she'd thought she'd seen a friend but then realized she'd made a mistake. Was that because she wasn't pleased to see me, or because she didn't want them to know how she felt about me? Did she still feel anything for me? God, I was so bloody confused—about her, about my feelings, about what I should do.

I stood up and said hello, even though I knew she wouldn't be able to hear me through the glass. She mouthed hello back but stayed where she was in the middle of the room as if she was afraid of approaching the glass screen. I knew I had to play it cool, too. They had only allowed me to see her because they thought I was on their side, that I wanted to study her, to find out what made her tick. Any sign of affection and they'd pull me out immediately, I was sure of that. God, I so much wanted to take her in my arms, to press myself against her and bury my face in her long, black hair, to seek out her lips with my own and kiss her until she couldn't breathe.

I motioned for her to sit down, and she shuffled forward, her hands slightly forward for balance, and lowered herself into the chair. She pulled the chair forward so that she was right up against the small shelf that ran under the glass partition. There was a matching shelf on my side of the glass, and I followed her example, getting as close to her as I could. I picked up the phone on my side of the glass, and there was a crackling noise like static. I nodded at her phone, and she picked it up gingerly with her left hand as if afraid it would give her a shock. She used her right hand to brush the hair behind her left ear and then pressed the receiver to it.

"Jamie, how are you?" she asked quietly.

"I'm fine, Terry. Just fine. How are they treating you?"

She looked deep into my eyes. Her right hand moved slowly on the shelf, making small stabbing movements with her extended index finger.

"I've been in better hotels," she joked. Her right hand moved up as if to brush the hair behind her right ear, but as she did she made a small cupping gesture. She was signing to me. The sign for "listen." *They listen.* She was telling me that the conversation was being listened to, though I'd already figured that out for myself. They'd be crazy not to monitor what was being said, and they'd be sure to record it, too, so that experts could go over it afterwards. I couldn't see any television cameras in the two rooms, but they'd been everywhere else, so I was pretty sure they'd be watching us here, probably through concealed cameras, in the ventilation grilles maybe. Terry had obviously realized that because she put her hand back on the shelf where it would be shielded by her body.

I nodded to let her know that I understood. "You're not hurt, or in pain?"

Terry began signing individual letters with her right hand. It was slow, but she couldn't use the normal word forms that made up the deaf and dumb language because they were very expressive and often required both hands, and the guards would have spotted it straight away. So as she talked she spelled out words, letter by letter.

"Sometimes, but there are lots of doctors here." I M-I-S-S Y-O-U.

"They feed you okay?" I signed back, keeping the movements to a minimum. M-E T-O-O.

"Yeah, but it's never the same with plastic cutlery, you know?" I L-O-V-E Y-O-U. "How long has it been, Jamie?"

That was one of the things I wasn't supposed to tell her because they were trying to disorient her sense of time. "How long do you think it's been?" M-E T-O-O.

She shrugged. "Eight years, maybe." C-A-N Y-O-U... "They don't have clocks in here."

"It's been a long time, that's for sure," I said.

"Not really, not for me." ...H-E-L-P M-E?

"What do you mean?" H-O-W?

"I mean it's not that long for me, in percentage terms." E-3-C-A-P-E. "For you eight years represents, what? A fifth of your life? Twenty percent? Have you any idea how small a part of my life eight years is, Jamie? It's nothing. It's the equivalent of you waiting for a taxi." P-L-E-A-S-E.

"Do you get bored?" H-O-W?

She shrugged. "I guess so, yeah." T-E-L-L T-H-E-M... "They let me have books. No newspapers. No television. No radio." ...W-H-E-R-E I A-M. "I asked if they'd let me have my cello a couple of years back, but they haven't decided yet." T-E-L-L T-H-E-M... "Do you think you could do anything about that?" ...L-E-V-E-L 1-8.

"I can try." T-E-L-L W-H-O? "Is there anything else you want?"

"Shit, Jamie," she said angrily. A F-R-I-E-N-D... "I just want to get the fuck outta this place, but we both know they're not going to allow that, don't we?" ...W-I-L-L V-I-S-I-T... "I'm here forever. You know, they don't allow me to have any visitors." ...Y-O-U S-O-O-N. "Not one. And they won't let me use the phone. Ever. In all these years I haven't seen one single person who hasn't been carrying a gun or wearing a white coat." T-E-L-L H-I-M... "Except for you. You're the first friend they've allowed in to see me." ...T-H-R-E-E O-T-H-E-R-S H-E-R-E... "I'm so glad that you came." ...A-L-L... "How did you swing it?" ...L-E-V-E-L 1-8.

Terry wasn't stupid. I knew that she already knew why I was there, she was just talking to cover the sign language, that it was the silent conversation which was the real one, but I still flushed, and the spoken answer was an embarrassment. "This isn't just a social visit, Terry." W-H-E-R-E... "You could help me with some research I'm doing." ...A-R-E W-E?

She frowned, and I realized she'd probably assumed that I knew the location of the prison. She had no way of knowing that even after all this time they didn't trust me completely and that it was only after I'd agreed to be drugged that they'd even let me inside the place.

"What sort of research?" she said frostily. M-A-R-I-O-N.

"It's for a paper I'm working on."

"What sort of paper?" P-R-I-S-O-N.

"For one of the clinical journals. I'm doing some research into aging and its effects on thought processes."

"Another computer program? Like the Beaverbrook Program?" I-L-L-I-N-O-I-S.

I nodded. I knew about Marion Prison, all right. It's the super-maximum security facility built by the U.S. Federal Bureau of Prisons to replace Alcatraz. Only the worst of the worst end up there, and all of them are kept in virtually permanent solitary confinement. At least two were cases that I'd worked on. Really bad cases. God knows how she expected to get out if they were keeping her eighteen levels below the prison. I'd seen pictures of the facility, surrounded by a double thirty-foot-high fence and bulletproof watchtowers. It was escape-proof.

She sneered, but her hand continued to talk. It was hard to keep the two conversations separate in my head. I kept wanting to answer her sign language verbally and vice versa. I was occasionally stumbling over my words and stuttering, and I had to force myself to keep looking at her face and not down at her right hand. She seemed to be having no problems, though; her voice sounded perfectly natural, and now she was letting her anger show.

"So that's what you're after, is it?" T-H-E-Y W-I-L-L… "You want to come up with a program that will pick out people like me?" .. R-E-S-C-U-E M-E.

"Something like that." W-II-A T T-H-E-N?

"And what do I get out of it, Jamie?" T-H-E-N Y-O-U… "Have you asked them that? Early parole, maybe?" …A-N-D M-E… "They'll let me out in two thousand years instead of two thousand five hundred?" …T-O-G-E-T-H-E-R… "What can they offer me, huh? They're never going to let me out, you know that. They're going to pick and probe at my mind and take samples and prod me and try to find out what makes me tick. They started from day one, you know." …F-O-R-E-V-E-R. "They analyze everything— my urine, my shit, they take blood samples every day, tissue samples when they want it. I've had more than one hundred spinal taps, Jamie—and they hurt me every bit as much as they'd hurt you. Ever had a spinal tap, Jamie? Have you?"

I didn't answer—I couldn't. The contempt in her voice was like a slap across my face, and I wanted to hug her and pick her up and tell her that it was all right, that I'd help her and that I loved her. But still, on the shelf, her right hand spoke to me.

"They've taken liver biopsies and pieces of my kidney." W-I-L-L Y-O-U... "They'll start scraping my glands next, and then they'll want samples of brain tissue." ...H-E-L-P... "They're going to take me apart piece by piece to see if they can find out what makes me tick." ...M-E? "It's going to be a death of a thousand cuts, Jamie."

"I thought you couldn't die," I said. O-F C-O-U-R-S-E.

"Not in the way you and your kind die, no. My cells live forever, but that won't do me any good if they're spread out across a dozen laboratories, will it?" I L-O-V-E... "I mean, it gives a whole new meaning to 'I Left My Heart in San Francisco,' doesn't it?" ...Y-O-U.

"I'm sorry," I said lamely.

"Sorry!" she spat, getting to her feet. "You're not fucking sorry, Jamie. You're here to help them. You're here to pull me apart, just like them. Okay, so you're not going to use a scalpel or a test tube, but you're every bit as much a butcher as they are. You make me sick, you really do."

The door behind her opened, and two guards came in, one carrying my laptop, the other with an assault rifle at the ready, his finger on the trigger. The man with the computer carried it over to the booth at the far side of the room and placed it down on the shelf in front of the glass. He kept a wary eye on Terry as he flicked up the screen and pressed the switch on the back, which powered it up and automatically booted the program.

"You expect me to run through one of your sick little computer programs, is that it, Jamie?" she yelled down the telephone. The two guards backed away and left through the door. It closed silently behind them.

"Calm down, Terry," I said. W-H-E-N W-I-L-L... "They've told me that if you cooperate, they'll allow you to see your friends." ...T-H-E-Y C-O-M-E? Not true that, they'd told me that she'd never again be allowed to be with her own kind. She'd know that too, but she'd also know that working through the program would buy her more time with me.

"They said that?" she said, frowning. S-O-O-N.

"If you cooperate," I said. "This research is important, Terry."

She looked at me through the bulletproof glass, and I tried to read her jet-black eyes. She smiled and flicked her hair out of her eyes. "Okay, Jamie, I'll do it." She put her telephone down and shuffled over to the computer. She looked down at the keyboard, her hair falling across her face like a veil, and tapped at the keys with one finger. I walked along the line of booths so that I was standing opposite her, but she didn't look up as she tapped away. She continued to sign as she worked, small hand movements that she shielded with her body. T E-L-L, T-H-E-M N-E-R-V-E G-A-S H-E-R-E, W-I-L-L N-E-E-D M-A-S-K-S. A-L-S-O T-R-A-N S P-O-N-D-E-R-S E-M-B-E-D-D-E-D I-N O-U-R N-E-C-K-S. M-U-S-T B-E R-E-M-O-V-E-D.

When she'd finished, she stepped back from the computer. She picked up the telephone in front of her, and I did the same. "There you are, Jamie. I hope they keep their side of the bargain."

"I hope so too," I said. I signed carefully. T-A-K-E C-A-R-E.

She smiled. The door opened behind her, and two more guards appeared. "It looks as if it's time to go," she said. She replaced the receiver and turned her back on me as two of the guards moved to either side of her. A third guard switched off the laptop and picked it up. Terry didn't look back as she left the steel tomb. I realized I was still holding my receiver in my hand and that I was gripping it so tightly that my knuckles had whitened and the tendons were stretched taut beneath the skin.

That was the last time I saw her. I was escorted back to the upper level, a man in a white coat gave me another injection, and when I woke up I was back in my own home, the laptop on my desk. That was this afternoon. I was groggy for an hour or so, and then I ran her responses through the latest version of the program. When I'd scanned through the results, I took the car, drove to the bank, opened the safety deposit box, and took out the manila file. It wasn't so much the case notes that I wanted, it was the picture. I wanted her picture on the desk while I waited. I kept checking the rearview mirror all the way home, but I couldn't see anybody following me. There was certainly no red pickup truck, but then I guess he'd be unlikely to keep the same vehicle for ten years, wouldn't he?

So, that's it. Now I just wait. I sit here at my desk, and I wait for them to come get me. It won't be long, I'm sure. The only question is who will get to me first. Her friend, who has obviously been following me for ten years, waiting for me to go to her, or the men in suits. And what will happen when they get to me?

I pour myself a drink with shaking hands and lift the glass to my lips. Some of it slops down my chin, but I manage to swallow most of it. As I put the glass down the lightning flashes and I nearly drop the glass. My nerves are shot to pieces.

Do I trust her, that's the question. Can I trust her? Or do I trust the men in suits? If she's being honest, then all I have to do is tell her friend where she is and wait for them to break her out. But how long would that take? Marion Prison is the ultimate prison. You can't get within ten miles of it without being seen. There are fewer than four hundred prisoners and thousands of guards, and even inside the double security fence and its coils of razor-sharp barbed wire you can't move more than a few yards without having to go through a steel gate or pass a television camera.

No one has ever escaped from Marion. It's not just a place to hold violent criminals, either. The government has a special holding unit there—seven cells in which they hold spies with information so secret that they can never be allowed to mix with other inmates. Ever. And Terry had told me that she and three others like her were being held eighteen levels below ground. How in God's name did she expect to escape? By being patient, maybe. By getting one of her own people into the prison system, by having them work their way into Marion Prison. But that would take years, decades probably, putting together a false work history, references, years in other prisons. I could be dead before they even came close to getting her out. Maybe they planned to get to one of the guards, blackmail him or kidnap his family. But I knew that the guards were specially chosen and positively vetted at regular intervals. It would be so difficult as to be virtually impossible. And what am I expected to do while they put together their escape plan? Am I to wait, getting older and older by the day? Greig Turner's turtle-like face flashes into my mind. How long do they expect me to wait? Would they trust me? Wouldn't they be better off killing me, so that they had all the time in the world?

The questions torment me, and I take another drink of whiskey. The lamp on the desk flickers, and a rumble of thunder rattles the windows as I pick up the bottle of capsules and break the seal. It makes a small popping noise. I push the cap in and twist it open.

Was she lying when she said that I'd be with her forever? The men in the suits said that it wasn't possible, that the phenomena was genetic and couldn't be passed on, that the vampire's kiss was a kiss of death and not the start of life everlasting. If she was lying, her friend would certainly kill me. I put the plastic cap on the desktop and pour out the red and green capsules. They sit in an untidy pile next to the bottle of whiskey, red and green, red and green.

They'll play back the tapes at some point, the men in suits. They'll sit there and listen to the conversation I had with Terry, and they'll play it through again and wonder why I was stuttering and why sometimes I appeared confused, and they'll look closely at the video recording from the cameras hidden in the ventilation grilles. I don't suppose they'll see much, otherwise they'd have seen it at the time and they'd never have allowed me to leave, but if they thought something was wrong then they might spot the arm movements, and maybe, just maybe, they'll put two and two together. If they did, then they'd come for me to find out what she'd told me. They'd do everything in their power to force me to tell them. And if they thought I was trying to help her, they'd kill me, I'm certain of that. They'd kill me, and then they'd move Terry and the others like her to another secure place, and this time they'd never have any visitors, or maybe they'd use me as bait and through me trap her friends. She'd think I betrayed her.

I pick up one of the capsules and swallow it. It has no taste. I wash it down with a mouthful of whiskey.

I've had plenty of time to think over the last ten years, and I'm pretty sure what happened now. Terry and her friends had been fishing for someone like me, somebody they could use to find out where the rest of their kind were being held. They'd had thousands of years of practice at covering their tracks, and yet it had taken me only a few days to find out who and what they were. That just couldn't have been possible unless they'd wanted me to find out. It was a setup from the start: the photograph of Greig

Turner, the Porsche, the bank accounts. All signposts pointing the same way, leading me to the basement where she was waiting. And all the time, never too far away, the redneck in the pickup, watching and waiting as she revealed the clues to me.

She allowed herself to be caught with Blumenthal's body, deliberately getting his blood on her face. She showed me her strength, her knowledge, her abilities, and then finally she showed me everything, knowing that she'd be found out and that the men from the government would come for her And she knew that I'd fall in love with her, that I'd move heaven and earth to be with her, and that eventually I'd get to see her. All they had to do was wait and watch. It was just a matter of time. And time was something they had plenty of.

So what are my options? Terry's friend kills me, the men in suits kill me, or nobody kills me and I spend the rest of my life waiting for her and getting older day by day. The liver spots on the backs of my hands are getting bigger. My skin is more wrinkled, and it's not as elastic as it used to be. My teeth, the ones that aren't capped, are starting to go yellow. Not much, you probably wouldn't notice even if I smiled at you, but I can see the changes. I'm getting older, and she's staying the same. I can't bear that.

I take another capsule and another mouthful of whiskey.

The study wall opposite the desk flashes a brilliant white, and the sky cracks again. From somewhere in the house I hear a noise, the sound of a chair being pushed in the darkness.

I love her so much, I don't want to betray her, and I don't want to get old and not be with her. I don't want to be abandoned. I don't want to be old and alone. I waited ten years to see her, and now that I've seen her I know for sure that she was lying to me. I couldn't see it in her eyes. I looked deep into her black eyes and saw nothing but love and the promise that we'd be together for all time. I wanted to believe her eyes, but I knew that what I felt was purely subjective and that the only thing I could truly believe in was the Beaverbrook Program, and that had been unequivocal. Terry was totally incapable of love—that's what the program had said. The questions I'd sprinkled through the psychological pro-filing appeared innocuous, but taken together with the response times and keyboard pressure they told me what my eyes had failed to see. She was using me, and her declaration that we'd be together was a lie. She loved me, in a way, that I'm sure of, but her loyalty to her own kind and her own survival were paramount. There was no way I could be with her forever. I would die, and she'd live on, just as Sugar said.

The capsules still have no taste, even when I swallow several at the same time. I wonder who will get to me first. The vampires. The men in suits. Or the capsules.

THE END

ABOUT THE AUTHOR

Stephen Leather is one of the United Kingdom's most successful thriller writers. His bestselling novels have been translated into ten languages, and his e-books have spent months on the UK's Kindle Top 100 list. Before turning to fiction-writing full time, he spent a decade working as a journalist for the *Times*, the *Daily Mail*, and the *South China Morning Post* in Hong Kong. He has also worked as a biochemist for ICI, a limestone-shoveler in a quarry, a baker, a petrol pump attendant, a barman, and an employee for the Inland Revenue. He has also written for television shows such as *London's Burning, The Knock,* and the BBC's *Murder in Mind* series. Two of his books, *The Stretch* and *The Bombmaker*, were adapted for TV. To learn more, visit his website at www.stephenleather.com.